To 1

MW01341059

Thank you
Good reading
Ron Roy

Thanks for your magic!
Barbara + Pierre

Harsh Magic

Harsh Magic

Ron Roy

Published by:
Four Season Mysteries

Printed by:
Walch Printing
Portland, Maine

Harsh Magic

Books may be ordered directly from the author
or by contacting the publisher at.
Four Season Mysteries
119 Hill Rd.
Dummer, NH 03588-5409
www.fourseasonmysteries.com
(603) 449-2210

ISBN: 978-0-9840224-6-5 (pbk)

Printed in the United States of America
Four Season Mystery rev. date 10/23/2013

To my brother, Richard, my sisters Barbara Ann and Cathy and my best friend, Girtha Pou

Acknowledgements:

I began this novel in a class at Southern Methodist University's Continuing Education Program. Thanks to Sally Kemp who worked with me on the first draft, long after the class had finished.

To Dr. Pat Vaughan, M.D for his help with the medical details and his literary advice.

To Ed Solar and Sue Solar of Four Season Mysteries.

ONE

The minute that Will backed into the room, he knew that things were bad. He paused as the door swung shut behind him and gave himself a moment to adjust to the humidity, kept high to compensate for the patient's fluid loss. He smelled the sweet odor of draining wounds, of sweat and antiseptics. He felt the fatigue and tension of the team, as well.

He glanced towards the monitors at the head of the table. The patient's blood pressure was almost non-existent. The anesthesiologists clustered at the head of the table. Bags of solutions dangled from the crosspieces of a half-dozen chrome intravenous stands and blood pumps. Fred Dean, the man in charge, selected a syringe from the row lying on his cart and made an injection through the IV line. He looked up and saw Will. He shook his head.

At the sterile field, Devin Shea, the surgeon, and his assistants jockeyed for position as they tried to place a skin graft. The lights focused on the patient's arm. It would have been a perfect specimen for an introductory anatomy class. At the edges of the wound, Will saw each layer of skin, then muscle laced with the thin, white bands of ligaments. At the wrist he caught a glimpse of bone.

He turned to the corner where Julie stood with troubled eyes. He walked over and leaned towards her, careful not to break his scrub.

“Are you all right?” he whispered.

"Was it like this last week?" she asked.

"It's been like this every week," he said. Will had already done Sheila Cole three times, but this was Julie’s first.

Looking over her shoulder, he placed the people who were scrubbed: scrub tech, surgeon, chief resident, two junior residents and two medical students.

"They should have given us a bigger room," he said.

"No room is big enough for this many doctors," she replied.

He smiled.

"Could you scratch my nose?" he asked.

She pushed the mask down off his nose, ran her finger up and down the bridge and slipped the mask back into place, adjusting the small, metal band that held it there.

"You've done this kid three times already?" she asked.

Will nodded.

"Well, I guess I should be able to do her once, then, shouldn’t I?"

"You'll be fine," he said, although he had his doubts. Sheila Cole was seventeen years old. She’d been trapped in her car when it had overturned in an accident. She had burns over 65% of her body. He wondered if Julie had the stomach for this one.

Will walked over to relieve the scrub tech, Barb Woodard, a very large and angry woman who’d worked in the OR for years. She backed away from the table and held a gown up for him. The eyes over her mask held their usual harsh glare. "So you won the jackpot," she said.

"I volunteered," he said, as he walked into the gown.

"You're a sick child," she said. She held a glove out for him and he stuck his hand into it.

Will nodded towards the table. "Not as sick as she is," he said.

For the next three hours, Fred Dean and his residents ran Sheila Cole through a steady stream of blood transfusions, IV solutions and medications. The surgeons did their work, trusting that Fred would do his. They sloughed away the layers of dead skin, took skin grafts from her few good areas and placed them where the damage was most severe. They evaluated her right arm and decided that they'd give the two fingers that they hadn't already amputated another week to see if they could be saved.

They asked for sponges, suture, staples and suction, six people in blood-soaked, sweat-stained gowns pressed together around the table. Will moved with them, trying to anticipate their needs. When he succeeded, he received no thanks. When he failed, they cursed him and he scrambled to catch up.

The orderlies beat a path to the blood bank. Fred needed medications from the pharmacy. Julie was relieved for break.

"Aren't you going to come with me?" She asked.

"I'll stick it out," he said.

"How much longer?"

"Maybe an hour."

She raised her eyebrows but left.

Finally, Shea backed away from the table. "Okay," he said. "Get the dressings on her and get her out of here."

He tore off his gloves and gown, dropped them on the floor and pushed out into the hall.

Julie, back from break, gathered up the bandages and creams that had been ordered and passed them to Will. She nodded towards the door.

“How come he gets to leave?”

"Rank has its privileges," he said. He, too, would have liked to go, but their work wasn't done, yet. Of course, surgeons also had to talk to the family, and Will didn’t envy Shea that task.

"It's so hot in here," Julie said. "I've about had it."

"We're almost done," he said.

The residents pulled the dull, green drapes away. One fell into the blood that had pooled under the table. A small, dark spot appeared in the center of the sheet. It grew larger, drawing the linen down. Will watched it for a few seconds, then pulled his eyes away, seeing the whole body, not just the wounds that they'd been working on today.

The red, raw flesh was like an alien landscape. Currents of molten rock swirled everywhere. Still, he saw that she was much improved. The grafts were taking on her back and thighs. A thin, white mesh of skin covered several gaping wounds that had been laid bare in the fire. The areas that they had debrided this afternoon looked better with the dead tissue cleared away. A thin layer of blood seeped over these, as if the body were trying to replace the layers it had lost. He nodded. They were getting there.

"Oh Jesus," Julie muttered. He turned to her. She shook her head. "Everybody talks about her," she said, "But it’s awful without the dressings."

"It is pretty rough."

"Hey, Will," Fred said. "Can we get these dressings on and get her out of here?"

"In a minute," Will said as he nodded towards Julie.

"I'm okay," Julie said.

"Are you sure?"

"I'm sure. Let's get this poor kid out of here."

On the drive home she was silent. Will thought back to his first week on the case and said nothing.

"She's seventeen years old," she said finally.

"What?"

"Sheila Cole is only seventeen, Will. She'll be down for surgery a dozen more times, and if she makes it through, she'll need years of rehab. She'll have scar tissue, contractures and pain. And when it's over, if she makes it, what's she going to look like, Will? She's a teen-age girl."

"I hadn't thought about that," he said.

"You've had three weeks of this," she said. "What do you think about?"

"I think about skin grafts and debridements," he said. "I think of how much better she is than on that first night."

"Better?" she said. "This is better?"

"Yes," he said. "It is."

When she didn't speak, he glanced at her. She stared out the window.

"Okay," she said. "I know you have to focus on the case, but do you ever think of her as a person. Do you ever wonder what it's like for her when she's not in the OR?"

"I wonder about the pain," he said after a few minutes. "What that must be like. They've got her on a morphine drip. She gets her pain meds through her IV continuously. You know. Drip. Drip. Drip. Fred says that without that kind of protection she'd go insane." He shook his head. "I wonder what that's like. The pain. The drugs. Battling back and forth inside her skull."

"Is that why you sleep so badly on Wednesday nights?"

"I guess."

"Martha could get you out of there next week, you know."

"I know. I don't want out."

"And you don't worry about what it'll be like for this kid when the surgeries are over?"

"No," he said. "Let's get her through them first, okay?"

She hesitated and he knew that she had more to say, but finally, she nodded.

"Thanks," he said.

That night he lay in bed after Julie had fallen asleep. She'd wrapped herself in two blankets, one around her legs, the second over her shoulders, the white fabric forming a cocoon around her body. The blanket around her shoulders edged up past her ears. Her blonde hair, cut close and teased up into sharp spikes, jutted out the top like tufts of dry grass. The red fringe of her teddy showed at the bottom.

He knew that what she'd said about Sheila Cole was true. What would her life be like once her surgeries were over? Why hadn't he even thought about that before today? He thought back to his first emergency surgery, a C-section with Lila Waznek and Fred Dean. Things had been so much simpler back then. Back then, surgery had seemed like magic.

That night two months ago, they'd taken a break on the roof outside the anesthesia office, waiting for the city's Fourth of July fireworks display. Will wondered if the fireworks would beat the thunderstorm threatening from the West. He watched the thick, black front sliding towards them, white bursts of lightning rippling through its crest.

Will sat with his back against the building. It was too hot. The air was heavy, expectant, waiting for the storm as much as they. Lila Waznek, his partner for the evening, sat on the window ledge, dangling one thick leg out onto the roof. The leg slapped against the wall beneath the window, beating time to the anger in her voice.

"I can't frigging believe it," she said. "It's the Fourth of July and I'm stuck in this frigging place. Don't get me wrong. I know the whole crew can't be rookies. Somebody has to know which end is up, but it sure as hell shouldn't be me. I've been here fifteen frigging years. I've done my time. Martha just has it in for me because I don't kiss her ass the way the others do. I shouldn't have to be a goddamn baby sitter. I raised six kids, for Christ's Sake. I don't even want to watch my grandkids."

Fred sat motionless on the roof in front of them. If Lila's tirade upset him, he didn't show it, but this was nothing new. Nothing ever seemed to bother Fred. Will wondered if there was anything that could get his blood going.

"Damn, it's hot," Lila said.

"It's not so bad," Fred said, his eyes still focused on the sliding, black curtain of the front. A small plane, its warning lights made brighter by the darkness, moved towards them, trying to outrun the storm.

"The frigging storm will probably break before they start, anyway," Lila said. "We won't even get to see the fireworks."

"Maybe, maybe not," Fred said.

"What do you think, Will?" she asked.

He shrugged. He had worked with Lila before and knew the best way to get her past her anger was to let her vent.

She might even forget that I'm the rookie she's here to baby-sit.

"What would you be doing right now if you weren't working, Lila?" he asked.

"We make a big deal of the Fourth out in Weston," she said. "The whole damn town gets together out on the green. We have a chicken barbecue and family games and a beer tent. The works. I went over for lunch, but I had to leave before things really got started. My husband's probably drunk on his ass, by now. I hope he lets our youngest drive them home. He can really be stubborn sometimes, though."

"Sounds good," Fred said. "It sounds like home."

Fred had been raised in Georgia. Lila smiled at Will. The nurses said that he acted as if he was on leave from the South and trying not to pick up any Northern habits, like moving fast, before he returned.

"What about you, Will," she asked. "You like to celebrate the Fourth?"

"Not really," he said. "I've never been that big on holidays."

"Well," she said. "That's a frigging shame. Holidays—"

"There," Fred said, tracing the path of a tiny, rising star with his arm. Suddenly, it exploded in a white burst that blossomed, hung for just a moment and faded quickly. They watched as the next made its slow climb into the sky, and exploded at its climax into a splash of red that formed a sparkling ribbon and rippled slowly towards the earth.

"Nice," Will said.

"Shit," Lila said and he turned to her. She pulled the OR cell phone from her pocket and raised it to her ear.

"OR, this is Lila," she said.

Will studied her face. He couldn't read her. Fred had better luck. He rose, shook himself, moved towards the window.

"Okay," Lila said. "Get down here as fast as you can." She pocketed the phone and wrestled her leg back through the window. Her scrubs caught on the window latch. She jerked them free.

Fred eased his huge frame back through the window as gracefully as Lila had struggled. Will took up the rear.

"It's a C-section," Lila said. "A fetal distress." Fred nodded, already headed down the hall towards the OR suites. "I'll have to crash her," he said.

Lila nodded. "Will," she said, "Go scrub while I set up the room."

"But I should help you."

"There isn't time."

He went right to the scrub sinks, leaving her to set out supplies from their emergency set-up. He scarcely had his hands wet when he heard the buzzer for the front door, the signal that the patient had arrived. He looked through the window that separated the scrub room from the OR. Lila waved for him to come in. "I've barely started," he protested but she just shook her head and waved for him again.

He backed into the room, slipped into his sterile gown and gloves and began to set up his instruments on the table.

Will turned and saw the patient on the stretcher.

"Fetal heart with multiple decelerations," said the delivery room nurse.

"Get her over on the table," Lila said.

"Here comes another," the patient gasped.

"It'll be fine in a just a minute," Fred said.

They moved her onto the table. Lila came over to Will.

"Have you ever done one of these?" she asked.

"Sure," he said. "Never an emergency though."

"This isn't any different," she said.

What was she talking about? The baby was in danger. Every second counted.

"It's happening too fast," he said.

"So slow it down."

"Slow it down?"

"In your head," she said.

Will turned back to the table. He focused on the things he had to do.

Suddenly, Jill Ackerman, the OB surgeon, stood beside Will, snapping her fingers for a gown. Will helped her into it and reached for a pair of gloves for her but she waved him aside. "I'll get them," she said. "You get her prepped."

Will grabbed a sponge-stick and a bowl of antiseptic paint. He leaned over the patient. "This is going to be cold," he said, but she was already under. Fred had crashed her, indeed.

He washed her bloated abdomen, spreading the thick, brown soap in a circular motion as if he were basting a turkey. As soon as he put the bowl down, Ackerman handed him one end of the surgical linen. Together they opened it and covered her umbilicus. They laid another at the base of her abdomen and two more perpendicular to these, leaving a rectangle of skin, dull yellow from the soap, in the center.

Ackerman held her hand out, ready to go. Will took a knife from the table and pressed the handle into her open palm.

She made the incision at the foot of the sloping belly. Blood oozed up along the line and Will pressed it dry with a sponge. He slid a retractor into the wound and tugged. He felt the skin's insistent pull against him, saw row upon row of cellulite, tiny yellow globules of fat, like the eggs one might find in the belly of a bulging brook trout.

Will saw a glimpse of purple in the wound. Ackerman held the uterus in her hand and made a tiny slit with the knife. Will eased the suction into the hole, and the amniotic fluid ran through the tubing, flushing red blood with a rush of clear fluid.

Will handed Ackerman the heavy-bladed bandage scissors. She slid them into the opening, rending the muscle for the baby's blossoming head: dark, black hair and purple skin, looming up like a whale's wide snout driving for the air.

Once she freed the baby, Ackerman handed it to the pediatric resident, clamped the cord and severed it. She turned back to the patient and Will stood frozen, staring at the child.

"Will," Lila said. He shook himself and turned back to the table, listening as the residents behind him struggled with the baby.

"Fred," the pediatrician said. "Can you give me a hand?"

Fred Dean crossed the space between them in two strides, flying from Will's vision. Bodies shifted as Fred moved in. Will had scarcely absorbed the shock of Fred's rush when a baby's cry filled the room, outraged, angry, but gloriously loud.

* * * * *

Later, Will had sat in the lounge as rain tore against the windows. He couldn't forget the sight of Fred wheeling the incubator down the hall towards the nursery, the baby peering suspiciously out from its tight, swaddling clothes.

Lila flopped into the chair beside him, driving it against his. "You won't forget that one for a long time, will you?" she asked.

"No, I guess I won't."

"I thought you said that was your first emergency C-Section?"

"It was," he said.

"You acted like a goddamn pro."

"What you said about slowing things down," he said. "It helped a lot. Thanks."

Blood flushed her face dark red. She looked away.

Lila embarrassed? Now that's a new one.

Lila looked at her watch. "I guess I'd better hit the road," she said. She stood and tugged off her OR cap, dropping the thin, blue sheath into the trash. Sweat pressed her dull, brown hair close to her skull. She fluffed it out with her hands. He hadn't realized it was so long. "I'm going to get out of these pajamas and into something more comfortable," she said. "How about you?"

"I think I'll stick around for awhile. I need to think about tonight, get my mind around it."

"Rookies," she said. She touched the top of his head.

"You did great tonight, kid," she said. "Don't mess it up by thinking it to death."

She went into the dressing room without looking back. He heard the shower running as he eased his head back against the chair and closed his eyes.

He felt a tap on his head. He opened his eyes.

"You fell asleep," she said. "If that's how you to process the night there might be hope for you."

He almost didn't recognize her. She stood over him, tugging at her mass of brown curls with a brush. Most of the women who'd worked in the OR more than a few years kept their hair cropped short. Lila's hair billowed out around her face. Why hadn't she chopped it off like all the rest?

The hair wasn't the only difference. She had on make-up. She wore a red tank top and matching shorts. She looked good.

"Hang around as long as you like, rook," she said. "Enjoy it while you can."

He watched her walk back across the lounge. The tight shorts hugged her butt. It was the first time he'd noticed that she had one.

"Lila," he said.

"Yeah," she said as she turned back to him.

"I couldn't believe it when the pediatric resident asked Fred for help."

"Well," she said. "It doesn't take long for most docs to figure out who to call at crunch time. Nobody can resuscitate a kid better than Fred."

"But he moved so fast. He usually moves in slow motion, but this time…."

"Who would have believed it?" she said. "You'd think somebody lit a goddamn firecracker and stuck it up his ass."

They'd stared at each other for a moment and then they laughed.

"I know what you mean," he'd said, "I feel a little funny down there myself."

"Way to go, rook," she'd said, holding her hand up for a high-five. "I couldn't have said it better myself."

And Will had known he wouldn't have said it at all if he'd never met her.

TWO

When it came to Will, things had never been simple for Lila. The night of that C-section, she had left him in the lounge and headed for her truck.

The levels of the parking garage, closely packed, trapped the heat, the exhaust fumes and the dust. Most nights, the crisscrossing concrete slabs weighed on Lila, as if she, not the pillars and the support cables, held them up

That night it had been different. The rain had cleansed the air. Lila took a deep breath. She felt light. But was it really the rain? Maybe it was the excitement of the case.

Yeah, right. You know exactly what it is, Lila Waznek. It's the kid.

She saw the cab of her truck jutting up above the roofs of the cars around it. Even without the running lights it would have dwarfed them. Something wasn't right, though. The cab leaned towards her. She came around and saw that the right front tire had gone flat.

She tossed her bag into the cab and climbed into the bed of the truck. She unlocked the toolbox to get the jack and unchained the spare. She tossed it out just to hear it hit the concrete. She threw a blanket down beside it.

Maybe this is a good thing. It might get my mind off the kid for a few minutes.

She pried off the hubcap with the bar, gently laid the shining metal on the blanket. She placed a socket over the first nut, whipped out the long bar and slid it into place. She gave the nut a nudge, knowing it wouldn't do a thing. She leaned into it and felt the first, satisfying twist as the metal gave. She repeated the move on every one, then slid the jack into place and hoisted the truck off the ground. She pulled her x-shaped tire iron from the back and twirled off the nuts. She jerked the tire off and dropped it to the pavement.

She paused to catch her breath. She wished her mind would do the same, but she couldn't stop thinking about Will. She'd had her eye on him for awhile, but watching how he carried himself in his first emergency was too much.

Why the hell did he come into my life, now anyway?

She had everything she'd ever wanted: a good man, kids grown and on their own except for Jerry, their baby, their mid-life mistake. Money problems were a thing of the past. Their house and land were paid for. They owned their cars outright, too. Once Jerry was out of the house, they'd be free and clear. Will Nathan was the last thing she needed in her life.

But what would be the harm in getting it on with him?

Everything. If she got caught, she'd lose everything. Everything she'd worked for.

Her husband, Ray, was a proud man. He'd never forgive her. Even if he did, she knew that it would break his heart. How could she justify doing that to her best friend?

Her best friend. That was part of the problem. Her husband was like a brother to her. Everybody said that's what made the best marriages, and she'd wanted to believe that. She always had, before Will came along.

How can I be in love with this child?

How she could be in love with Ray might be a better question. They were practically twins. Same height. Same build. Same brown hair. That was one of the reasons she refused to get it cut. She knew that if she cut it short, only their friends would be able to tell them apart.

Then there was Will. He was six feet tall. He kept his blonde hair cut short and his beard trimmed neatly like a lawyer or a college professor.

Kid, my ass.

This kid was all man. It was obvious he worked out. Not like Ray, whose muscle came from real work. This kid had a chest on him and six pack abs. And legs?

Jesus Christ, what legs.

She jerked the spare up into place and hand-tightened the nuts.

She remembered the first time she'd seen Will's body. He'd shown up for an evening shift in a tank top and shorts after running. He wiped the sweat from his face with the tail of the tank top, revealing those abs. Martha chewed him out for showing up for work like that, but that was just Martha.

As if the patients getting wheeled into the OR cared that the hunk glistening with sweat might be working on them in a few minutes. They were just happy to look at him. One young blond had reared up on her gurney and grabbed Will's arm, "Whatever you put in my IV, Doctor," she'd slurred to the Fred Dean, "Give me a little more, I want to be able to dream HIM up whenever I want."

And Martha, that hypocrite, had led the discussion in the locker room later that night about just how hot Will was.

Lila tightened the nuts and let the jack down. The truck dropped back to earth. She stood up and felt the tightness in her chest and in her arms for the first time. She gasped for air. The dust scratched her throat.

She saw her reflection in the side mirror and slapped it out of line. She was a sight. She could feel her hair fizzing out. A good thing Will hadn't walked out with her.

She climbed into the cab, gunned the engine and wheeled the truck down the ramp.

She took her time in the neighborhoods around the hospital. They seemed deserted, but she couldn't afford any more points on her license.

When she hit the outskirts of town, though, she put her foot down. She knew the cops had better things to do than patrol the back roads to Weston.

At Weston Common, the street lamps took over again, illuminating the remnants of the celebration. The clean-up crew would be back in the morning. Trash drifted across the grass and snagged on the gazebo. The banners waved above the beer tent. Chip Lander's cruiser stood in its shadow.

That's a good one, our illustrious alcoholic sheriff guarding the goddamn beer.

She dipped back into the darkness. The clouds had come back in after the storm, maybe spoiling for another. She couldn't see a thing beyond the range of her lights.

She took the turn-off to their property, and followed the narrow drive deeper into the woods, until it opened up on their front lawn.

Her husband liked to call their place "Wazneck Manor". He had earned that right. When they'd bought it, it wasn't much, but together they'd made it into one of the best properties in town.

She parked the truck behind Ray's Mustang. In the kitchen the keys to the Mustang hung on the hook over the counter. Ray must have let Jerry drive home after all.

She looked in on Jerry. Ray could wait. He'd be sleeping it off.

Snoring so loud he'll sound like the truck when the plugs are fouled.

She wished she could sleep on the couch, but sometime during the night he would wake up and find her missing and track her down wherever she was.

She took another shower, this time for her bout with the tire and the dust from the garage. Once she got in she stayed a long time.

She walked into the bedroom. Something was missing. The snoring. She went over to the bed and flipped on the lamp on the bedside table.

Ray lay still, his breathing shallow. Even in the dim light, she saw his skin was blue.

"Ray," she had said. She'd poked him, but he hadn't moved. "Jesus Christ, Ray. What the hell have you done?"

THREE

Will came to work early every day, pausing for a moment just outside the double doors that separated the OR from the rest of the hospital. He saw the front desk through the glass, the row of white coats hanging beside it. Sometimes there would be a patient on a stretcher in the hallway, a surgeon or anesthesiologist leaning over them.

He'd scan his badge and the door would open. He'd feel the faint rush of air escaping and hear voices at the front desk. He'd nod to his co-workers as he slipped by. He'd go to the locker room, change into his scrubs and wander over to the ICU to get a cup of coffee.

At 2:45 he'd sit down in the lounge, stretch out and wait for report with the coffee balanced on his stomach, wondering what Martha Givens, his charge nurse, had in store for him that day.

He'd come a long way from his days spent working in fast food restaurants and convenience stores and he planned on enjoying every minute.

The day after he and Julie worked Sheila Cole together, Will got his coffee and found his seat in the lounge. He'd always thought of the lounge as no-man's land. It might have been its dim lighting, or maybe the space, itself, long and narrow, more like a corridor than a room. Chairs lined each side and a lamp stood on an end table, one bright spot in the low light. The door on one end opened into the lockers rooms. Bright light streamed in from the door that led out into the OR. Will always felt a surge of excitement when he walked into that light.

He'd left home just before noon so he could go to the gym before work. Julie was still in bed. A restless sleeper, she'd shed her blankets and lay with a sheet draped across her hips. He ran his fingers down her body. He loved that she was all curves and angles, no cover girl, no skinny, untouchable manikin. She stirred at his touch, but didn't wake. He pulled the covers back over her, kissed her spiked hair and left.

Tim Murphy came into the lounge. They touched fists. Murph was Will's age, but his curly black hair and pale skin made him look as if he should still be in high school. They'd worked out together a few times, had a few beers after work. Murph was okay.

Kathy Rogers came in and sat beside Murph. Her hair hung down her back almost to her waist. Report for her was about taming her hair, getting it into the OR cap. When she'd finished with her hair, it weighed down the thin blue paper of the cap, framing her face like the hood of a cobra. She looked like an Egyptian princess.

Kathy spent every summer afternoon sunbathing in her back yard. Her skin was chocolate brown from Mid-July until October. Will wondered what she would look like when she was fifty-five, when it was time to pay the price for her addiction to the sun. He pictured her face with wrinkles and blotches and patches of dry skin.

Perhaps she'd never have to pay up, though. She'd marry a dermatologist, better yet, a plastic surgeon. While most lost the battle with aging, Kathy would have every resource at her disposal.

Will looked at Murph sitting beside Kathy. He pictured him at fifty-five. His curly, black hair receded as if in a time-lapse photograph. His face collapsed into a double chin. Coarse, gray hair sprouted from his ears while Kathy stayed herself beside him.

The guys often joked that certain nurses were "Doctor Material". Kathy was one of those nurses. The image of Murph and Kathy at fifty-five brought that home for Will. They were from different species. They could no more mate for life than a gorilla and a hummingbird. It was no accident that God told Noah to line the animals up two-by-two when it was time to load the Ark.

Lila would have normally been sitting right beside Kathy, but she'd taken a leave of absence after her husband's heart attack and heart surgery. Will understood, but he missed her. He'd felt close to her after that C-Section and then she'd disappeared. She'd been out for almost two months.

Julie came through the door, carrying her shoes in one hand and her scrub cap in the other.

"Hey," Will said.

"Hey," she said and brushed her hand across his shoulders. She nodded at Kathy and Murph and took a seat beside them.

Melanie Sanchez was the last regular member of the crew, although no one had ever been able to figure out why she was an OR nurse. She was young, pretty enough, but the unhappiest person that Will had ever known. She never smiled, even in the lightest moments.

You'd think she was working on an assembly line for all the joy she gets out of her work.

Martha entered and took the biggest chair, a green upholstered lump that looked as if it had been picked up at a yard sale. Martha lay the OR schedule over one arm of the chair like a doily. She opened the folder where she carried the evening assignments.

She pulled off her OR hat. Her short hair was a harsh shade of red that God might never have intended, but she somehow managed to pull off. Her face was thick with freckles that flowed down into the V-neck of her scrubs. Will had never been able to figure out how old she was, somewhere between thirty and fifty.

"Good evening," she said. "Room 18 is Mixter's second heart," she began "A coronary graft with five jumps. They attempted an angioplasty in the Cardiac Cath Lab, but decided they needed the OR, after all."

Will leaned forward in his chair. These cases could get pretty hairy, as hectic as any fetal distress. He wondered how this one had gone down.

"The trip from x-ray went smoothly," Martha said. "The patient is stable and on the pump. Mixter is confident that things will stay that way. Kathy and Murph, this one is yours, of course."

Will wondered why she even felt the need to say it. Those two were the heart team and everybody knew it. He was curious about hearts. He'd asked Martha if he could spend some time in them, and she'd promised that his time would come.

"In Room 5," Martha said. "Doctor Jamison will be doing a debridement and external fixation on a compound fracture of the right femur. The patient was in a motorcycle accident. We'll flush out the debris and clean up the tissue around the wound. The femur is a mess, though. I wonder if even Jamison can pull this one out.

"Will," she said. "You'll be the scrub on this one. Julie, you circulate."

Martha ran through the rest of the cases: a small bowel obstruction, a cataract and two ankle fractures. Most would be done by seven pm and would be finished up by the nurses already in those rooms who were working the middle shift.

"Melanie," she said. "That leaves you with me as the emergency team. Get started on room restock. I'll let you know when another team is available and if I have anything for you."

Melanie shrugged. That was her reaction to everything, be it busy work or the wildest emergency.

All right," Martha said. "Let's have a good shift."

Murph and Kathy headed to their room. Melanie followed them. Martha headed back to the front desk. Julie didn't get up, so Will slipped into the chair beside her.

"Howdy partner," she said. She leaned over to tie her shoes. They were heavy, white nursing models. Like most of the nurses, Julie wore bright socks in contrast to her dull scrubs. He saw white specks on aquamarine. He realized they were seagulls. Her gold ankle bracelet rested just above the colors.

"So we get orthopedics, today," she said.

"Yeah, Doc Jamison."

She stood up and offered him her hand.

"The good doctor awaits," she said

"Good doctor?" he said as she pulled him to his feet. "Have you met Jamison?"

He stopped in the scrub room to wash his hands. Julie pushed through into the OR.

He turned away from the sink as he scrubbed, watched through the window at what was going on, at the surgeons around the bed and the array on instruments laid out on the back table.

Lila said that surgeons were like the members of different kinds of trade unions. Vascular surgeons were plumbers. Neurosurgeons were electricians. Orthopedists were a toss-up between carpenters and blacksmiths.

Whatever trade they belonged to, surgeons loved their tools. Orthopedic surgeons had the most. They used mallets and chisels and vise grips. They put bones back together with plates and screws. They loved their power tools, their saws and drills and reamers.

Will backed into the room. He dried his hands and slipped into his gown. Julie came over and tied him up in the back. "Martha wasn't kidding about this guy," she said. "His femur is a mess."

They cleaned the wound, first, flushing out the debris, clipping the rough tissue. Then they worked on the bone. With the brown solution splashed across the skin and the lights focused down, it looked like broken china.

Jamison set the bone with an external fixator. He pierced each fragment of bone with a sharp pin that jutted straight out. He arranged the fragments and attached a crosspiece to each pin. He attached wing nuts and swivel joints to each pin. Then he ran a small framework of metal tubes through the cross pieces at right angles to the pins, forming a miniature scaffolding. Will imagined tiny cartoon workmen scrambling over it.

Jamison tried a dozen different combinations, as if he were piecing together a puzzle. He rearranged the bone fragments. Will handed him the pieces of the frame. Half the time Jamison tossed them back. Once he winged one across the room. It missed Julie by six inches as it smacked against the wall. She looked up but didn't say a word to Jamison. She just rolled her eyes at Will.

They were used to Jamison's antics. Will was happy to put up with it to be around cases like this. Even Lila respected the guy. "He's an ass," she said. "But if I break every bone in my body, he's the one I want to put me back together."

"I think we're almost there," Jamison said finally. Will looked down. The pile of broken fragments was perfectly aligned. Jamison stood back and studied his handiwork. Julie stood up and came to the edge of the sterile field. She winked at Will.

"What do you think, children?" Jamison asked.

"It's beautiful," Will said.

"What did you want to close with?" Julie asked.

Jamison drew the skin together until the scaffolding was all that was visible above the skin. It would remain there until the bone had healed, an erector set jutting out of the man's thigh.

"Sometimes the patients bitch when they wake up with this tinker-toy on their legs," Jamison said. "That's why I send the boys here," he nodded towards the residents, "To talk to them when they come out of the anesthesia. We explain to people what we're going to do every time, but I guess some of them just can't believe it."

Martha had come at six to offer Will his lunch relief, but it wasn't a good time in the case, so he waited. Only when Jamison turned the case over to the residents to close did Will send Julie to let Martha know that he was ready to scrub out.

At the end of the shift, Will sat in the lounge with a cup of coffee balanced on his stomach. One of the night nurses had called in sick and Julie had agreed to work a double. The rest of their crew had gone home and her partner for the night, Chuck Segal, was running late so she'd asked Will to wait until Chuck showed up.

The phone rang. Will sipped his coffee and set it back on his stomach.

Julie burst through the door of the nurse's locker room.

"Ruptured Triple-A," she said, hurdling his legs. "It blew in the ER. They're coming right up."

The words jerked Will to his feet as if she'd taken both his hands and dragged him. His coffee spilled and he pulled his scrub top away before it could soak through. Julie went out the other door without looking back, knowing he would be there in her wake.

In an a ruptured abdominal aortic aneurysm or Triple-A, the aorta, the large artery that delivers blood to the entire lower body weakens and blows in the abdomen, flooding the cavity with blood. Once the vessel bursts, the patient bleeds to death in minutes.

They ran into the room to get set up, opening packages in a controlled frenzy. Will slid into his gown, no time to scrub, and pulled on a pair of gloves. He tore open the wrapper for his tray and set the instruments out on the stand. He armed the knife blades. He heard Lila's words in his head.

Just slow everything down.

They came through the door with a med student straddling the patient on the stretcher, doing compressions, the kid's face as grey as the patient's. Will held out a gown and gloves for the vascular surgeon, Rick Davis. Fred Dean called out the blood pressures. " "70/palp, 65, 60..."

Davis walked into the gown and plunged his hands into the gloves that Will offered. Julie doused the belly with paint. Will pressed the knife into Davis' palm. He slit the smooth, brown skin. Blood oozed up through the incision. The belly overflowed. Davis plunged a retractor into the wound and pulled the belly open. Will placed a metal, ten-quart basin on the edge of the wound and began to bail out handfuls of clotted blood with his cupped palms. When they had bailed out enough to see the bowel, Davis pushed it aside, coil after coil of pink and yellow tissue.

With two suctions going, they could finally see the aorta, flush with the spine in the base of the cavity. Will handed Davis the longest vascular clamp he had. Davis slipped it over the pulsing vessel just above the rupture point and clamped down hard. The blood eased to a manageable flow. He leaned back and sighed. "I think we got it in time." He looked around at the room. He smiled. "The fun's over gang," he said, "Now we've got work to do."

He nodded at Will but then focused just past his shoulder. "Nice of you join us, Chuck," he said.

Will turned. Chuck Segal stood just behind him. He shook his head. "Talk about lousy timing," he said. "The rookie gets the good part and I get mop-up duty."

"Maybe Will deserves the good part," Julie said. She winked at Will, her eyes bright over her mask. "Maybe next time you'll show up for work when you're supposed to."

"She's got a point, Chuck," Davis said. "This kid has what it takes."

Chuck scrubbed in and took his place beside Will.

"Will you be okay for a minute, Chuck?" Julie asked.

He nodded.

Will peeled off his bloody gown and gloves and he and Julie walked out together. Just outside the room, she slumped against the wall, but he paced back and forth.

"Hey," she said. "Calm down. It's over. We'll slap in a graft, replace his blood volume and he'll be fine."

"I know."

"You did luck out," she said. "There's nothing like those first few minutes of a ruptured aneurysm."

She glanced down the hall. No one was in sight. She kissed him.

"I'll see you in the morning," he said.

"Why don't you stick around awhile?" she said. "You need to wind down. Sit in the lounge, put your feet up."

"That's what I was doing before you dragged me into this," he said. "I'm wired, now. I need to keep moving."

"Suit yourself."

He went into the locker room, pulled off his scrubs and slipped into shorts and a tank top. He slammed his locker door and went to the elevator. He punched the button, hit it again and decided on the third try to take the stairs. He went down the stairs two at a time, taking the last five in a leap. He burst out the door by the ER into the cool night air. He ran. He didn't stretch as he normally did, but started out on a dead run. At the point when he should have been gasping, falling apart, he just kept going, moving easily. He felt strong. He kept getting stronger. He glanced up at the sky and the stars were everywhere. He tilted his head back. His head reeling, his legs pumping, he careened on.

His foot slammed into concrete and he stumbled. He caught himself. Reluctantly, he brought his eyes down to the pavement, accelerating again, moving over sidewalks pushed skyward by bulging oak roots.

He'd lost all sense of time. He realized that he was on his street. An hour's walk covered in twenty minutes.

He sprinted the final hundred yards. Leaning past his driveway, he toppled down on his front lawn, landing on all fours, then flipped over on his back. His lungs heaving, his arms outstretched upon the grass, he watched the rivers of stars flowing in the sky.

He lay on his back until his lungs were quiet, until his head was clear. He felt the cold sweat on his back, the moisture of the grass and earth. He stood and climbed the stairs unsteadily, like a giddy drunk who has finally come down from his high.

At the top of the stairs, he paused. He frowned and walked back to the window overlooking his parking space. It was empty. He laughed out loud. He'd run home, even though he'd driven his car to work that afternoon.

FOUR

The first few days after any major surgery are frightening. In the doctor's lounge, away from the civilians, Mixter had probably summed it up best. "Having major surgery is like falling off a five story building. The only difference is that in surgery a team of doctors, nurses and techs are standing at the bottom, so that as soon as you hit the ground, they pick up the pieces and put you back together."

Lila had tried to prepare her family after Ray's surgery. She couldn't give them Mixter's version, of course, but she warned them that Ray would look pretty rough the first few days. Like most kids, they wanted their dad to be indestructible. Before this, he'd always managed to pull it off.

Thanks to new methods for open hearts, things were better than they once were. Ray lay intubated and on the respirator for only a few hours. Before he would have been hooked up for days. There was much less drainage from his wounds. The most important change was in the pain level.

Lila rubbed her chest. Once, this surgery would have resulted in a scar down Ray's chest from his neck through his breastbone. The thought of the saw tearing through the bone, of the spreader jacking the ribs apart still made her wince.

Instead, they'd worked through a port cut between his ribs.

If you had to screw up your heart, Ray, at least you got the timing right. You waited long enough. They didn't have to split you wide open.

It was still rough on the kids. They didn't care about ancient history, about advances in medicine. They just knew their father was broken and in pain. They wanted their father back. Only time would give them that.

All six of her boys were there along with their wives and her nineteen grandchildren. They'd filled the surgical waiting room, a solid mass of humanity, sipping coffee and soda, staring at the walls. They hadn't read the magazines or newspapers that were spread around the room. They hadn't talked. Even the kids were quiet. See them at the family gatherings and they were a force of nature, careening into each other on the wide lawns of Waznek Manor, but they seemed to understand that this was different, as an occasional sign or bored whimper was quickly hushed by the older children.

She loved her family. She knew that she'd never have gotten through this without them, but so many times in those few days, she'd thought that she might scream.

There wasn't enough oxygen in that goddamn closet to support 5000 pounds of Wazneks.

"I thought they'd never leave," Ray had said a few days after the surgery when he and Lila were finally alone. His voice rasped from the irritation of the ET tube.

The kids had gone home, having finally seen enough progress to get back to their lives. They could go back to work and school and visit him in shifts, but first they'd needed to see the color come back to his face, needed to hear the words from his own mouth, "Go home before I smack the lot of you."

They'd each hugged him gingerly, tying to avoid the center of his chest, until the hugs became gentle pats, as if he were a giant baby who needed to be burped.

"They just needed to be sure," Lila said. "You scared the sit out of them. First the heart attack, then you ended up in the OR. Things haven't exactly been going according to plan, you know."

"I know," he said. "I'm sorry, babe." He smiled at her. It was a sheepish grin, as if he knew that since the worst was over, he was in for it. With the grin and his soft, brown curly hair, he looked like a child.

"It isn't just the kids, you know," she said. "You scared the frigging hell out of me, too."

"I know."

"How many times have I told you to cut down on your goddamn drinking? I asked you to watch your diet, but you keep eating junk. You might as well be smearing your arteries with grease, for Christ's sake."

"I know, I'm sorry. Somehow life isn't the same without a burger and a beer every now and then."

"Every now and then?" She tried to jerk her hand away but he held tight.

"Okay, okay," he said. "I know I eat and drink the wrong stuff all the time. What can I say, Babe? I'm weak."

"Weak?" she said. "You're the strongest man I know."

He shrugged. He flexed his arms. The tattoo on his bicep flashed "Semper Fi".

"I'm not talking about muscles, babe," he said.

"And neither am I. Everything we have is because of you. You built our goddamn house from the ground up. You work fifty hours a week and then come home and work another forty around the house. You've kept these frigging mob we call a family in line, kept the boys from running wild."

Tears ran down her face. He leaned towards her and tried to swipe them away. One thick finger jabbed her eye. She jerked back. She pulled her hand from his and covered her eyes.

"Jesus, Ray."

"I'm sorry. Are you all right? I'm such a clumsy—"

"Will you cut with the bullshit?" she said. "You're not clumsy. You're not weak. You're a rock. You're my goddamn husband and I don't want to lose you. You have to start taking better care of yourself."

He held out his hand, but hers were still over her eyes.

"Are you crying?" he asked.

"Of course I'm crying. You stuck your frigging finger in my eye."

He laughed. She pulled her hand away.

"What's so goddamn funny?"

"You are," he said. "I didn't build everything we have by myself. You were there, too. You're just as strong as I am."

"We did it together," she said. "So what the hell would I do if you died on me, asshole?"

"You'd survive," he said. "You'd start over. It's what I'd want you to do."

"Are you trying to get rid of me?"

"No," he said, he patted the bed beside him. "Come here. Stop acting like a crazy woman."

She crawled up on the bed beside him.

"So," he said. "Tell me about what they just did to me."

"Mixter explained it all, weren't you listening."

"Of course, I listened. I just want to hear it from you."

"You want it in laymen's terms."

"I want it from you."

She explained the procedure to him. It wasn't exactly a bedtime story, but somehow it calmed him. His breath came easily and she thought he was asleep.

"Sounds like a pretty big deal," he said.

"It is," she said. "And it'll all be a waste if you don't change your goddamn diet and cut down on your drinking."

"Why can't they just give me a new heart?' he asked. "It took me fifty years to ruin this one. That means I'd be at least 100 before the second one gives out."

"You're frigging hopeless," she said.

"I know. I'll try to be better, babe, I promise."

His breathing soothed her and she thought they might doze off together, but he fooled her again.

"Maybe you should take off, too."

"I'm not ready to go home.'

"I didn't mean home. Maybe you could go down to the OR and see your crew.

I know how tight you are. Jerry said a lot of them stopped by when we were in ICU."

"Yeah. It was good to see them."

"I thought I knew most of them," he said. "Jerry mentioned Martha, Murph and Kathy, even that sourpuss. What's her name?"

"Melanie," she said.

"That's right," he said. "But he mentioned someone else. Some kid? Jerry said he came by more than anyone, but I didn't recognize his name."

She couldn't look at him. She prayed he was still dozing, half asleep, that when she looked at him his eyes would still be closed, that she wouldn't have to wonder how much her face betrayed.

"What did he say the name was, Bob, Bill…?" he mumbled.

She finally took the chance. She looked at him. His eyes were closed.

"Will," she said as she took his hand.

"How long has he been working with you?"

"I guess a couple months. He graduated from tech school in May."

"You've never mentioned him. You usually talk about the new ones, the 'fresh meat'?"

It was true. She always told him about all the young studs that came to work with them. It was a game they played. She'd get wound up talking about them. Foreplay, that's what it was.

In the end, though, it was just she and Ray. She'd never been one to close her eyes and pretend that her husband was someone else.

"I'm sure I said something," she said. She ran her fingers though his hair. "You just forgot."

He pulled his hand away from her and covered his eyes with his forearm. "Maybe," he said. "My brain is pretty messed up these days."

She touched his cheek. He placed his hand over hers.

"You know how clogged up your pipes were," she said. "Maybe you're not getting enough oxygen to your brain."

"Maybe I need brain surgery, too?"

"That might not be a bad idea," she said. She touched his throat. Her fingers rested on his carotid artery. She felt the sure and steady pulse. She let it calm her.

"Maybe I could get a brain transplant," he said. He chuckled. "Maybe they could just replace everything and we could start from scratch."

His breath grew more even. Soon it was as steady as his pulse. This time he was asleep.

Ray rolled over and the lines on the monitor jumped for an instant, then settled back.

It's a good thing those aren't strapped to me. I'd be sending them right off the charts.

She stroked Ray's hair, smoothing down the rough tangles.

What was she going to do? He'd mentioned Will and she'd gone crazy. At first, she thought he was figuring things out, but why would he be suspicious? She'd never given him reason to be. Thirty-five years together and she'd never been unfaithful to him.

He wondered why she'd never told him about Will. She wondered why she hadn't used Will in their game. Will pushed more buttons for her than anyone ever had.

Because he isn't a game, something to prime the pump for me and Ray.

Anything that started with Will would have to end there. She didn't want him in the bed with she and Ray, she wanted him all to herself.

She'd never played around. She'd played the game with Ray, talked with the girls in the locker room, but that was it. Will was the first one who'd ever made her want to act. Talk about bad timing.

She'd known she had to put these feelings away, bury them deep down where no one else could see them. She'd lived without Will Nathan for fifty years. Just like that transplant heart Ray wanted, she could manage another fifty.

That was when she had decided to take a leave of absence. It was as much about putting distance between she and Will as taking care of Ray.

FIVE

As he drove to work the following Wednesday, Will hoped that Martha wouldn't assign Julie to work with him on Sheila Cole. They hadn't spoken about the case all week, but he didn't think that silence would survive another round.

In the lounge, Murph and Kathy were already in their seats.

Kathy began the battle with her hair, tying up the ends, coiling it around her head. She held it in place with one hand and slipped the cap over it.

"Are you doing that Sheila Cole kid, today?" Murph asked.

"She's on the schedule," Will said.

"But are you going to be in there again?"

"Yeah. You know it's my case, now."

Murph shook his head. "Don't know how you do it, man. Burns give me the creeps." He shuddered "And this one really is the pits."

"You get used to it," Will said. Julie walked in the door as if on cue. She brushed his shoulder and sat beside him. Melanie sulked across the aisle.

"Good evening, everyone," Martha said as she came though the door.

"Good evening," Will answered for all of them.

"It's Wednesday," Martha said, "So that means Sheila Cole is back. Will, I want you down there, of course. Julie, I need you to work with him."

"Can't you assign somebody else?" Julie asked.

The lounge fell silent. Martha looked up from her papers.

"Is there a problem, Julie?" Martha asked.

Julie blushed and played with the fringe of her ankle socks, cream colored with lace and sequins.

"No problem," Julie said. "I just wondered if you could put somebody else in there tonight. It's a nasty case. It only seems fair to rotate people in and out."

"Well," Martha said. "I might have done that if you'd mentioned your problem sooner."

Julie flushed. She glanced at Will, but he looked at the floor.

What does she want from me?

"I told you, Martha," Julie said. "I don't have a problem. I just want things to be fair." She looked around the room, but no one met her gaze.

Only Martha would look at her. "All right, Julie,' she said but the frown on her face was the opposite of agreement. "I'll talk to the rest of the crew and see how they feel. Perhaps some of the seven o'clock people would be able to do the first half of the case from now on. Tonight, however, you're doing the case and that's final."

Martha ran through the rest of the assignments. Will hadn't seen her this angry for a long time.

When Martha left the room, Will leaned in towards Julie, but she jerked away.

"Hey, Julie," Murph said. "Don't let Martha get you down. I know just how you feel. I was telling Will earlier. That room is a regular freak show."

"Thanks, Murph," Julie said.

"Of course, we can afford to be sympathetic," Kathy said as she stood up. She offered Murph her hand and pulled him to his feet.

"We know where we're going to be every night and it isn't with Sheila Cole," she said. "You won't make too many friends with the rest of the crew, though, if you suck them into that quagmire."

"But it's only fair," Julie said.

Melanie got to her feet. "I guess it is," she said, "If by fair you mean that everybody gets fucked over equally."

She walked out of the lounge.

"Hey," Julie yelled after her, but she didn't look back. Murph and Kathy shifted uncomfortably on their feet.

"Don't mind her," Murph said. "You know she's always got a stick up her ass."

Julie covered her face with her hand. Kathy caught Will's eye and jerked her head in Julie's direction.

Like I can fix this mess.

He waved at Murph and Kathy to leave. They went out the door.

He put his arm on Julie's shoulder. This time, she let him.

"Melanie?" She said. "The nastiest bitch in the OR is telling me that I'm screwing everybody?"

"Don't listen to her Jules. You know—"

She stood and shrugged his arm away.

"As if you don't feel the same way," she said without looking at him. "Come on, let's get this nightmare over with."

She stormed out of the lounge. Will stared at the doorway. He watched the light from the hall stream into the dull grey of the lounge.

Why does she have to be this way? Is she trying to ruin everything for me?

SIX

Lila stayed with Ray for two months after his surgery. She was restless after the first few weeks, but she stayed.

"Please," he said finally. "Go back to work. Talk to Martha before we kill each other. You know the reason our marriage has worked for thirty years is because we both do our own thing. You've had my back these last few months and I love you for it, babe, but enough is enough. You know you miss it. You miss the work. You miss your people. I'm fine. The doctor says I'm good as new. Get your life back. It's time."

My man. He thinks he knows me so well. I would have gone back after that first month, but I'm afraid to see Will. But it's not like I can hide from this forever.

She kissed Ray and climbed into her truck. She headed for the hospital, even though it was after nine o'clock. Things would be winding down and she'd have a chance to talk to Martha.

And Will.

Julie and Kathy were sitting in the lounge when she got to the OR. They didn't notice when she came in.

"I'm on my break," Julie said to Kathy. "I just needed to get out of there for awhile."

When she saw Lila, Julie glared defiantly, as if she expected a comment.

"How's it going ladies?" Lila asked. "Sounds like they're messed up for you, Julie. Anything I can do to help?"

Julie seemed shocked by the question, but she rallied.

"No," she said. "Not unless you want to suit up and head down to Room Ten. We've got this burn case we've been doing for the last month and it's nasty."

"Those can be rough," Lila said as she sat down beside them.

"At least you're getting used to it," Kathy said.

"I knew I'd get used to it," Julie said. "It's not really the blood and gore that gets to me. It's just seems so pointless. All the work we're doing and the kid's still going to be hideous. I wonder if she'll end up thanking us or hating us."

"It's a good thing we don't work for gratitude," Lila said.

Julie glared at her. Lila hadn't meant it as a put-down.

"Didn't Will want to take a break?" Kathy asked.

"You know how he is. He doesn't want to leave if it's a rough spot in the case and this is just one big rough spot."

That's my boy.

She looked up and Julie was watching her. She seemed to be daring Lila to speak.

She probably thinks I'm pissed off because she left Will in the room. Hell, she did him a favor. Her relief, whoever it is, has to be an improvement over her whiney ass.

"Will's pretty intense about this stuff," Kathy said.

Julie waited. They both looked at Lila.

"He is wound a bit tight," Lila said. "But that's part of what we like about him."

"That and those abs," Kathy said.

They all laughed together, bound by their feelings for Will.

What they don't know won't hurt them.

When Julie went back to work, Lila visited with Kathy until Martha was free. They agreed she'd start again the following Monday. She was done by ten-thirty but she waited for Will.

As if that wasn't always the plan.

She didn't see him until the shift was almost over. She found him in the lounge slumped in a chair. She sat down just across from him. He didn't open his eyes. She heard his breath, slow and even. His skin was pale, his head tilted to one side. Drool trickled out the side of his mouth.

That's my stud.

She leaned towards him and ran her fingers though his hair.

He stirred. He opened his eyes. He smiled.

"Hey, Lila," he said. He frowned. As if there was something he was trying to remember.

"You're not supposed to be here," he said. "You're on leave."

"I'm coming back. I stopped by to set it up with Martha."

"That's great," he said. "I still remember that C-Section we did just before you went on leave."

"I remember it, too."

He closed his eyes and she thought he'd fall back to sleep.

"Rough night?" she asked.

"Yeah," he said without opening his eyes.

"That burn patient sounds like a rough one."

"Yeah."

"I'm sure Martha would let you out if you asked."

"She already offered. I'm going to stick it out. I know it better than anybody. It gets a little easier every week."

"If this is easier, I'm glad I didn't see you after the first night."

He smiled. He opened his eyes.

"I'll talk to Martha," she said, "And have her put me in there with you from now on."

"That'd be nice."

"I'm way behind, though. You'll have to help me get up to speed."

"It'll be my pleasure."

SEVEN

Will and Julie had separate apartments but spent every night together. Wednesday nights they stayed at his place. Julie was quiet on the drive home. He hoped she'd stay that way. He didn't need the "Why are we wasting our time on Sheila Cole?" debate tonight.

Still, he could see by the expression on her face that it was coming, that tonight would to be a rehash of last week's argument.

She looked in his direction.

Here it comes.

"Lila can be such a bitch, sometimes," she said.

"What do you mean?"

"She came into the lounge before she talked to Martha. I tried to talk to her about Sheila Cole. I told her that sometimes I wondered how Sheila would feel when all this was over. Would she thank us or hate us. Do you know what Lila said? 'It's a good thing we don't work for gratitude.'"

He reached across the seat and covered her hands as they rested in her lap.

"That's just Lila," he said. "You can't take it personally."

She jerked her hands away.

"Of course you'd take her side," she said.

"Her side? What are you talking about?"

"I don't know which of you is worse," she said. She turned away from him and stared out the window. "You both think you're better than the rest of us."

"Come on, Julie. Where's this coming from?" He put his hand on her shoulder and tried to pull her back. "This isn't about taking sides. It isn't about being better than anybody else. Lila's hard core. You have to look past it, that's all. If you worry about it, you'll drive yourself nuts."

"So what's your excuse?"

"My excuse?"

"Sure," she said. "At least Lila's looking down on me from thirty year's experience. Why are you all holier-than-thou? Won't take your lunch break unless 'the time is right'. Volunteer to do Sheila Cole every week when the only sane thing to do is get the hell out of there. Sometimes, Will, you make me sick."

Don't hold back girl, tell me how you really feel.

They drove the next block in silence. Will stared straight ahead, stunned by the vehemence of her anger. He waited for it to pass, for her to come down, to hear her own words and apologize. He looked at her, but she glared at the dashboard.

He glanced into the rear-view mirror and whipped the car into a U-turn.

"What are you doing?"

"Taking you home."

"We're almost home."

"I meant your home. I'll drop you off. I don't want to stay with you tonight."

He felt her hand on his shoulder.

Too little, too late.

"Are you serious?" She asked.

"Of course I'm serious," he said. "I make you sick. Why would you want to be around me? I'm doing you a favor."

She didn't speak, at first, but as they got closer and closer to her apartment, perhaps she realized that this wasn't a bluff. Perhaps she finally realized she'd gone too far. He could feel her fidgeting in the seat beside him. He glanced over. She picked at the lace fringe of her ankle socks. When she looked at him, he looked away.

He pulled up outside her apartment building and idled at the curb.

"Turn off the car," she said.

"I'm not staying."

She reached across to turn off the ignition and he pinned her hand. They glared at each other. He released her hand and turned the key himself.

"You're really leaving?" she asked. "You're serious?"

"Weren't you?"

"Look," she said. "I'm sorry. Sometimes work makes me a little crazy, but nothing ever seems to bother you. It's not normal. Lila's the same way. I can't compete with that."

"Compete? Who said anything about competing?"

"We work together, Will," she said. "We work together and you're a fanatic about the work we do. I'm competing whether I want to or not."

"I don't see it that way."

"Of course you don't. You don't even think about it. You don't think about breathing, either, do you?"

She took his hand. He fought the urge to jerk it away. Still, he couldn't pretend everything was okay.

"Come upstairs," she said.

"No. This is too weird for me Julie. You should have heard yourself. It was like you hated me."

"You know what they say, 'There's a thin line...'"

She smiled at him, but it was little comfort.

"I'll be over tomorrow," he said. "We can have lunch." He knew they'd have to talk before work. He didn't want this hanging over their heads on the job.

Maybe I should just go in tonight. Settle it now. Who am I kidding? That's not the kind of settling we need.

"This is just what I was talking about," she said. "You'll go home and be up all night wondering how you ever hooked up with the likes of me. Forget lunch tomorrow. Forget the whole thing. Why don't you call Lila and have a good laugh at my expense? Oh, wait, she's home with her husband. At least somebody won't be sleeping alone tonight."

She shoved her door open.

"Come on, Julie. You started this..."

"If that's what you think, than we really are in trouble," she said as she slammed the door.

He watched her as she climbed the stairs. Even in anger, she walked the walk. It took everything he had not to follow her.

He turned the key, put the car in gear and hit the gas.

Julie was right about one thing. He knew he couldn't call Lila, but it would have nice to have somebody to talk to, somebody who'd understand. Lila would have been the best choice, maybe the only choice. What did that say about his life, these days that his best chance for empathy was from a fifty-year-old woman?

He had friends, of course, but they pretty much broke down into two groups. Half of them were scattered at colleges across the Eastern seaboard. The rest of his old crew had regular jobs, anything that paid the bills. He still hung out with them. Not as much since he'd been with Julie, but he knew they didn't hold it against him.

These guys just weren't talkers. Besides, if he told any of them that he was feuding with a fine woman over his job, they'd tell him to get his head examined.

So, who else was there? Murph? He wasn't much different than the old crowd. He was someone to work out with, have a few beers. He cared about the job, but he'd found his place in the heart room. He'd be on Julie's side with this one, anyway. Sheila Cole gave him the Willies.

Julie had good questions about this case. That's why he didn't like to talk about it. Should they have just let this girl die after they pulled her from the wreck? Were they fixing her just because they could?

Wasn't his refusal to discuss those questions proof that they were valid? The only thing different about he and Julie was that she asked questions so she wouldn't have to do the job. He didn't ask them so he could keep doing it.

And what would Lila say if he asked her about all this?

Quit your frigging jawing. We've got work to do.

He and Lila didn't need to debate the merits of the case. Next week they'd be doing it together while Julie slid back to something less confusing. Maybe they'd all be able to get back to normal. But could they really? Julies' feelings about Sheila Cole were valid. Her contempt for him was another story.

What in hell am I going to do with that?

EIGHT

Trouble in paradise?

Lila studied Will and Julie at report the next afternoon. They weren't sitting together. Will glanced at Julie once or twice, but she stared sullenly ahead. Melanie slumped in the seat beside her. She'd seemed as surprised as everyone else to find it empty.

Julie's angry scowl mirrored Melanie's usual look.

Double your pleasure.

Lila and Will got a hip with Jamison, an eighty-three-year-old man who'd fallen at his nursing home. They'd fix it with a plate and compression screw.

"You doing okay?" she asked him as he scrubbed. She turned towards the window and studied the room.

"I'm fine," he said.

"Trouble at home?"

"You could say that."

"Then it's a good thing we got Jamison. You won't have time to think about it for awhile."

"Sounds good to me."

True to form, Jamison kept them hopping and Lila could see the tension drain from Will's face.

Nothing like the job to get one's mind in the right place.

They took their break together after the case. Julie was in a room. She and Will usually swapped around to go together, but Will didn't say a word to Martha. They went out on the roof. They hadn't been out there together since the Fourth of July.

Hard to believe that it was two months ago. My butt parked on the window ledge, him sitting with his back against the wall. Those are the only things that haven't changed.

"So," she asked. "Do you want to talk about it?"

"It's complicated," he said.

"You don't think I can handle complicated?"

He stood up and walked to the edge of the roof. He turned back towards her. The surface of the roof was crushed rock embedded in tar. He squatted down, picked up a loose stone. He stood up and tossed the stone a few feet in the air, then caught it. He tossed it up in the air again and winged it out into the wide green lawn that ran behind the hospital.

"You know that Julie's freaking out about Sheila Cole," he said.

"Yeah," she said. "Even Melanie busted her chops the other day."

"I don't blame Melanie," he said. "The way Julie's whining, the way she wants to drag everybody else into working on Sheila. I don't like it much myself."

He bent down to pick up another stone. This time he tossed it at a large rock at the edge of the lawn, a gray spot in uncut green. The rock disappeared harmlessly into the grass.

"Her whining is bad enough," he said, "But it isn't the worst thing. Now, she's tearing me up because I'm not freaking out like her."

"You've got to be kidding me," Lila said. She slid down off the window ledge. She scooped up a stone as she walked towards Will and took aim at the same rock that he'd targeted. She threw the stone and missed.

"She went off on me last night on the way home," he said. "You should have heard her. She says I'm a freak because it doesn't bother me. Like I'm too cold to ask questions about what we're doing."

This time anger fueled his arm and his shot sailed ten feet past the rock.

"Do you ask questions?"

"Not out loud."

"But you ask them?"

"Of course I do. I'm not an idiot. I'm not an insensitive bastard, either."

"I doubt that she called you that."

"Pretty much."

"So what if she did? Screw her. This isn't about you, Will. It's about her. She can't handle the case, but she can't admit that. It's easier for her to tear you down."

She picked up another stone and tossed it. It soared over the rock, still rising as it plunked into a tree.

"Then what am I supposed to do?"

"Tell her to kiss your ass."

Will laughed and shook his head. He winged one stone after another as he zeroed in. Finally, he hit dead center.

"All right," he said and turned towards her with his hand outstretched for a high-five. She smacked it.

"I was right about one thing," he said.

"What's that?"

"You really don't do complicated, do you? Come on. Martha's going to send out a search party if we don't get back."

NINE

The week went by too quickly. Lila rested her arms on the window ledge in the scrub room as Will washed his hands, steeling himself for another bout with Sheila Cole.

He and Julie were still at odds. They'd had lunch the day after their fight, but they hadn't settled anything. It seemed as if she didn't understand anything that mattered to him. He couldn't believe that she had worked in the OR for so long and learned so little.

I guess she's right about one thing. I am looking down on her.

They'd finally just stopped talking about any of it. They both seemed to sense that they were close to the kinds of words that couldn't be unsaid.

Although I wonder if we really have a choice.

Will glanced at Lila, but she was focused on the room. They hadn't talked about it all week either.

"Things don't look so bad," Lila said. "There's too many doctors in the room, but I guess we can handle that."

"You know you can't really tell from this side of the glass," he said. "You can't feel anything."

She tapped her fingers on the glass and looked back over her shoulder. She smiled and he realized he'd practically called her a rookie.

"Are you ready?" she asked.

"Yeah, could you scratch my nose?"

She pulled the mask down to the tip of his nose and ran her finger up and down the bridge, surprising him with the gentleness of her touch.

“How’s that?” she asked.

“That’s nice.”

She slid the mask back up into place and pushed through the door. He followed her.

He was right about the glass. When he moved into the room, the humidity, the odors, and the feelings were all there, as if he'd never left. He took a breath. It was different. The tension he had come to recognize had changed, replaced by something new. He looked to Fred and the anesthesia team. They were talking quietly, seemingly at ease. The monitors were good. The girl was stable. The surgeons were the ones this time. They seemed angry about everything, as if for the first time they knew the girl was going to live, and it really was the quality of her life that they were holding in their hands. Maybe touch-and-go was better than whatever this day was really all about.

At five Martha offered to relieve Lila for lunch. By now she knew better than to ask Will. Lila turned her down, as well.

“You don’t have to stay,” he said after Martha had left the room. Even she was shaking her head at them.

“We know what’s what,” Lila said. “We might as well stick it out.”

At ten Shea pulled off his gloves, slumped down onto a stool and rolled back into the corner. "Get the dressings on her," he said. "Leave her lying on her right side the first four hours." He stood up. "Thank you, Lila, Will." He left the room.

Lila had the dressings ready and he held them up for Will.

"Damn, I'm beat," he said.

"The worst is over," she said.

When the dressings were complete and the linen pulled away, Will looked down at the girl. Only her face was left uncovered, her breathing tube in place, her eyes taped shut so they would not dry out while she was under anesthesia. He touched her forehead. It was one of the few places without a burn, without a bandage.

Their work complete, the residents slipped away, leaving Lila, Will and Fred Dean to get her to the Intensive Care Unit. They transferred her from the OR bed to the ICU model she'd been transported on. They pushed her back to the Unit.

The charge nurse took one look at them and groaned. "She's supposed to be lying on her left side," she said.

"Shea said the right," Lila said.

"Well, he was just here," she said. She flipped the chart open and showed Lila the orders. "He wants her turned every four hours, and he said he wanted her to start her on her left side. You should have turned her in OR when you had a lot of help."

"He must have changed his mind on the way over," Lila said. "Let's do it."

They wheeled her into her room. There was room enough for her bed and for perhaps two people to get around easily. Here, too, the humidity was high. In the smaller room it seemed much warmer. Everything seemed magnified. "It's so frigging hot," Lila said. Will nodded. He'd been holding himself together for too long. He knew how many steps it was from the OR to Intensive Care, and he had paced them off. He had promised himself that that would be it, and now he had to go a little farther.

The ICU charge nurse came back in with two of her nurses. Martha was just behind them. "I thought I'd make sure there weren't any problems," she said.

"Now, there's a thought," Lila said.

The ICU nurses lined up on one side of the bed and gently slipped their arms beneath Sheila's body. Lila, Will and Martha stood across from them, pressed together, their arms straight out before them, forming a bed to receive her. Fred Dean stood at the head. "Just say when," Will said.

"Okay," Fred said. "On three. One, two, three." The nurses lifted her in unison, brought her up level with Will and the others. "Ready," Martha said. Fred gripped her shoulders and rolled her slowly onto their waiting arms.

"Okay," the ICU charge said, "Hold her there for a minute while I straighten out her linen."

They held the body out before them as the nurse tugged and smoothed the sheet. The heat closed in on Will. The film of sweat upon his face was no protection. He held his muscles tense and tight. He felt them where they joined: forearms, biceps, shoulders, lower back. He felt Lila pressed against him along his left side, Martha on the right. The bandages were warm against his forearms. The smell was sweet inside his nostrils. Martha's perfume, laced with sweat, jockeyed for position in his skull. So much, he thought. So much.

"Okay," the nurses said. "All set. Let her down easy."

They set her down. Will lingered for an instant, his face inches away from her, then pulled his arms away reluctantly, as one by one the sensations slipped away, until he was left only with the trembling of his muscles and an absence that he could not bear.

* * * *

"So how were things with Sheila Cole," Julie asked him as they drove home that night.

Will didn't answer. How could he tell her that he'd loved today, that he ached for the feel of Martha and Lila against his side, of Sheila Cole resting lightly on his arms, the air pressing in around him? She'd be right back to calling him a freak.

He knew he couldn't tell her. He needed Lila.

"It went okay," he said.

"What was that mess about in the ICU?" she asked.

"Shea changed the orders on us, so we had to turn her," he said.

"Shea is such an asshole," she said.

"Aren't they all?"

TEN

Lila came to work early the next day. She got her assignment from Martha before report and went down to her room to talk to the daytime circulating nurse. Once that was out of the way, she'd be able to wait with Will while he scrubbed. It would be their time.

"So how did you sleep last night?" she asked him when they were alone.

"Like a baby," he said.

She leaned on the window ledge, her back to him.

"Things went pretty frigging smooth yesterday, didn't they?" she asked. "Except for that screw-up in the ICU."

"That wasn't so bad," he said.

"What are talking about?" she asked. "That was insane."

"It's complicated," he said. "Maybe we can talk later."

"Okay," she said. She pulled his mask down and scratched his nose. "Ready to go?" she asked.

He didn't answer. She looked up at him. He seemed puzzled. She realized that she'd scratched his nose without being asked.

"Sorry," she said.

"No," he said. "It's fine. You read my mind, that's all."

As long as you don't start reading mine, kid.

They didn't have time for complicated the rest of the night. They did a knee with Jamison and an intracranial pressure monitor. Will took his breaks with Julie, of course.

Lila sat with Will at the end of the shift, but she knew they'd only have a minute before Julie was ready to head home. She was going to have to make the most of those visits in the scrub room.

Will's going to have to learn to talk fast.

"I guess our talk will have to wait," she said.

"I guess so."

"Well, you know I'm here for you, when you're ready to talk, I mean."

"I know that. Thanks a lot."

She went into the locker room and changed. She studied herself in the mirror. She wore a tight black sleeveless top and a denim skirt. The top should have been a belly shirt if she really wanted to be in style. She ran her hand over her stomach. She felt her stretch marks. Delivering six boys would do that. No amount of sit-ups could make them disappear. That's why there were tummy tucks. Another advantage to being doctor material, an advantage she'd never really know.

She heard Julie's voice. She headed towards the door.

The wind blew in the parking garage. As always, it seemed stronger here, pressed between the layers of concrete. It made her regret her short sleeves, but she was grateful for the stiff denim. She wasn't ready to do a Marilyn Monroe impression as she walked to the truck, wrestling with her skirt.

She shivered, hugged herself and walked faster.

"Lila, wait!"

She jumped. The voice was too close, right behind her. She realized that it was Will. She turned to him.

"Did I scare you?" he asked. "I'm sorry."

"You surprised me," she said. "I figure there might to be weirdos lurking out here late at night. A voice in my ear is pretty much proof of that."

"I'm sorry. I never thought of that."

"Don't worry about it." The breeze picked up, swirling a bright orange scrap of cellophane past their feet and under her truck. She shivered.

"You're cold," he said. He slipped out of his sweatshirt and draped it over her shoulders.

"Did you have to go right home?" he asked.

"Of course, I do. If I'm not in the door by one, Ray has the state troopers scouring the trees along the side of Route Nine for wrecks."

He pulled the collar of his sweatshirt snug around her throat.

"Maybe you could call him," he said. "Tell him you're going to be late."

They'd reached her truck. She rummaged in her purse for her keys.

"Why am I going to be late?" she asked, "And where's Julie, anyway?"

"She's working a double. Chuck called in sick at the last minute."

Lila leaned back against the truck. The sweatshirt and her top bunched up in the back and her bare skin brushed the cool metal. She jerked away, pulled the shirt down, leaned back.

I need to lean on something. I don't trust my legs to hold me up.

"I just figured that with Julie working, it would give us a chance to talk about last night."

"Sure," she said. "Just let me call Ray." She got her phone out of her purse. She looked up and he was still right there. "Back off a bit, will you? I don't like to talk in front of people."

"Sure," he said. He walked ten feet away, turned and raised his arms.

"Far enough?" he asked.

"That's fine," she said. She turned her back to him. She dialed the phone. It rang a half dozen times before Ray picked up.

"Hello," he said.

"Hi Ray."

"Hey, babe. What's up? You okay?"

"Yeah. I'm just going to be late. Chuck Segal called in sick, so I have to hang around until they get somebody else in here. It shouldn't be later than two or three."

"Why do you have to do it? Can't they find somebody else?"

"It's just my turn, Ray."

"I suppose. You guys need a union, somebody to stand up for you," he said. He paused, caught between anger and sleep.

What am I caught between?

"I have to go," she said.

"Okay. Call me if it's going to be later than you said."

"Okay."

"Don't work to hard."

"I won't."

How can I even say the words? Why don't they stick in my throat?

She hit "end" and turned back to Will. He came towards her as soon as she put the phone in her purse.

"Now what?" she asked. "Did you want to sit in the truck?"

"No way," he said. "Let's go someplace warm. Let me buy you a beer."

They went to "Jack's Pub", the hangout for the hospital. It was crowded.

"I think I'll just go up to bar," Will said, "It'll probably take forever for a waitress to find us. What'll it be?"

"Get me a Fosters.

"The big can?"

"You know it."

She scanned the room for familiar faces. Surprisingly, Kathy and Murph weren't here. They must have gone straight home. She saw Melanie in the corner.

Melanie must have felt her gaze. She looked at Lila, and then her glance slipped over to Will at the bar. Lila waited for some reaction, but nothing came. Melanie turned back to the guy across the table from her, who'd been talking the whole time. She gave him the same look of bored indifference that she wore every day at work.

Maybe it was time for them to reconsider their view of Melanie as a short-timer in the OR. She'd probably be with them for a long time.

If she carries that look with her everywhere, than no Prince Charming is going to save her from a life of blood and guts.

Will returned with the beer. He'd gotten a large can for himself, too. Four beers for the price of two. If this were a fast food joint, they'd say he'd supersized their order. The cans sat in a bucket of ice. She picked up hers, cradling the cool metal in her hands. She took a long pull and felt the cold, smooth liquid run down her throat. She waited for it to settle her. Nothing.

She looked at Will and he was watching her. She nodded in Melanie's direction. He looked over and smiled.

"A face only a mother could love," he said.

"You got that right. I was just thinking that we might be stuck with her for a long time."

"I don't know," he said. "Some guys like the sullen types. They're a challenge."

"You've got to be kidding me."

"No. That guy probably thinks that he's the only man in the world who could ever make her smile."

Lila glanced back over at them. The guy was working hard, but he didn't look upset. Maybe Will was right.

She took another sip. It was getting warmer in the place, so she slid his sweatshirt off her shoulders. She glanced at her watch.

"If we're going to talk, we'd better get started," she said. "What's so important that you had to kidnap an old lady and mess with her beauty sleep?"

"Don't talk that way," he said. "You're not so old and you look great. You should give yourself more credit."

She blushed.

Okay, Lila, it worked. You went fishing for a compliment and you hit pay dirt.

"I know," she said. "That's just talk."

"So cut it out," he said. He reached across the table for her hand. She pulled it away.

"Enough about me," she said. "We came here to talk about you. Why aren't you upset about what happened in ICU last night?"

He leaned back against the stiff black leather of the booth. He took a long pull from his beer, the same kind that she'd taken when she'd sat down.

"Do you ever just love the work Lila?"

"Love it? Sure, why else would I do this? Where's this coming from, anyway?"

"From working with Sheila Cole."

"I get that," Lila said. "Things are going well. She's going to make it. She'll have it rough for awhile, but--"

"That's not what I'm talking about, Lila. I don't care about any of that. I don't care about *her*. Everybody thinks I'm some kind of hero, but I'm not. I don't sign up for this one because of Sheila Cole. I don't do it to spare my co-workers. I do it for myself, for the way it makes me feel. I can't get enough of it. Does that make any sense?"

Lila sat stunned. Of course it made sense. It was what kept her going, but she'd never met anyone else who was willing to talk about it.

"Go on," she said.

"Like yesterday," he said. "The case went on forever. It took everything I had to keep on top of things, and I knew, I just knew that I was the only one in the entire crew who could pull it off."

"You did good work. You were proud of yourself. That's only human."

He shook his head. "I know that. It's more than that. After the case, when we took her to the ICU, I knew just how far it was, how many steps even. I counted them last week. This week, I counted the steps and I knew that I was just going to make it, that once we got her in the door, I'd be done. I knew I wouldn't be able to do another thing. We'd hand her off to the ICU nurses and then I'd crash."

"And then we weren't done," she said.

"That's right, but when we had to turn her, when you and me and Martha were holding her up, it was such a rush. I felt so alive. I didn't want it to stop. And when we put her down, when we walked away, it was like somebody shot me, like I was dead.

"One minute I was working on every cylinder, my senses in overdrive and then, nothing. I hated the way that felt. I wanted the good feeling back."

He stopped, as if he'd died again. As if there wasn't anything left. He grinned, as if now that he'd finally gotten it out, he wished that he could take it back.

Too late for that.

"Does any of this make sense?" he asked.

"Of course it does," she said. "The work is rough, sometimes. We need to focus and we need adrenaline to pull us through. Sometimes I think it's addictive."

"I suppose."

They finished their beer in silence. On the drive back to the hospital they made small talk. He walked her back to her truck. She snuck a glance at him. He looked so sad, but what did she expect? He'd given her mystical and she'd answered with "whatever it takes." He fancied himself something special and she'd told him he was just another adrenaline junkie.

Why had she done it? She was watching out for him. She wanted to make sure he didn't burn out before his time.

But he hadn't really asked for her protection. He felt something and wanted to know if she felt the same way. He wanted a partner and she'd given him a mother.

She always chastised herself for wanting him, always reminding herself that she was being foolish, that they were too different, but when he'd held his hand out to her, she'd slapped it away.

When they reached the truck, she didn't get in, but leaned back against the door on the driver's side.

"I'm sorry," she said.

"Sorry?" he said. "What are you sorry for?" The sad look disappeared. He seemed puzzled. He leaned against the truck, his shoulder touching the metal at a right angle to her. She felt his warmth in sharp contrast to the cool metal against her back.

"I know it took a lot for you to talk about all this and I pretty much shot you down."

"You were just being—"

"Let me finish. You're right about all of this. We do get caught up in the work. We have to. We forget everything, even the people that we're trying to fix. What you said about Sheila Cole, that you didn't care about her, would scare most people, but I know exactly how you feel. That's why I'm sorry. I should have told you that I understand."

"You're the only one I could tell," he said.

"I know," she said. "You deserved better from me."

She dug into her purse and found her keys. She unlocked the door. "I should stop trying to protect you."

"Protect me." He touched her shoulder. "Why would you try to protect me?"

"Maternal instinct, I guess."

He kept his hand on her shoulder. He squeezed. "I don't want you to be my mother," he said.

She turned into him and he kissed her. His hand slid down and caressed her stomach. She cringed as his fingers slid beneath the smooth fabric of the top and found the rough ridges of her stretch marks. He hesitated. She thought he would pull away, but he spread his fingers, stroking gently.

She reached down and pulled his hand away. She turned her face away from his. They stood for a moment, pressed together against the truck.

"I'm sorry,' he said.

"Don't be," she said. "I've wanted you to do that for a long time. It's just that I've got Ray and you've got Julie."

"I don't think that's going to last." He slid his hand down to her stomach, grazing her breast. She didn't stop him. Her hands rested on his chest.

"Why won't it last?" she asked.

"She doesn't understand the work," he said. "She's a good nurse, but I think this is just a job to her."

He caressed her stretch marks.

"Don't," she said. She pulled his hand away, laced her fingers through his and held them down by her side.

"What?"

"I know my stomach is gross," she said.

"No, it's not," he said. "It's just a part of you."

"Yeah, the tired, worn out part."

"I told you not to talk that way." He tried to free his hand, but she clamped down hard. He smiled, but pulled harder. They could have been arm wrestling.

"I'm just being honest, kid."

"Will," he said.

"What?"

"Don't call me a kid. My name is Will." He jerked his fingers away. She blocked the route to her stomach, so he caressed her cheek. He kissed her again. This time she didn't fight.

"What about your husband?" he asked when they finally broke apart. "Do you think that's going to last?"

She laughed, jarring herself from the soft haze of the kiss. "You mean for another thirty years?"

He nodded, accepting the humor, it seemed, as easily as he accepted everything about her.

"Ray's not a part of this," she said, "Whatever happens here is separate from my life with him."

"What if I don't want to share?"

She slid away from him. He fell against the truck. "Then nothing happens," she said.

"Okay."

He kissed her again, and this time it was her turn to let her hands explore. She ran her hands up and down his arms, caressed his abs. They were everything that she'd thought they'd be.

If only the girls in the locker room could see me now.

She grabbed the drawstring of his scrubs and pulled.

"Whoa!" he said as he pulled away.

"Too much?"

"We are in a parking garage," he said. He pulled the scrubs tight again.

"We could go to my place," he said.

We sure as hell can't go to mine.

"Okay."

"I'll give you the address. I'll get my car and meet you there." He fumbled in his pocket for something to write on.

"No," she said. "I'll ride with you. We can come back for my truck."

"That's crazy, Lila. Why do you want to come back here? What if somebody sees your truck and wonders why you haven't gone home? What if they see us together when we come back?"

She frowned. She hadn't thought of that. She hadn't had any experience with sneaking around. As far as wanting to ride with him, it was simple. She was afraid that if she had time to think about it, she'd take the turn on Route Nine and head for home.

She took his hand. "I just never thought you and I would end up here," she said. "I want to enjoy every minute."

"But—"

"Don't," she said. She figured he was going to say something about having plenty of time, but they didn't. She knew that. Just a few hours because her husband was asleep, because Julie was doing a double shift. There was nothing promised after tonight.

They walked to his car. After they got out of the garage, she slid across the seat and pressed against him. She hadn't ridden this close to Ray since high school.

Because you grew up, Lila. Because you got a life.

But wasn't this life, too? She felt the kid's warmth, smelled him. He shifted in the seat beside her. He looked at her, his face flushed and she understood that his body was reacting to hers just as hers was to his. She put her hand into his lap for confirmation.

"Come on, Lila," he said. "I'm driving here."

Great. We'll run off the road and the EMT's will find me with his dick in my hand.

It all came back to her. Lying to Ray on the phone. Will worrying that someone would see her truck. Was it worth it?

The kid smiled at her.

Oh yeah.

She liked his apartment. It was a real bachelor pad, a place to make a pit stop every now and then.

But there were also signs of Julie, everywhere. Her toothbrush in the bathroom, a pair of panties bunched up on the floor beside the toilet. When he led her to the bedroom, she knew that the fuzzy yellow bunny slippers that jutted out from under the bed weren't his. It made her wish they'd gone to a "rates by-the-hour" motel.

She looked away from Julie's things, but then she forced herself to look again. She catalogued each piece: toothbrush, panties, fuzzy slippers.

There's a reason why they call it cheating, Lila.

"What's wrong?" Will said as he moved up behind her. He put his arm around her neck. She felt his body pressed against hers.

"Nothing," she said.

Everything, but it doesn't matter.

She turned to him, never breaking contact. His arm rested on her shoulders. She put both arms behind him and pulled him closer. She kissed him.

She felt his hesitation, as if he sensed hers, as if he didn't want to push. He pulled back.

"Lila," he said.

She covered his mouth with hers, plunging her tongue between his lips. This time, he came back at her with equal force.

She pulled her hands from his back and jerked at the drawstring of his scrubs. She took his penis in her hands. He moaned.

She pushed him towards the bed. He fought. He steadied himself with one hand on the dresser. The other found the spot between her legs. They jockeyed for position. She squeezed. He closed his eyes.

She planted her shoulder in his chest and he went down, losing his grip on the dresser and on her. She pinned him to the bed. She pushed his scrub bottoms down and mounted him.

He came up to meet her, smiling, laughing, then both were gone and his face mirrored hers, desperate, intent, unyielding.

They came together and she collapsed on to the bed. She closed her eyes. She fought to get her breathing back, but before she could, she felt his hands caressing her breasts, her stomach and thighs. His fingers slipped across her lips and she bit him.

"Ouch," he said, but he didn't pull away and the smile never left his lips.

"That was insane,' he said.

"You think?"

"This time," he said as he slid his fingers inside of her, "We'll have to go slow."

They fought in the car on the way back to the hospital.

"I'm not just going to drop you off in the street," he said. "I'll take you to your truck."

"I don't want you to do that."

"What about the weirdo stalkers?" he asked. "You're the one who mentioned them before."

She smiled in spite of herself. "Don't try to throw that back in my face," she said. "That was earlier, that was before."

Everything is different, now.

"You're the one who didn't want me to leave my truck in the garage in the first place," she said. "Now you want to cruise through at three in the morning with me in the front seat beside you? Why don't we just pop up to the frigging OR while we're here and you can let Julie sniff my crotch?

"Jesus, Lila," he said, but without the anger she'd hoped to bring. She wanted to remind him what was at stake. She wanted to remind him just who she was.

He smiled. It was as if he knew exactly what was going on. She was just being Lila, after all. It scared her.

They pulled up in front of the hospital. She expected him to pull into the main drive, but he did what she'd been asking, drove by and pulled into the service drive, just beyond the range of the harsh red glow of the lights for the garage. He took the corner and stopped at a side entrance, beyond a line of trees that further blocked the light. He killed the lights and left only the dashboard on. The street light over them was defective, its energy concentrated in one, bright red coal.

"What happens now?" he asked.

"Damned if I know," she said.

"It won't be easy for us to get together."

"No it won't."

She knew it would probably be easier for her. She and Ray went their separate ways, but Will and Julie were still in that newlywed phase. Of course, if he broke it off with Julie that problem would be solved.

And mine would be just beginning.

"Do you think the crew will figure this out?" he asked.

"We can't let that happen. Relationships among the crew are pretty common, even if they are a bad idea, but married people screwing around is still frowned upon."

"We'll have to be careful."

"You'll have to stop giving me goo-goo eyes."

"Giving you what?"

"Goo-goo eyes. The only place I've seen a man look as sappy as you do now was in the movies."

He glanced into the rear view mirror, as if he wanted to see the expression that she was talking about.

"I can be cool," he said.

"We'll see."

Now his look was wounded, as if they were back on uneven ground, as if she were the adult again, and he, the child. She knew it was a lie. They were both children, selfishly taking what they wanted regardless of whom they hurt.

"I have to go," she said.

"Okay," he said. He slid his hand under her skirt and caressed her thigh.

"Hey," she said, "You call this being cool?"

"As cool as I can be," he said. "What I really want to do is kiss you, but someone might see that. This way all the action is out of sight. We're just a couple of co-workers saying good night after a long shift."

"Uh, huh," she said as his fingers probed deeper. She bit her lip. It was all that she could do not to throw her head back against the headrest.

He pulled his hand away.

"Thanks," she said.

"I can be cool," he said. "It won't be easy, but I'll try. See you tomorrow."

She stood in the shadows and watched him drive away. She'd taken a shower at Will's. She'd had to brush aside a pair of Julie's ankle socks to turn on the hot water. A breeze ruffled her hair. She hadn't had a chance to dry it. She shivered.

She wished she still had Will's sweatshirt. She cursed the sleeveless top, was thankful once again for the denim skirt. At least it was some protection. She thought of Kathy's wardrobe, leather mini-skirts or tufts of red and blue that barely covered her butt.

There's a price to pay for being stylish.

She wondered what the price would be for what had just happened between she and Will.

ELEVEN

Will laid in bed and stared at the clock. Six o'clock. What would he say to Julie when she got home? Things had been strained between them the last few weeks because of Sheila, but breaking up would probably still be a shock. He wished that he could tell her about Lila, but he knew he couldn't. He hated having to lie. He wasn't used to worrying about jealous husbands, ex-girlfriends and hiding his true feelings from his co-workers.

Work was his refuge, the place to go and put everything else aside. Now he'd turned it into a soap opera.

When Lila had returned to work, she'd watched Kathy and Murph in report and told Will that they were an item. He hadn't suspected a thing

"No good will come of it," she'd said. "You should never mess where you eat. Even pigs have a section of the pen set aside as a frigging bathroom."

He hadn't taken her seriously at the time. Why should he? How could they not date the people they worked with? It was the natural thing. Those were the only people who could understand what they were all about.

He'd made a mistake with Julie. He'd fallen for her because of her looks, her body and her ankle socks. He should have waited until he'd seen what lay beneath.

And Lila, how could he not want her when she was the only one who understood what the work was really all about for him?

She must feel the same way because she's breaking her own rule. Whatever happens, I'll just have to deal with it.

He just wasn't ready to deal with it, yet. At six-thirty, he got out of bed and pulled on his running gear. Julie would be home within an hour. He left a note for her on the kitchen table.

Outside, the air was cool and he was underdressed in a tank top and shorts. He knew it wouldn't take long to change that once he got started. Gooseflesh dotted his skin, but he forced himself to stretch.

Some people use running as a chance to let their minds wander. For them this run would have been a continuation of the night's thoughts, but he pushed those aside, focused on his breathing and his stride. He needed something that was his own, especially now that he'd messed up the OR.

He got into a solid rhythm and left his problems behind.

They were all still there, of course, when he got back to his apartment. He climbed the stairs, hoping that Julie would be asleep, that he'd be able to crawl in beside her and put off a confrontation until the afternoon.

When he walked into the kitchen, his note was still on the table. He walked into the bedroom. She wasn't there. He felt a mixture of relief and anger.

He didn't want to see her, but she didn't know that. What was going on here, anyway?

He walked back into the kitchen and saw the light blinking on the answering machine. He hit the button,

"Hey," her voice said, "I'm pretty beat. Guess I'm getting too old to work double shifts. I figured I'd just crash at my place. I'll see you at work."

He stood looking down at the machine. Now he was really confused. They hadn't spent a night apart in the last two months, except the night after their first fight about Sheila. She couldn't know about he and Lila. It had to be a weird co-incidence.

Maybe she was just questioning things, too. Just as he questioned her commitment to what they did, maybe she couldn't get past his fanaticism.

If that was the case, it was surely for the best. Work was the best thing in his life, and being with Lila had been incredible. There was no way this combination could be bad.

He wished it were only about he and Lila. There was no way he could handle everything at once: Lila, Julie, work, their crew. He picked up the phone and dialed the hospital.

"Yeah," he said. "This is Will Nathan. Could you please tell Martha I won't be in tonight. I'm pretty sick. I guess I picked up some kind of bug.

TWELVE

You'd think that facing Ray would have been the hard part.

Lila stared at the door of her locker, trying not to look at Julie, who sat on a bench across the locker room, doing her make-up.

Of course, Ray had been asleep when she got home. She'd crawled in bed beside him, as she'd done a thousand times before. He'd shifted his body and put one leg over hers without waking.

She told herself that what happened with Will was separate from them and it worked, somehow. By the time Ray woke her for breakfast, she'd hugged him and they talked about their plans for the day ahead.

Lila glanced at Julie. The girl looked like hell. She dabbed at the bags under her eyes as she tried to get some color in her cheeks. She caught Lila looking at her and clipped her compact shut. She stuffed it into her purse, slammed her locker shut and went into the lounge.

She looks as if she's been rode hard and put away wet. No wait, that was me fucking her boyfriend in their bed.

She hated herself for that and for what she'd done to Ray.

But my heart's still beating like crazy at the thought of walking through that door and seeing Will. I'm like a frigging schoolgirl.

She studied her face in the mirror on the door of her locker. She ran her fingers through her hair. She'd changed it when she was out on leave, going with the spikes that the kids wore these days. Ray hated it, but Will liked it. Maybe it helped him forget how old she was. She slammed the door and headed for the lounge.

She entered with her eyes down, fighting the urge to seek Will out. She brought her eyes up slowly and started on the opposite side of the lounge from his chair. She nodded hello to Kathy and Murph, found Martha, skimmed over Julie who stared at the floor, finally came to Will. At least to Will's chair, where Melanie sat.

Lila scanned the room in confusion. Where was he? She focused back on Julie. The look on her face made Melanie look cheery. Had she and Will fought? Did she know?

Martha smiled. "Have a seat, Lila," she said.

Lila had expected things to be turned around today, but if Martha was the only friendly face in the room, then she knew she was in trouble.

"We've got our hands full tonight," Martha said. "We have a full schedule and Will called in sick. Knowing how he feels about this place, he must be half dead. Has anybody talked to him today?"

Everyone turned to Julie.

"Julie?" Martha asked.

Julie looked up and met Martha's eyes. Her face flushed, but the sullen look never left her face. "I haven't talked to him," she said. "He seemed fine when he left last night." She seemed angry that Martha had even asked.

"Okay," Martha said. "Let's move on." She glanced at Lila. Lila thought she saw the trace of a smile on the edge of Martha's lips. She seemed to be enjoying Julie's anger. Perhaps she didn't approve of Will's choice of partners, either. What her face would look like if she knew the truth?

Lila looked at Kathy, whose eyebrows went up a notch. "What's up with those two?" she seemed to be asking. Lila shrugged.

Martha put Julie and Lila together. Maybe she thought that only the best partner would keep her in line.

At least they had good cases: first a fractured hip and then a wrist with Jamison. Next came a ruptured spleen, although that was pretty much a free-for-all with every spare hand pitching in. She knew that Will would be sorry he missed it.

Julie held up well. Lila tried to give her the benefit of the doubt. People who knew what they were doing probably scared her because she didn't think she'd ever be one of them.

One of us.

By the end of the night, Julie's anger had faded. She looked at Lila once or twice. She even smiled. It was a miracle sometimes what the work could do.

Just my luck. The work is the only thing keeping Will and Julie apart. So, I let her pick my brains for awhile and they'll be back fucking like bunnies.

Where was Will, anyway? She still couldn't believe that he'd wimped out. Mostly, though, she just wanted to see him. She was angry that he didn't feel the same way.

He was waiting by her truck when she got off work.

He came to me first.

"Hey," he said.

"Hey, yourself."

He opened his arms and she entered his embrace. He rested his chin on the top of her head. Maybe that was why he liked the spiked curls. He wanted to crush them.

"You'd better not let Martha see you. She thinks you must be half dead," she murmured into his chest.

"Nice of her to give me the benefit of the doubt."

"More than the bitch ever did for me," she said. "I guess she never had you figured as being a wimp. Neither did I."

"I just needed today," he said. "I wouldn't have done right by anybody today: you, Julie and the work. I'll be ready tomorrow."

She pulled back and locked forearms with him, holding him away from her.

"Tomorrow won't be any different," she said.

"Sure it will. Today I would have had to walk into the lounge cold. This way I get to talk to you, I get to talk to Julie. I'm not saying tomorrow will be easy, but at least everyone will know where they stand."

"And where's that?" she asked. "What's going on with you and Julie? Martha asked her how you were feeling and she said she hadn't seen you. Didn't you guys talk when she come home this morning?"

"She didn't come home," he said as he reached out to smooth the spikes in her hair. "I went out running about the time she would have and when I got back there was a message on my machine. She said that she was beat and that she was just going to crash at her place." He smiled. "I guess the honeymoon's over."

"Didn't you call her?"

"No," he said. "I know how it is after a rough shift. I figured I'd let her sleep. I called her at work and told her I'd see her at her place tonight."

"So, we're on the clock," Lila said.

"But we were anyway. Didn't you say your husband worries if you're not home by one?"

Had she said that? Of course she had, but that was yesterday, back when she was trying to save her old life.

Today she'd parked her truck on the top floor of the garage, the last place to fill up, so they'd be less likely to be seen if they'd come up here after work. She'd never thought of herself as a fast learner, but she was already figuring out the finer points of this cheating business.

"We've got a few minutes," she said. "Why don't we sit in the truck?"

When they climbed into the cab, she expected a wrestling match, but he leaned back against the door on the passenger side. In the full-sized cab, he seemed miles away.

"I don't have any regrets about what happened last night," he said. "I want it to keep on happening. I know you're married. I know you want to stay that way. I'm willing to do whatever you say."

Lila smiled. This was her Will: all business. She hoped that she could be the same way.

"It isn't just me and Ray," she said, "You've got Julie."

"I won't after tonight," he said.

"You're joking," she said as she tried to hide her excitement. She was also afraid. "What if I tell you that nothing else is going to happen between you and me?" She said.

"That won't change a thing between me and Julie. I made a mistake. I can't be with somebody like that."

"Like what?"

"You know."

And of course, she did. She just didn't understand how he could. Could he really be twenty-one?

"And you understand that you breaking up with Julie has nothing to do with me and Ray. You and I can have an affair, but that's all it can ever be."

"I already told you that your decision has nothing to do with mine," he said. He finally reached across the distance between them. He pulled her to him. She turned her face up to his and kissed him. He responded, tentatively, at first, but as her tongue probed his mouth, he wrapped his arms around her and pulled her to him.

She tugged at his belt buckle.

"Hey," he said. "Slow down. Line of sight, remember." He waved his arm at the windows. "Somebody's going to see us."

"They might see you," she said, "But who said I'm going to stay in the line of sight?"

THIRTEEN

It was almost three o'clock before he got to Julie's. He had to swing by his house to take a shower. There are some scents that shouldn't be on the body when breaking up with a woman.

He thought she'd be asleep, but she was sitting up in bed, her back against the headboard. Her skin was pale, her hair matted down. She wore only a faded, white t-shirt. She was usually a silk teddy kind of girl.

He was the one who'd called in sick, but it wouldn't have been a lie if she had done the same.

She had a notebook in her lap. It looked like she'd been writing.

"What's that?" he said, nodding towards the rumpled pages.

"I've been working on a pros and cons list."

"For what?"

"You and me."

"How's it going?"

"Not so good."

"Can I see it?"

"No," she said. She stuffed the notebook under her pillow. She shivered and pulled the blankets up around her shoulders. He remembered all the times he'd seen her this way, wrapped in blankets, forming a cocoon. He nudged her and she pulled away from the headboard. He slid behind her and she leaned back against him. He wrapped his arms around her.

"Do you remember when we started working together?" he asked.

Julie had worked the night shift when Will started in the OR. He'd stayed after hours with her. They'd spent hours at the front desk as Chuck Segal slept on a stretcher down the hall. She'd wrapped herself in a cocoon of blankets, even then, whiling the time away until an emergency case came through the doors and they'd fly into action.

She was a sight to see when the shit hit the fan.

After he and Julie had started dated, she'd transferred to evenings so they could spend more time together after work.

"Yeah," she said. "It's funny. The job brought us together, but now it's tearing us apart. I've been in the OR for three years and you've been here nine months, but you treat me like a rookie. I swear you want to break up with me because you don't think I'm a good nurse. Who does that? Tell me you don't want me. Tell me you met somebody else. No one else I've ever dated even cared what I did for a living. They just wanted to get their hands on me. Some of them still do, even though you and I are together."

She parted the blanket for a moment, pulled his hands inside and ran them down her body. Even with their Sheila Cole, issues if it hadn't been for Lila he might have wavered.

He knew what he should tell her about Lila. Even though Julie had attacked him first when she freaked out about Sheila Cole, they might have worked things out. But she'd drawn a line, put he and Lila alone on one side of it. That had been the breaking point. Since he couldn't tell her about Lila, he didn't say a word.

"It doesn't have to be this way," she said. "Everybody knows you're good at this, that you've got something special. It doesn't mean you have to look down on the rest of us. I worked with Lila tonight and we did fine."

He was glad that he was sitting behind her. His knew his face would have given everything away.

"Everybody knows Lila is the best there is," she said. "If she can treat me right I don't know why you can't. We're good together. We have a lot of fun. Are we really going to break up because of the job?"

"I'm sorry."

"I don't want you to be sorry. I want us back the way we used to be."

Before Sheila Cole. Before Lila.

"I don't think I can do that."

She pulled away from him and looked into his eyes. She shook her head.

"I'm just trying to be straight with you,' he said.

"Fair enough," she said.

He pulled her closer to him, wrapped the blankets around both of them and leaned back against the headboard. She burrowed into his chest and closed her eyes. He rested his head on top of hers and did the same.

They awoke as they'd done a hundred times before. He had his arm around her, his leg over hers. They'd thrown the blankets off, but they didn't need them. The warmth that radiated from them was enough. He traced the line of her body, ran his fingers up one slope and down another, even though he knew he had no right to.

She stirred and turned to him. He expected anger, resentment, but got only a smile. "Once more for old times sake?" she asked.

"Really?"

"No."

She leaned past him and plucked the blankets from the floor where they'd settled in a pile. She wrapped them around her shoulders and moved to the other side of the bed.

Again with the cocoon. Maybe she wants to remind me of what I'm losing. No, if she wanted to do that, we'd be making love right now,

"Now what?" he asked.

"We break up," she said. "Good thing we kept our own apartments. Maybe we both learned a lesson. We never should have mixed work and dating. What's that Lila always says, 'Don't mess where you eat.'?"

"Yeah," he said, "That's what she says."

Those words were with him when he got to report the next day. It would probably be easier not to date his co-workers if they weren't all good looking, each in a different way. He watched Julie as she tugged on lemon yellow ankle socks, Kathy as she spun her hair on the top of her head with that practiced hand. She pulled the OR hat over it and the blue edges sagged into their royal hood. Murph caught him looking at Kathy and smiled, mimicking her gestures, thinking this was about sharing a laugh.

Martha didn't have her hat on, yet. Will studied her short red hair, her freckles as they ran down between her breasts. What was her body like? She'd never married, never had kids. Was her stomach as smooth as a teenager's, never weighed down by the burden of a child?

He looked at Melanie. Was it possible to make her smile? Could he really be the first one to ever make that happen? Was that a lottery he wanted to buy a ticket for?

Then Lila came through the door and those thoughts went away. All that mattered was the look on her face, the shyness, the fear of what the room would think as she scanned the faces. Mostly, it was the joy he saw when she found him. Whatever happened, he was going to enjoy this while it lasted.

FOURTEEN

She didn't think she'd make it through the weekend and she dreaded walking into the lounge on Monday. This time she knew that Will would be there. A few days reprieve was all she'd gotten. Today was the first day of a new life on the job. She'd always managed to keep things separate. There was work and there was everything else. Once she came in the door, she gave everything she had. Once she walked away, it was Ray and the kids and the house.

Today was different. Will was here. Work was here. She somehow had to make this work while juggling the two. She'd often watched the others battle with their social lives within the confines of the job, while she floated along above it all. Now it was her turn to find out what that was all about.

Martha looked up, nodded to acknowledge her entrance, then looked back down at the notes in her lap, putting the final touch on her report.

Next, Lila looked for Julie. She wanted to look at Will, of course, but she didn't want to be too obvious. She figured she'd learn just as much by studying Julie's reaction. No luck there, though. Julie just smiled. She still seemed to have the same good feeling that she'd had after they'd worked together on Friday.

If Will broke up with her, he obviously kept my name out of it.

"Okay, people," Martha said. "I have an announcement to make before I start report.

"Julie just told me that she'd like to go back to the night shift. While part of me is sorry to see her go, I'm happy about her decision. I haven't found anyone half as competent as she is to take her place on nights. It takes a special kind of person to run the night shift and Julie fills the bill."

Kathy applauded. "Way to go, Jules," she said and the rest of them joined in.

Lila snuck a look at Will as all the others focused on Julie. He seemed to be studying her with a newfound admiration.

"Half the work on nights is keeping Chuck in line," Martha said. "Someday you'll have to share your secret on that one, Julie."

Julie nodded.

"As most of you know by now," Martha said. "When we go through changes like this, I always take a chance to reexamine our teams. When Lila was on leave, for example, I used Will more as a float person, something that Lila had always done for me. With Will in that role, I'm going to use Lila as a training person, actually a mentor. Not just with the raw recruits, but with everyone on the team. I think you'll all benefit from some time with her."

"Here, here," Julie said.

Martha smiled at Julie.

What the hell is this? Is it really just a chance to realign or is she just trying to keep me and Will apart? Has she noticed anything?

Lila shook her head.

Get a grip woman.

It didn't matter if she knew or not. She was doing them a favor. Things had gotten too crazy, too fast. This would be a chance to get back to normal while they were at work.

"So," Martha said. "Lila, I want you to work with Melanie."

Lila looked around the circle. Will met her eyes for the first time. He shook his head. Maybe he wondered about Martha's motivations, too. Or maybe he just knew that working with Melanie would be a pain. Did Martha really think she could straighten out that sour child?

Good luck with this one. I'm good but nobody ever said that I'm a frigging miracle worker.

Jamison had his own ideas on the subject. He smiled at Lila when he came into the room but when he saw Melanie the smile vanished. His face was almost as sour as Melanie's.

"What is this child doing in my room?" he said, even as he walked to Melanie and stepped into the gown that she held up for him. Most people would have dropped their voices, but his filled the room. He turned back to Lila as Melanie tried to tie his gown. He walked back towards Lila. Melanie trailed behind him, fumbling with the strings.

"Martha's experimenting with the crews," Lila explained. "She wants me to work with Melanie for awhile. She seems to think I'll be a good influence on her."

She winked at Jamison. He shook his head.

"A noble experiment," he said. "But I don't see why I have to be dragged into it. Work your magic on the child while you're with the plumbers and electricians. We have serious work here to do, here."

He turned back towards Melanie and slid his hands into his gloves. He still wouldn't look at her. It was as if the gown and gloves were hanging in the air waiting for him.

"What can I say, Doc?" Lila said. "If you want me, you get Melanie."

Jamison seemed to ponder this as he snapped his gloves tight around his wrists.

"This is a dilemma, Lila," he said. He stood over the table and scanned the fractured bone that had been laid bare by his residents. The anger faded from his face as he pondered the dilemma that it posed.

Just be quiet, Lila. Give him one more minute and he'll be hooked. He won't care who's passing him the tools. Then all I have to do is keep Melanie one step ahead of him, and I might just pull this off.

Lila's plan worked. Things didn't go as smoothly as they would have if Will had been her tech, but Jamison seemed content.

She knew that judging things by how she and Will did as a team was living in the past. If Will had been in the room, she probably would have been the one giving Jamison fits. Martha was doing him a favor by keeping them apart.

The night passed quickly. She forgot about Will. Then she stepped though the door into the lounge at eleven o'clock, saw him sitting in his chair and all was lost.

"Hey," he said. "How did your night go? Did Jamison try to choke Melanie?"

She slid into the chair beside his, nudged his shoulder with her own.

"It actually went pretty well. Luckily, the first break we had to fix was a real challenge. The old boy made a lot of noise, at first, but once he got into it, he pretty much forgot she was there. After that, we kept things flowing, so it worked out okay."

"So," he said. "You can make Melanie a tech even Doc Jamison could love. It's official, you are a miracle worker."

He put his arm around her shoulder. She pulled away.

"Hey, watch that," she said. "Anybody could come in."

"I'm sorry," he said. "It's hard. You shouldn't sit right next to me."

She stood up and went to the farthest corner of the lounge. "How's this?" she said, flattening herself against the wall.

"Better," he said. He stood up.

"Keep your distance, sir," she said. She pressed her wrist to her forehead. "Come one step closer and I'll scream."

"Suit yourself," he said as he sat back down. "I can wait until I get you back to my place tonight."

Her smile disappeared. "Tonight?" she asked. "I can't come to your place. I can manage a late night here and there, not every day."

He frowned. "So what's it going to be, a few minutes in the truck? We're not in high school, Lila."

"No, we're not," she said. "You're at least two years removed from it and the last Prom I went to was my son Richard's."

His face flushed. "Why do you always do that?"

"I have to," she said. "We're not kids. I'm married remember? We're having an affair. We have to be careful."

"I know," he said as he sank back down into his chair. "I just want to make love to you the right way in a bed."

She nodded. She walked to him, rested one hand on his shoulder. He looked up.

"You know," she said. "There's more than one kind of bed."

"What are you talking about?"

"Give me five minutes and meet me down in Room 12A." She stepped through the door and into the OR.

She hurried down the hall.

What the hell am I doing?

Room 12A was in the farthest corner of the OR from the front desk. It was used only for overflow cases and the smallest general procedures. Put an orthopedic guy or a neurosurgeon in there and the whining would be audible all the way across town.

Room 12A was also the safest place to have sex in the OR at night or on weekends.

Fear and excitement battled in her. Excitement got the upper hand.

She glanced over her shoulder as she got closer to the room, wanting to make sure no one saw her. The halls got darker as she got closer to the room, everything shut down and buttoned up for the night on this end of the OR.

What the hell am I doing? Have I lost my frigging mind?

She went through the scrub room and on into the room, itself. The lights were off. With the hall lights down, the table, the monitors and anesthesia machine were indistinguishable in the darkness.

She backed into the corner just inside the door. She waited, her heart racing.

Something blocked out the light in the small, square window to the scrub room and then a shape stood beside her.

"Lila?" Will said.

She groped in the dark, found him and put her hand over his mouth.

"Who else?" she hissed.

He shrugged. "You never know. This is the fuck room."

She sagged.

What the hell am I doing?

"I never expected to be here," he said.

"That makes two of us."

"I don't care about any of that," he said. "I just want to do this right." He kissed her, but she could sense his indecision, as if he had one eye on the door.

She got down on her knees and fumbled for something to stop the door. The rubber wedge was right where it should be. She jammed it under the door.

She knew that they were safe. Most of the evening crew was gone. Martha would be giving report to the night nurse. Chuck Segal, the night scrub tech, was probably already sacked out somewhere.

The dim lights in the hallway gave her Will only as a dark shape. Everything was touch and taste, heightened by the absence of the light. She put her fears aside and focused on what she had.

When they were done, she lay on top of him, their bodies stretched out of the OR bed. He ran his fingers over her stiff spikes. She caressed his abs.

The last bit of light vanished. A face blocked the window. A hand hit the door, then a body. She heard cursing at the unexpected resistance. She heard Julie's voice.

"What the hell?" Julie said.

"I guess we should have made a reservation," a second voice said. It was Steve Dempsey one of Fred's anesthesia residents.

Lila was off Will in an instant. She grabbed his hand and jerked him from the table, fixing her clothes as she dragged him towards the back door of the room.

Why didn't I wedge this door, too? What if they had come this way?

Will resisted her, grabbing for something on the floor.

Someone put a shoulder to the door.

"Chill out, Julie," Dempsey said.

"There's somebody in there," Julie said.

"We're the only ones left besides the night crew," Dempsey said. "Somebody must have wedged it earlier and forgot to remove it."

Lila led Will through the back door. In the darkened hallway she did a quick scan of both their clothes. They were acceptable enough to get them down the hallway into the supply room where they could do a more thorough check.

She forced herself to walk slowly. Will stayed beside her.

She didn't want anyone to see them together, but there wasn't time for Will to wait.

They reached the supply room and ducked inside. She leaned against the wall.

"That was close," Will said. He threw his arms around her. Safe, the tension broken, they laughed together.

Everything's a joke as long as you don't get caught.

She took his hand and led him between a line of shelves that blocked the view from the hall.

"Fix your clothes," she said.

"Check for stains and snotty noses," he said.

She laughed in spite of herself. The fear of getting caught couldn't kill the high of being with him.

She heard a cough from behind the next row of shelves. Her legs got weak. Her stomach roiled.

They stood silently. They heard another cough and a sputter. A body turned and relaxed. The sputters wound down to silence and stopped. Finally, they heard snoring. They stared at each other.

"Chuck," he mouthed.

Lila stuck her head around the corner and saw Chuck Segal asleep on a stretcher. She exhaled.

They checked and straightened their scrubs. They checked each other's faces and smoothed each other's hair.

"I'll go first," he said. "I'll meet you at your truck."

"Okay."

She listened to Chuck's breathing after Will left, ready to bolt if the rhythm changed, but it stayed steady. When she thought enough time had passed, she went to her locker.

As she eased down the hall, she thought of all the different ways she could be caught. Julie and Steve might be finished in Room 12A. Martha's report might have dragged on and she'd be in the locker room when Lila arrived. She'd wonder why Lila hadn't left. The night nurse might be waiting behind the front desk.

She thought she'd be all right if Will had already made his escape. As long as no one saw them together, they'd probably be okay.

She blushed.

As long as nobody mentions his name or makes me think of him.

The locker room was empty. She decided to take a shower. That would put some distance between she and

Will. He could run out the door, but she needed to erase the evidence before she went home to Ray.

She stood under the stream of hot water and let the steam focus on her right calf that she'd strained while balancing on the table. She massaged it until the pain receded.

I guess this is penance. If it's all I have to pay, then I'm a lucky woman.

She rode the elevator to the top floor of the garage. There were only a few cars up here at this time of night. She looked to the back row and saw Will leaning on her truck, in a dark spot where the pools of light from the lampposts barely intersected.

I figured that pretty well.

Every step closer, she felt her excitement rise. She wanted him to look her way, to share in her excitement, but he didn't seem to notice her.

"You're deep in thought," she said when she was still a few feet away. "Thinking about how close we came to getting busted?"

He jumped.

He never even saw me. So much for sharing the love.

"Sort of," he said.

She walked into her arms. He hugged her absently.

"It's okay," she said. "We're safe."

His mood puzzled her.

"What was Julie doing with Steve Dempsey outside the fuck room?" he asked.

"Who knows?" she said. "They probably had a good reason. It isn't just that kind of room, you know."

"Steve said that they should have made a reservation, Lila."

"Okay, maybe that's why they were there. Why do you care? You dumped the girl, remember?"

"Of course, I do," he said, "But it was only yesterday. "

He disengaged himself from her arms and went to the back ledge. The back of the garage looked out on a wild bit of undeveloped land. He stared down at the treetops.

"So what's the problem?" Lila asked. "You want the girl to be pining for you? You want her to be miserable? Come on, Will, that's not fair."

"I guess I just wanted her to wait a day or two before—"

"You didn't. You were with me before you'd even broken up with her."

"I know that," he said, "But that's different. We've got something, here. What can she have with Steve Dempsey? He's a real jerk. You know he's screwed half the nurses in the OR. Why would she be with him?"

"Maybe it's because he's a jerk. Maybe she just wants something easy and uncomplicated. You said things got messy for you two at the end, work and your relationship and Sheila Cole all rolled into one. Steven Dempsey certainly isn't complicated. Isn't that for her to decide, though? Besides, you have to admit they're a great looking couple. Dempsey's the only guy in the OR who's almost as good looking as you."

"Thanks a lot," he said. "Does this mean you'll be chasing after him next?"

"Not a chance," she said. "This thing we've got is more than enough for me."

She looked out over the trees. Through a hole in the canopy, she saw a line of raccoons heading for a dumpster.

The wildlife made her think of being home with Ray, lying in bed, listening to the birds and the crickets.

But you're not in Weston anymore.

She shuddered.

"Are you cold?" he asked. He pulled off his sweatshirt and draped it over her shoulders.

She pulled the sweatshirt tight around her neck. "What's going on, Will?" she asked. "Why do you care about Julie and Steve Dempsey? Are you still into her?"

"Of course not."

"Than stop acting like a jealous boyfriend."

Is that really it? Now that we've been together is he comparing me to Julie? How can I compete with that sweet young thing?

"I know it's crazy," he said. "I guess I just want her to miss me for a little while, and I want her to end up with somebody decent."

He looked at her and smiled. It all washed over her. She and Will at his place, in the truck, in Room 12A. If that was their reality, than why should any other coupling surprise them?

"There's no accounting for taste," she said.

She hugged him and his hands dropped to her buttocks. She pulled away.

"You're killing me," she said. "I have to get home. Are you going to be all right?"

"It was a shock, that's all. Everything happens so fast these days."

"Too fast," she said.

"Do you think they'll ever slow down?" He asked.

"I hope not," she said.

They'd better. I think it'll kill me if they don't.

FIFTEEN

Martha was full of surprises. On Wednesday, she paired Lila and Melanie on a laparoscopy, Kathy and Murph in the heart room and told Will she didn't have a case for him.

"But it's Wednesday," Will said. "Where's Sheila Cole? You can't assign someone else to her. I'm the only one—"

"Sheila is already back in ICU," she said. "They found an earlier slot for her in the schedule and she was only down here for about five hours today. Shea said she's turned a corner. She'll be coming back to the OR for a long time, of course, but I don't think we'll be seeing her again. Frankly, Will, I would think you'd be relieved. I left you in there because you asked me to, but those kind of cases do take a toll on us."

"I guess I just got used to it," he said. "It was a challenge."

"And you met that challenge beautifully," she said. "Now it's time to move on."

He shrugged.

"How can I move on if you don't have a case for me?"

"Well," she said. "I'm short on orderlies tonight. You could pick up a patient in the ER ."

Pick up a patient? Now she wants me to talk to people?

She responded to the look on his face. "Unless you want to scrub the case the patient is having done," she said, "It's the laparoscopy I gave to Melanie."

Will frowned. Laparoscopies were the most boring cases in the OR as far as he was concerned. They were done through a series of small incisions in the abdomen. The surgeons used a camera and viewed the inside of the abdominal cavity on a video monitor. Will called it remote-control surgery. Martha understood how he felt about these cases. She'd done him a favor by not assigning him. He knew he had to repay that kindness.

"I'll get the patient," he said.

"I thought you might."

He went to the back of the OR where the gurneys were stored. He got fresh linen, flapped the sheet out over the mattress and tucked it in, careful not to leave any wrinkles.

"That's one of the things I like about you, Will," Lila said. He turned and she was behind him.

"Martha sticks you with scut work and you still do it 100%."

She pulled a quarter from her pocket and tossed it on the sheet. It bounced.

He scooped it up and dropped it in the front pocket of his scrub top.

"My dad always told me that every job was important," he said, "That it deserved to be done right."

"He wasn't worried you'd end up doing scut work forever?"

"No," he said. He ran his hand over the sheet, smoothing out wrinkles that weren't there. "He also said that doing a job right didn't have to keep you from looking for something better."

"He sounds like a smart guy," she said. "No wonder you turned out so good." She looked over her shoulder. No one was in sight. She gave him a quick peck on the cheek.

"Do you think Martha's on to us?" he asked.

"Why do you say that?"

"She split us up. She made me an orderly."

Lila shook her head. "Even if she did know, Martha would never do that. All she cares about is the work. Look at Murph and Kathy. She never messes with them."

He grabbed a pillow from the linen cart, slipped it into a fresh pillowcase. He got a cover sheet and tossed the folded square in the middle of the stretcher.

"Of course," Lila said, "Everybody treats the Heart Team differently. They could join a cult that practices frigging human sacrifice and nobody would say a word."

"You've got that right," he said. He smiled at Lila, but her face had grown serious.

"What's up?" He asked.

"No Sheila Cole today," she said. "That must bum you out."

"It feels weird," he said. "I psych myself out for her days, so I'm pretty wired"

"Did you ask Martha why she isn't here?" she asked.

"She said she came down earlier today, but also that she's turned a corner. There probably won't be any more marathons that run into our shift."

She took his hand.

"You know that's best for the poor kid," she said. "Besides, they'll be plenty more nightmare surgeries for you."

"Thanks," he said. "Give me something to look forward to. I'd better go."

"Good idea. You don't want it to look like you think you're too good to be lugging patients around."

"Even if I am."

In the ER he got the room number for his patient and knocked on the door.

"Come in," a small voice said. He paused. The chart said the patient was twenty-five, but this sounded like a small child. He pushed through the door.

She lay on her side with her back to him. Her hospital gown fell open in the back, revealing pale skin and bright red bikini panties. A sheet was bunched up around her feet.

"Miss Eldridge? I'm here to take you to the OR."

She rolled over, saw him and grabbed for the sheet. She grimaced and held her stomach, still pawing for the sheet, not able to bend enough to reach it.

He leaned over and pulled the sheet up past her waist.

"Thank you," she said.

"You shouldn't try to make any fast movements."

"I know," she said. "A girl has to have her pride, though, don't you think?"

"Of course," he said. He looked down at the chart, not wanting to stare into the blue eyes that seemed to cut right through him.

He read the diagnosis: nausea and vomiting for four days with pelvic pain. Ackerman wanted to do an exploratory laparoscopy. They'd make a tiny incision in her abdomen, insert a scope and look around for problems. There were several possible problems: endometriosis, a ruptured ovarian cyst or an inflammation of the lymph nodes.

He looked up and she still watched him. She was beautiful. Pain couldn't hide that. If anything, her pallor accentuated it. Her features were delicate. She might as well have been a porcelain figurine. Her black hair was cut short and spiked high, like Julie's, like Lila's.

"Are you a nurse, Miss Eldridge?" he asked.

"Call me Monique," she said.

"Okay, Monique. I'm Will."

"Hello, Will," she said. "I'm not a nurse. Why do you ask?"

"Your hair," he said. "Most of the OR nurses cut it short because of the hats we have to wear all the time."

She pointed towards a leather bag on the chair besides the bed. "Look at the magazine in there," she said.

He pulled it out. It was a fashion magazine. There were dozens of models with their hair close cropped. One was bald. He glanced at her clothes, crumpled in a ball underneath the magazine. Grey sweats.

"Hey," she said as her eyes followed his gaze. "Give me a break, I'd been vomiting for four days before I finally dragged myself in here. I'm not at my best."

"You still look great."

"Thanks." She smiled, but it was cut short by another grimace. She clutched her stomach.

"Take a deep breath," he said.

She closed her eyes, inhaled.

"Hold it in," he said. "Now, let it out slowly."

"That's better. Thanks. It helps to have somebody around."

"Are you here alone?" he asked. "Don't you have family? A boyfriend?"

"My family doesn't live in town," she said. "My boyfriend dropped me off." She held her stomach, took several more deep breaths. “He had plans with friends. They made them a long time ago.”

“Oh.” He wanted to ask what kind of plans would make anyone desert someone this beautiful, but he knew that wasn’t his place.

“His friends are from out of town,” she said. “They’re only going to be around today. I made him go,” she said, as if it was important that he understand.

“Look,” he said. “It isn’t my business. You probably didn’t feel this bad when he dropped you off.”

“Actually,” she said. “I’ve felt like hell for three days. I hate hospitals. I wouldn’t be here if I wasn’t sure that I’m about to die.”

“And he still left you?”

“Well, I never told him how bad I felt. I didn’t want to come here. By the time I realized I had to, it was too late to tell him the truth.”

Tell him? Why would she have to tell him? All he had to do was open his eyes. What a jerk. She deserved better.

“You shouldn’t talk about dying,” he said. “This surgery is minor. You should be back to normal in a couple of days. They do the procedure through tiny incisions. You won’t even have a scar.”

She smiled at him.

“So, I’ll still be able to wear a bikini?” She asked.

Oh yes.

He nodded.

Her smile faded. She clutched her stomach.

“Can we get on with this?” she asked.

He looked back at the chart. “We have to wait a few more minutes. The general surgeon needs to talk to you, a second opinion, you know?”

It was just a formality. The general surgeon would rubber stamp Ackerman's opinion and they'd be on their way.

Just then, Nolan Baines, the general surgeon, came into the room. He was old school. He'd soon be forced into retirement because he had no desire to learn how to do surgery through a scope. If he had to look around inside someone, he wanted to cut them open and check things out with his own, two hands. Until then, he was hanging on, giving second opinions and specializing in the types of cases that were best done open.

His thick gray hair spouted wildly from his skull and ears. He wore thick glasses and his face was pockmarked with acne. Everyone called him Noley, not out of affection but from disrespect. Will handed him the chart, but he waved it away. "Not so fast," he said.

He turned to Monique. "So, young lady," he said, "Tell me what your problem is."

"I've been throwing up for three days and I have terrible pains down here." She ran her hand over her lower abdomen.

He nodded. "Diarrhea?"

"I had some at first, but it's been so long since I kept anything down, it dried up."

"Perfectly normal," he said.

He moved closer and lifted her gown. As he poked and prodded her abdomen, she squirmed. Will wanted to pull Noley's hands away.

Why does he have to be so rough?

Baines nodded and backed away. She pulled her gown back into place. He held his hand out to Will who gave him the chart.

"So," he said as he read the chart, "They want to do a laparoscopy, do they? They think it's lady problems."

"That's what Dr. Ackerman thinks," she said. "What about you?"

"Well," he said, "If a laparoscopy is the new cure for gastroenteritis than I'm all for it."

"What did you say?"

For a moment Will was afraid that the question had come from his mouth, but it was hers. Had Noley Baines just contradicted another surgeon in front of a patient?

I guess he doesn't have much of a future in second opinions.

"I said you've got the flu, my dear. It's a severe case. You've neglected it far too long. If you were my patient, I'd admit you, give you medication and an IV, but if you want to let someone poke around inside you with a telescope and half a dozen sharp sticks, then by all means have a scope."

He offered his hand. She took it and he shook it briskly.

"Good luck whatever you decide, dear," he said. He turned and left the room.

She lay without speaking after he'd left, staring at the door. She looked even smaller than she had when he'd come in.

"Did he just say that I don't need an operation?" she asked. She looked right at Will. He looked away.

"What should I do?" she asked.

"I'll get Dr. Ackerman back in here," he said.

"I don't want her," she said. "I asked you."

He looked back at her. He saw the confusion and anger in her eyes. He understood both. She'd been dumped here by her boyfriend and told she needed surgery. Now Noley Baines had then told her it was the flu. She needed someone to be straight with her, someone to watch out for her. She wanted him to be the one to do it.

He looked away. "I can't really say," he said.

Liz Ackerman came through the door. She looked as angry as Will had ever seen her. Obviously, she didn't appreciate being undercut by Noley Baines. Even worse, now she had to justify herself to a patient.

"Could you step out a moment, please," she said to Will.

"Can't he stay?" Monique asked.

It was almost too much for Ackerman. She eyed Will as if he were part of an age-old conspiracy. She'd been hearing this for years. Just because she had a vagina and uterus was no reason to let her fix another woman's.

"It would be better if we had privacy," she said.

"All right," she said, but she begged him to stay with her eyes.

"I'll be right outside," he said.

He left the room because he didn't want a confrontation with Ackerman, but once he got into the hall, he knew that would have been easier than having to face himself.

How quickly things change. A few minutes ago he'd been angry at Monique's boyfriend for deserting her. Now, he'd done the same.

Did she really need surgery? He didn't know. Noley Baines was old school. He hated scopes. They were taking away his livelihood. What would he say if he were cutting her open the old-fashioned way instead of poking her with sticks?

Then there was Ackerman. Will knew that this had nothing to do with her being a woman. She was a surgeon. She needed to cut. The flu wasn't very sexy, after all.

A few months ago, he'd have been right on board with that, before Lila's husband, before Sheila Cole, before this girl. Now there was another face to go with a surgery.

Being an orderly really sucks.

He'd never appreciated how perfectly positioned the scrub techs were. They didn't have to make the decisions. They didn't have to face the people. They just showed up when it was time to work, when the patients were hidden underneath a curtain of blue linen. They did the job and moved on to the next case.

What could he have told Monique? Nothing really. That wasn't his job. If he was assigned to her case, he'd do everything he could to make sure the procedure went smoothly, but here he was useless to her.

Her idiot boyfriend would be more help. At least the guy could ask if they should listen to the crazy old doctor or the bitch.

Ackerman came out the door.

"She's ready, now," she said.

"She's going to have the surgery?"

Ackerman glared at him. "Of course, she's going to have the surgery. She needs it. Goddamn Noley…" She paused, as if she'd forgotten for a moment that she was talking to the hired help and needed to keep her cool no matter how angry Noley Baines had made her. Now, she remembered. They had to keep the dirty laundry in the family. Everyone isn't doctor material, after all.

"Just get her to the OR," she said.

"Yes Mam."

She walked away. If she noticed his attempt at sarcasm, she let it slide.

Walking back into her room was probably the hardest thing he had to do that day. He wondered if she'd even look at him. How could she forgive him after the way he'd let her down?

Her eyes focused on him. "I guess I'm going to do this," she said.

If Noley Baines had made her shrink, she was making a comeback, now. Or maybe it was because he felt so small. He looked at the floor.

He reached over to adjust the rails on her stretcher. He felt her hand on his. He looked back into her eyes.

"It's hard to know what to do when even the doctors can't agree," she said.

"That's true," he said.

"I think the safe thing to do is have the surgery. And you did say the procedure is minor."

He couldn't believe it. He'd run from the decision with his tail between his legs and she'd still found a way to include him.

She squirmed. "Besides," she said. "I don't think I can wait on that old guy's conservative approach."

"Let's do this, then," he said. He checked the side rails and pulled the blanket up to her chin.

"All tucked in," she said.

I hope when I have kids I do better by them than I have by her.

He was happy to get out into the hall. Since he was pushing the stretcher, he could stand at the head of the bed and didn't have to look her in the eye.

She, apparently, had other ideas. She craned her neck back, looking at him upside down.

"So tell me exactly what they're going to do," she said.

"Okay," he said, happy to be back in his own territory. "First, we'll get you transferred from this stretcher to the OR table. We'll get you situated and then they'll give you the anesthesia. Dr. Dean is doing that today. I think you'll like him."

By the time they got to the OR, he felt more like himself. What had made him think it was his job to make the decision for her?

Right now, his job was to help her relax and get her to surgery. He'd get her situated for the case and then he'd move on to his real job. Everything else was pretension.

Lila met them at the door of the OR room. He glanced past her and saw Melanie setting up the table.

"Miss Eldridge," Lila said. "I'm your nurse for today. Let's get things started."

"Is Will going to be here, too?" Monique asked.

Lila's eyebrows arched up above her mask. "For a few minutes," she said. "He'll stay until we've made you comfortable, then you're stuck with me."

Monique looked at Will. "You're not a nurse?" she asked.

"He's a scrub tech," Lila said. "But just for today he's a transporter. Normally he'd be over there." She nodded towards Melanie.

"Oh," Monique said. "You don't usually bring people down to the OR?"

"No," he said. "I'm usually just one of the people behind the masks."

"Well," she said. "I guess I got lucky."

This time Lila's arched eyebrows aimed directly at Will. Melanie glanced over her shoulder at them.

The vibe must be really strong if even Melanie is picking it up.

"Well," Lila said, "Let's get started."

"Good afternoon, Mam," Fred said. "I'm Doctor Dean and I'll be your anesthesiologist today."

Mam?

Will studied Fred's eyes. There was no trace of irony in them. Were all females "Mam" to Fred once he got them on the table? Was that what it took to do this job?

"Will told me about you," she said.

"Don't believe any of it," Fred said.

"We'll be doing a general," he continued. "I believe one of my colleagues discussed it with you in the ER?"

"Yes, they did."

"Okay, let's slide you over on to the table."

They steadied her as she made the transfer. Once she was on the bed, Will pulled the stretcher away and pushed it back out into the hall.

When he returned, Lila had pulled the sheet back up over Monique's legs.

"It's pretty cold in here," Monique said.

"Would you please get Miss Eldridge a warm blanket, Will," Lila asked.

"Sure," he said.

He went back into the scrub room and pulled a blanket from the warmer. He held it to his chest for a minute. He absorbed the warmth and smelled the hospital's disinfectant in the fibers. He looked back and Lila was watching him.

So now I'm getting touchy-feely with the linen. I need to get back with my instruments.

He went back into the room and covered Monique with the blanket, avoiding Lila's eyes.

"That feels nice," Monique said.

Lila went over to Melanie. "You need anything, hon?" she asked.

"No, I'm fine."

She came back to Will and touched his arm.

"I've got this, Will," she said. "You'd probably better check to see if Martha needs you for anything else."

"Okay," Will said, but he didn't move.

Monique looked up at him. "Thanks for everything," she said.

"I'm just doing my job," he said.

"I don't believe that for a minute," she said as she turned back to Fred.

"You and me both," Lila said as she pushed past him.

Martha put him in with Jamison. It was a relief. He threw himself into the case.

He saw Fred later in the lounge.

"How'd things go with the girl I brought up from the ER?" he asked.

"Everything went fine," he said. He smiled. "You certainly are a lucky man, though. First time Martha sends you to pick up a patient and you get that sweet, young thing. I could tell you two connected. It must be nice to be young."

"She was in a lot of pain and Noley and Ackerman were squabbling over her. I felt bad for her."

"Oh really? And I guess she took to you because you were a friendly face?"

"I guess."

"I like my version better," he said. "Then again, I'm a romantic."

Fred a romantic? This guy is full of surprises

"So," Lila said later as they walked to her truck. "I thought I'd just have to worry about you around your ex, but it turns out I have watch you with the patients, too."

"Come on, Lila? You know you can trust me."

And how many of the patients are going to look like Monique?

"How do I know that?" she asked. "You and I have been doing this for less than a week. Last week you were with Julie and yesterday you got jealous when you found out she might be with somebody else. You're screwing me and carrying a torch for your old girlfriend. Apparently, you've not the man I thought you were."

"Jesus, Lila," he said. "Cut it out."

He reached for her, but she slapped his hands away, hard enough to leave him wondering if she was serious.

"So tonight you walk into the ER," she said, "And the patient you've been sent to pick up might just as well have stepped off the pages of a fashion magazine. Bang, you're off again."

"It's not like that," he said. "I'm not like that. She was sick. She needed a friend."

"Are you sure about that?" she asked.

She batted her eyelashes in an exaggerated manner, her voice soft, out of breath. Marilyn Monroe was alive and well. "You mean you don't usually bring the patients down, Will?" she said. "I'm just SO lucky!" she said.

"Cut it out, Lila," he said.

"Touchy, touchy," he said. She jabbed her finger into his arm. "I think I hit a nerve."

"Don't be such a bitch," he said. "She was messed up. She was sick and her boyfriend dumped her here and left. Noley Baines and Ackerman were fighting about whether or not she even needed surgery."

This time he reached for her and she let him hold her hand.

"Frigging Noley and Ackerman," Lila said, "They shouldn't have done that shit in front of the patient. Noley's just pissed off because he knows his time has passed and Ackerman has a chip on her shoulder because she knows she's never going to get to be one of the good old boys. You need a penis for that."

"That's what I thought," Will said. "How was I supposed to tell Monique which one of them was right?"

"You had no way of knowing," Lila said. "That's the thing about exploratory surgery. You have to cut to find out that you didn't really need to."

"What do you mean?"

"Noley Baines was right," she said. "That girl needed surgery like I need a couple more grandkids."

He squeezed her hand. "So are we all right?" he said. "I was just doing my job."

"If you say so."

But after Lila drove away that night, he went back into the hospital. He slipped into Monique's room and sat in the chair beside the bed. She opened her eyes.

"Hi," she said.

"Hi."

"You disappeared," she said.

"I had to get back to my regular job," he said. "How are you feeling?"

"Better. Dr. Ackerman said everything's in order. I guess that old guy was right, after all. It was just the flu. Hard to believe since I felt so bad."

"Did your boyfriend ever make it back?"

"He did," she said, "But I sent him home. I was hoping you'd come back." She glanced at the clock. "Does that say two am?" she asked.

"Yeah."

"You work this late?" she asked.

"I got off awhile ago. I just wanted to check on you before I headed home."

"So this isn't an official visit?"

"No."

She closed her eyes and nodded. "That's good," she said.

He studied her face. The color had returned to her cheeks.

"So why did you send your boyfriend home?" he asked.

"Because he's not my boyfriend, anymore. I've had my doubts about him for awhile, but today pretty much cemented them. Good riddance."

He didn't want to speak. How could he tell her how happy the news made him when he was still with Lila?

"I appreciate everything you did for me," she said without opening her eyes.

He winced.

"I didn't do anything," he said. "I couldn't advise you on whether or not to have the surgery. I pretty much screwed everything up."

She opened her eyes. She seemed puzzled. She patted the sheet beside her. "Come here," she said.

He sat on the bed beside her. She leaned against him. She touched the dressings on her abdomen.

"I guess I see why you think you messed up," she said. "You wouldn't say anything about my having the surgery or not, but I understand that. It might have caused a problem for you with the doctors if you had. Still, I needed a soft touch before the others got down to business. You gave me that."

"But you didn't really need surgery," he said.

"That's easy to say, now," she said. "I could have been all turned around inside. No one can say. Isn't that why they call it exploratory surgery?"

"Of course."

But he wasn't so sure after today. Now he was wondering if exploratory surgery was a doctor's way of saying "Baby needs a new pair of shoes." Was it just something to tide them over until they had real lives to save?

The world needed Ackerman for fetal distress C-sections. Maybe exploratory scopes were payback for those services.

It's easy to get self-righteous, now. Where was all this when Ackerman was all up in my face?

"Are you always so hard on yourself?" she asked.

"I hadn't thought of it that way, but I guess so."

"You're going to burn out before you're twenty-five. You need to develop some defense mechanisms."

"Yes, Mam," he said and smiled as Fred Dean's words came from his mouth.

She adjusted the linen on her bed, pulled the sheet up to her chest and smoothed the edges down over her form, accentuating her narrow hips, her slim legs.

He didn't usually need defense mechanisms. The surgical linen was usually enough. It draped the patients. It screened their faces. He was fine as long as he stayed behind the screen. Too late for that with her.

"I'm glad you came back," she said.

"I felt badly the way things ended. I wanted to make sure you were all right."

"You knew I'd be fine," she said. "You said yourself that it was a minor procedure."

"That's true. I just wanted to see you again."

"I'm glad."

He inhaled. Her body, scrubbed clean, smelled only of the OR. "I really shouldn't be here," he said.

"The nurses won't bother us," she said. "They told me the last time they checked on me that they wouldn't have to wake me up again until six. We've got plenty of time."

He ran his fingers through her hair. "I'm not talking about getting caught by the nurses."

"Ah,' she said. "I'm sorry," she said. "I don't usually read things this badly."

"You didn't. It's just..."

"Just because I have an idiot for a boyfriend who abandoned me in the ER, that doesn't me that you're unattached," she said.

"That's right," he said. He stood. He sat back in the chair

"She's a lucky girl," she said.

He winced at the word girl. How had things gotten this complicated? Once his only concern with a woman was if she'd look good under her make-up. Now he'd found a girl who was drop-dead gorgeous lying on an ER stretcher and he had to push her away because he had feelings for a married woman twice his age.

"I'd better go," he said. He leaned over and kissed her on the top of her head. He lingered for a moment.

"Thanks again," she said. She reached over to the bedside table and scribbled on a scrap of paper. She slipped it into the front pocket of his scrubs.

"That's my number," she said. "If things ever change for you, I mean."

"Okay."

In the hall he read the number a dozen times, as if he wanted to commit it to memory. He knew that he should toss it away. He saw her face, a dozen different versions from the day. He knew it wouldn't be going away anytime soon. He slipped the number into his wallet.

Outside, he took a deep breath, bent down, scooped up a handful of stones from the gravel walk and winged them one by one at the rock on the edge of the lawn. Each hit dead center and bounced away. He pumped his fist and smiled.

In the parking garage, he paused at the bottom of the stairwell. He saw Monique's face again. He took the stairs two at a time, buoyed by the image. At the top of the stairs, Lila's face replaced Monique's and he stopped. He slumped against the concrete ledge.

What was wrong with him? He was with Lila. She was married and risking everything for him while he was acting like a lovesick teenager. He stared out over the dark lawn.

Is this the guy I want to be?

He turned from the ledge and walked to his car. By the time he reached it, he had his answer.

SIXTEEN

Lila had watched for Will from her truck, parked under the trees, sheltered in the darkness as they'd been a few days before. She hadn't wanted to be there, but she had to see if he'd gone home.

After they'd said good night, she'd watched as he walked over to his car. Something about the way he'd stood beside it, made her think that he wasn't ready to leave. She'd driven down the levels and gone out the gate, but had waited there for his car to come out. It never had. She knew that he'd gone back to the hospital to check on that girl.

Everybody had patients who stuck with them. She'd had them herself. Most people came and went without even making a blip on the radar screen, but some stood out.

It only made sense that this girl had attached herself to Will. She was scared and alone. What must she have thought when he came through the door of the ER? And it made just as much sense that he felt it, encouraged it. She was beautiful, vulnerable. He'd have to be made of stone not to feel something.

She told herself that she was being paranoid. Maybe he'd just forgotten something and gone back to his locker. Maybe he'd taken the back exit to the garage. Maybe he was home in bed while she waited here under the trees.

Even if he had felt something for the girl, maybe he knew it for what it was, a transitory thing. It was intense but it wouldn't last. Will had always been ahead of the curve when it came to the job. Maybe tomorrow they'd talk about this girl the way they'd talked about Jamison's most recent fractured femur or a ruptured aneurysm. Everything would be back to normal.

But the longer she waited in the darkness, the more she knew that this wasn't just bonding with a patient. Will had felt something for this girl. Why shouldn't he? She was his age. She was beautiful. She was every young man's dream.

It was insane for me to think that anything could ever last between us. Last? Why would I even use that word? We've been together three times. It's only been a few days.

Lila waited. The large rock on the edge of the grass shone in the moonlight. It was the only thing that held the light. Everything else was dark. It suited her.

Finally, Will emerged from the side entrance of the hospital and headed for the garage. She watched him cut across the grass.

He bent down, picked up a stone and winged it at the rock. He threw three more. Each hit in the center of rock and bounced away. He pumped his fist and headed into the garage. She watched as he took the steps two at a time, his form visible through the spaces in the stairwell.

Lila rested her head on the steering wheel.

Damn, damn, damn.

As she drove the road to Weston, Lila let her feelings wash over her.

What was going on with Will? He said that he cared for her, but he'd gone back to visit this patient and he was jealous of Julie and Steve Dempsey.

As far as Julie was concerned, wasn't it better that he was jealous? What would it say about him if his feelings for her had died so easily? If he was that fickle, if he could move so easily past Julie, than maybe he'd do the same with her and move on to this patient.

Or maybe he'll just flit back and forth between the three of us like a goddamn hummingbird.

And why shouldn't he? Why shouldn't he experience it all: sexy young co-worker, savvy OR Vet, fashion model waif on a stretcher?

The next thing you know, he'll be screwing Ackerman. Of course, if he wants to stick his dick in ice water, best of luck to him.

As she drove past Weston Common, as her truck took the curves on the road to Waznek Manor, as she climbed the stairs to her bedroom and slid into bed beside her husband, she felt Will tugging at her, drawing her back to him.

What the hell is wrong with me?

Will might flit around for awhile. That was part of being young, but it wasn't as if she was the place that he would settle when the time came. She was just a stop along the way. She knew that. She'd always known it. So why couldn't she accept it?

Because you've never been that kind of girl.

Ray stirred beside her.

"Hey, babe," he said. He wrapped his arms around her.

"Hey," she said as she settled into him.

"How was your night?" he asked.

"Good."

"Just good?"

She pulled back so she could see his face. "You got a problem with good?" she asked.

He shrugged. He wouldn't meet her eyes. He looked up at the ceiling. One hand stroked her back while the other traced the top of the headboard.

"You used to bitch to me every night," he said. "There was always something: Martha didn't appreciate you. Jamison was an asshole. If that little bitch Melanie didn't wipe that sour look off her face, you were going to smack her. Now all you ever say is good."

"So you want me to be screwed up, pissed off, beaten down?" She grabbed his hand from the headboard, pressed it to her chest.

"Of course not," he said. "I just want you to talk to me," he pulled his hand away from her and covered his eyes.

"I want you to stop protecting me," he said.

"Protecting you?" she said. "What the hell is that supposed to mean?"

He uncovered his face and sat up, leaning back against the headboard.

"It's hard for me to believe that suddenly your job is perfect, that's all," he said. "I think you've stopped talking about it because you're afraid it'll upset me. You walk on eggshells when you're around me. Something's not right."

What could she say to that? She didn't trust herself to speak. Luckily, he wasn't finished.

"I had a heart attack, okay," he said, "Most of that was lousy diet and bad genes. Some of it might have been stress, but it was my stress: work, money, real stuff.

"Listening to you bitch about work isn't stressful. I'm supposed to be there for you. You want to talk about stress? Just be inside me when I feel like I'm not doing my job, not being your husband. Sometimes I think my chest's going to explode."

"I didn't know," she said. "Why didn't you tell me sooner?"

"Why should I talk to you if you won't talk to me?"

She saw the sadness in his eyes. Of course, she'd been quieter, but it was because of her feelings for Will. The less she talked about work, the less chance there was for her to slip. He knew that she was shielding him from something, but he thought it was from the problems that she had at work. Their life had been so solid for so long, he couldn't imagine what was really going on.

Lucky for me.

She slid across the bed and nestled against his chest. "This is crazy," she said. "I guess I have stopped bitching but it isn't because I'm protecting you. Things really are better since I got back from leave. I think they'd been taking me for granted, you know? When I was missing in action for two months, they finally figured out how much I did around the goddamn place."

"It's about time."

She ran her fingers over his chest, caressing the thick hair. Her fingers traced his sternum.

"Martha's been much better," she said. "She treats me almost like an equal. Even Jamison seems to finally appreciate me, and that asshole treats everyone like crap."

"What about the rest of the crew? Is that girl Melanie still there?"

"Oh, yeah."

"And is she still a sourpuss?" he asked.

"Pretty much. Martha wants me to work with her more closely, now. I think she wants me to straighten her out."

"Doesn't that bother you?" he asked. "She used to drive you nuts."

"I'm trying to make the best of it," she said. "She can't help it that her mother locked her in the closet when she was a kid."

He chuckled, tightened his arms around her.

"That's part of what I miss," he said. "You used to bitch a lot, but you were funny as hell."

"I'm sorry to ruin your fun, but I'm just happier, now. We've got a good bunch, now. Kathy, Murph and Will." She was happy to be able to slide his name in last.

"And I just appreciate everything more, now," she said. "Isn't that what they say when you come close to losing everything, it makes you appreciate what you have?"

"I'm the one who had the heart attack," he said.

"And I'm the one who worried that I'd lose you."

They lay for a few minutes in silence, thinking of how close they'd come to losing the life they knew.

"I do appreciate things more," he said, finally.

"When you're not being paranoid about your wife being happy?" she said. She smacked his chest.

"Okay," he said. "You made your point. I do miss the bitching, though. Like I said, you were pretty funny sometimes."

"I could make stuff up," she said.

"That would be nice. Tell me something bad about that kid, what's his name, Will?"

She stiffened. "Not much to say," she said. "He's perfect."

"Oh, come on. You said you'd make stuff up. You're not even trying."

"I'm not making this up. That's what's bad about him. He's young, he thinks he's invulnerable. He's so damn full of himself, you know?"

"Yeah," he said. "It was awhile ago, but I remember."

"Youth is wasted on the frigging young," she said.

"You got that right."

Ray fell back to sleep and she lay with her head on his chest. How many more nights would she do this, lay beside her husband and think of Will? Maybe everyone would be better if she broke it off with Will. He could go back to his young stud's life, be with this patient or go back to Julie if he wanted. She could give her husband the life that he deserved. She couldn't do anyone justice this way. She needed to make up her mind before she hurt them all.

Or maybe, Ray was the one that she should leave behind. Maybe Will's thing with the fashion model was just because she wouldn't commit to him. Maybe if she took a chance he'd do the same for her. He was a stand-up guy, he always had been.

You're the problem, Lila. You need to shit or get off the frigging pot.

Ray stirred, rolled away from her. She slid up against his back and lay one leg over his. She closed her eyes, felt his warmth, his solid frame. Suddenly, her eyes popped open. She pulled back and sat on the edge of the bed.

You want to leave this man, but your body follows him across the bed. You want Will to be with you, to ignore all the pretty faces around him, but you can't give him what he wants. You are certainly one hell of a hot mess, Lila Waznek.

She lay back down with her back to Ray. She pulled the covers over her and tried to sleep.

SEVENTEEN

Room 12A looked different in the light of day.

It really is more a broom closet than an OR, though. No wonder everybody uses it as the fuck room. It isn't good for much else.

When they'd arrived at report, things had been so quiet that Martha didn't have a case for them. She'd sent him off to check and restock rooms.

Will heard the door open behind him. Suddenly, he felt a hand slide down the front of his scrub bottoms.

"Whoa," he yelled, as he jumped forward. He turned. Lila put a hand over his mouth.

"Keep it down," she said. "Martha's just across the hall." She pulled her hand away from his mouth.

"What are you doing?" he whispered.

She didn't answer, just tugged at the drawstring of his scrubs and took him in her hand again.

"Jesus, Lila," he moaned. "Martha could walk in on us."

"Fuck her," Lila said.

She took him in her hand and worked him hard.

"Ouch," he said and she eased up. Her hands were gentle, coaxing. Then the intensity returned. His head fell back against the wall. He closed his eyes and waited for the rush.

"What was that all about?" he asked after she had finished, not opening his eyes.

"It's called a hand job," she said. "What it's about is that red glow on your face."

"Come on, Lila," he said. "You know what I mean. Why here? Why now? I thought we were going to be careful."

"We were," she said, "Before yesterday."

"Is this still about Monique?" he asked, happy that the red glow in his cheeks would hide the blood that rushed to them. "I told you it was nothing."

His hand touched his wallet where Monique's phone number lay neatly folded among the bills, his driver's license and his credit card.

"It's not about that," she said. "I mean it is, but it's more about me."

She opened a cabinet beside her and began to check off the supplies. He put a hand on her shoulder.

"I already checked those," he said. "Come on, Lila, talk to me."

"I am jealous of that little girl," she said, "Even though I know I have no right to be. I gave you shit about her last night but I went home and slept beside my husband. He woke up and complained that I don't talk to him anymore."

She shook her head.

"He thinks I've stopped bitching to him about work every night because I'm trying not to stress him out," she said.

She slapped her hand into the metal edge of the cabinet.

"Isn't that a frigging joke?" she asked. "I don't talk to him about work because I'm afraid he'll see the look on my face if I slip and talk about you. Poor guy, he doesn't have a clue."

Will smiled. He touched her face.

"What are you smiling about?" she asked.

"I know it's weird, but I'm happy that he's suspicious," he said. "Not about us, I mean, but that he knows something's wrong. Sometimes I wonder how you can just go home and act like everything is normal. It makes me think that what we're doing doesn't matter to you."

"Are you kidding me?" she asked. "Of course it matters. Why else would I hassle you about Julie, about this patient, Monique? The problem is that I'm crazy about you but I love my husband, too."

"So what are you going to do?" he asked.

"I don't know," she said. "I know I have to do something before I screw this up for all of us."

The intercom on the wall came alive with a burst of static. They both jumped, but then they laughed together.

"Lila and Will, please report to desk," Martha announced.

"Well, duty calls," Lila said.

Lila got a case with Melanie. Will got a fracture with Jamison. He was grateful for the distraction, happy for anything to help forget the mess that they were in.

He wondered if Lila felt the same way.

He didn't see her again until almost ten o'clock. He found her in the lounge. Melanie sat in the corner with her eyes closed. He thought, at first, that she was asleep, that maybe it would be safe to talk to Lila, but then Melanie opened her eyes and looked at the clock. She scowled, angry, perhaps, that so little time had passed. Her eyes slid shut.

He looked at Lila, nodded in Melanie's direction. She shrugged. It was a different shrug, more tolerant, as if she accepted Melanie, scowls and all. One more thing to ask her about when they were alone.

Martha came through the door. "There's an abdominal anuerysm in the ER," she said.

Will jumped to his feet, but she put an arm on his shoulder.

"Whoa, cowboy," she said. "I'm sorry, but it's not that kind."

Will slumped back into his chair.

"I'm sorry," Martha said. "It's a Triple A, but it hasn't burst. The patient is stable. They're going to do a few tests and bring him up in fifteen or twenty minutes."

"Next time wait for the word rupture before you go into overdrive," Lila said. She winked at him, but it didn't help. It just made him feel foolish. She seemed to realize this. Her face flushed. She looked at the floor. What else could she do with Martha around?

"I'm giving this one to Lila and Melanie," Martha said. "I'll keep you in reserve, Will. Why don't you help them get set up?"

"Okay."

Martha left the lounge. Lila came to him and offered her hand. She pulled him to his feet and turned back towards Melanie whose eyes were still shut. Will wondered if she'd even opened them when she'd heard Martha's voice.

"Let's go girl," Lila said.

Melanie eased to her feet.

"How many aneurysms have you done?" Lila asked her.

"Two or three," Melanie said.

"Did you have to do them on the fly or could you take your time?" Lila asked.

"They were scheduled cases," Melanie said. "I took my time."

Will watched as she slunk across the lounge. Of course she'd taken her time. He doubted that there was another option.

They gathered their supplies and went down to the room. Melanie went into the scrub room.

"Martha gave you a real shock before," Lila said, as she tugged the pack open. She drew the edges down over the table, establishing the sterile field.

"I know she didn't do it on purpose," Will said. He stood beside Lila and opened packages onto the table.

"She's like me," Lila said. "Sometimes she forgets you've been here less than a year. You fit in so well, we think you've been here forever.

He heard an unfamiliar sound in the hallway. Someone was running.

"What the hell?" Lila said.

Something hit the door. It jerked open, then fell back into place. Something hit again and the foot of a stretcher slipped into view. Steve Dempsey pushed a skinny, gray man through. He shoved the stretcher across the last few feet between them, as if he were trying to rid himself of it, as if it had attached itself to him like a leech.

"He stopped breathing on the elevator," Dempsey said. His face was bright red. Sweat poured off is forehead.

Will caught the stretcher before it slammed into the OR table. Lila touched the old man's throat. "He doesn't have a pulse," she said. "Will, start compressions."

Will dropped the railing on the stretcher and then dropped the head down flat. He tried to position himself over the chest, but he couldn't straighten his arms because the stretcher was too high. He set the brake, climbed on and straddled the chest. He laced his fingers together, measured one palm up from the bottom of the sternum and began to pump.

Lila grabbed the bag from the anesthesia table and slapped it over the patient's lips. They were gray, just like the rest of the guy, but also had a tinge of blue. Will had never seen anyone so old.

Lila pumped the bag as Will counted his compressions. Melanie stood at her table methodically arranging her instruments.

Her cool would be impressive if it wasn't just that she doesn't give a shit.

Dempsey stayed in the doorway.

"What the hell is going on here?" Fred Dean shoved past Dempsey, then turned back to him and jammed his hand into his chest.

"He just stopped breathing—" Dempsey said.

"So what the hell are you doing over here?" Fred asked.

"But I was alone, on the elevator. I was alone," Dempsey said.

Will stared. He didn't want to, but he couldn't look away. Dempsey was usually a jerk. Where was his swagger, his arrogance?

What the hell happened to his face? He's ugly. I know the guy is beautiful. How could that change?

Fred turned away from Dempsey with a finality that made Will lose his count.

Lila took over and they didn't miss a beat.

Fred came towards them and Will flinched, but the anger was gone from Fred's eyes.

"What have we got Lila?" he asked.

"Cardiac arrest," she said. "We've only been at it a minute or two. I'm not sure how long he was down before that."

"Can't be too long," Fred said, "Since it started on the elevator."

Dempsey was at Fred's shoulder. "It's been five minutes tops," he said.

Fred glared at him.

"I'm all right now," Dempsey said.

"Too late," Fred said.

"But I was alone on the elevator," Dempsey whined.

"You weren't alone when I walked into this room," Fred snapped. "You had the best damn team in the OR to direct and you were standing in the doorway. Get out of my room. I'll deal with you later."

"But this is my patient."

"Not any more."

Davis, the surgeon, came through the door. "What the hell happened, Fred?" he asked.

"Your guy crashed on the elevator. The crew initiated CPR."

"How long?"

"Just a few minutes."

"So let's move," Davis said.

Will glanced towards the doorway. Dempsey was gone.

Something cold splashed Will's forearms. He looked down. Melanie was prepping the belly and had gotten as much paint on him as she had on the patient. The thick, brown soap trickled down his arms.

Melanie held a drape up to Davis, but he waved it away.

"Just give me a knife," he said.

Melanie dropped the linen, reached behind her and grabbed a knife from the mayo stand.

Davis made the incision a few inches below Will's laced fingers. The knife sliced through the skin. Will braced himself for a second splash, warm blood from the abdominal cavity, but nothing came from the wound except the normal oozing from the skin.

"What the hell?" Davis said.

Melanie slid a retractor into the incision and pulled back. Davis plunged his hand into the wound. He pulled it back out and stared when his glove came back dry.

He dove back in, groping through the abdominal cavity, probing towards the spine where he knew he would find the aorta.

"What have you got?" Fred asked.

"An aneurysm the size of a football," Davis said, "But it's intact."

He eased his arm back out.

"Stop compressions, Will," he said.

Will stopped. Davis lengthened the incision. He cut through the diaphragm and reached into the chest cavity. He found the heart

"Damn, these coronary arteries are nasty," he said. "I've never felt so much calcification. This guy's been walking around dead for months. He just refused to lie down."

"Sounds like my old man," Fred said.

Everybody laughed. Will looked at Lila. She joined in, but he could see in her eyes that it was forced. Too close to home. None of them should be laughing, of course, a man was dead, but this was just a case to them. They didn't have a loved one who'd just had work done on his heart. Procedures were definitely easier than people.

If Will's first abdominal aneurysm had been about high drama and adrenaline, than this one was the opposite. The old, gray guy was dead and there was nothing they could do. Davis pronounced time of death and they sewed him up.

Fred and Davis left the room. Melanie gathered up her instruments and took them across the hall to be processed. Will helped Lila clean up the old guy for his family. Will cleaned the blood from the belly, but the yellow stain of the paint wouldn't go away. He knew it would take awhile to wear off his own arms, too.

Will looked at the patient, at his body, small and gray and shriveled up.

If Dempsey had made any mistake, it was not accepting that the guy was just old. He should have left him in peace when his eyes rolled back in his head. That's what they all should have done.

Will remembered the rush he'd had when Dempsey came through the door. Those next few minutes had been the best, but it was all for nothing. Sometimes people just died. The excitement had nothing to do with this patient. It was really all for them.

When he and Lila wheeled the old guy from the room, Fred Dean and Dempsey stood in the door of the doctor's lounge. Fred waved a finger in Dempsey's face. Dempsey stared sullenly ahead.

Will studied his face for other emotions, embarrassment, regret, but there was only anger. He was still ugly.

GQ won't be calling him anytime soon.

He felt Lila's hand on his arm.

"Don't stare," she said as she pulled him away. "You probably rubber-neck at car wrecks, too."

In the truck after work Lila seemed distracted. Will thought of the old guy and his heart. He knew that it must make her think of her husband. He wanted to say something, but it was just too weird.

How do I talk to her about her husband when her legs are lying across mine?

"Can you believe Dempsey?" she asked.

"That was pretty sad," he said.

"At least I won't complain for awhile about God not being fair."

"What does that mean?"

"Sometimes it bothers me because it seems some people get so much while others get the short end of the stick," she said. "I always thought Dempsey got more than his share of looks and brains and personality"

"But he didn't get everything." Will said.

"No," she said. She reached down between Will's legs and cupped his scrotum. "He is definitely lacking in one department. What a waste."

"I felt bad the way Fred chewed him out."

"I felt that way, too," she said, "Until I saw the look on his face after the case. He should have been embarrassed, upset with himself, but he was just pissed off at Fred. You can't learn from the bad stuff if you just get mad at everybody else."

She gently squeezed Will's scrotum.

I guess the philosophical part of the discussion is over.

"It is rare to find someone who has the complete package," she said. "That's why I like you."

"I'm not rich."

She laughed out loud and squeezed harder. "So you know you've got everything else?"

"I didn't say that. I thought you did."

She pulled her hand away and took his hand, instead.

"I don't think I can really be trusted on this subject," she said. "I'm not exactly objective. Besides, it's just a matter of time until you're rich."

He laced his fingers through hers. He roughed up the spikes on the top of her head.

"What are you talking about?" he asked.

"You won't be a scrub tech forever. I figure you'll do this for a year or two and then start thinking about medical school. It's inevitable."

"I don't know," he said. "Doctors have to go to school forever. I think I'd go nuts."

"You don't have to stop working. You can scrub while you're premed. You can do it right up until you start your hospital rotations in medical school. It'll keep you off the streets and out of trouble."

Maybe she's right. It might even keep me from falling in love every other day.

"Maybe you're right," he said. He stroked her legs, gradually moving higher.

"Don't change the subject," she said.

"Why not?" he asked. "It's not like I'm going to decide anything tonight. I've never thought about it before."

"You're kidding," she said.

"No, I'm not. You're doing it again, Lila, acting like I've been a scrub tech for twenty years. I'm still learning this job. I'm not ready to move on. Let me enjoy this, will you, before you shove me out the door." His hand slid up her leg again.

"Okay," she said, "You're right." She didn't try to stop him this time.

Decisions about Ray and medical school were all in the future. They settled for the moment.

EIGHTEEN

After Will walked away, Lila drove down the ramps and parked in the grass beneath the trees. She needed to see if Will went home tonight. Laparoscopy patients often went home on the first day post-op, but she wondered if Monique had been kept for one more night because she'd been so ill. Would Will go to visit her again? She had to see for herself.

What right do I have to be jealous as long as I'm still with Ray? Maybe that's what this is all about. Maybe Will's forcing my hand.

She knew that was crazy. Will wasn't like that

She thought about their conversation. She couldn't believe that Will had never thought of medical school before today. She'd always thought it must be part of his plan, but you couldn't fake the blank look he'd given her when she mentioned it.

Maybe he isn't the total package. Maybe ambition is missing from the mix.

Was that a bad thing? Weren't half the people in the world driving themselves crazy because they couldn't be happy where they were? Was it so terrible that Will was smart enough to savor what he had? It didn't mean that he'd never think about moving on, he just hadn't, yet.

What was wrong with her, anyway? Why put the idea in his head? Why turn his eyes to the future? She knew she had no place in it.

She knew she'd said it because she wanted the best for him.

Again with the motherly thoughts. He doesn't want a mother, remember? He just wants to fuck somebody he can respect.

Maybe he was the wise one in their relationship. He accepted them for what they were. Why couldn't she do that? Because she knew it wasn't always possible to live in the moment.

She remembered battling with Ray Jr. and Roland when they were in high school. They both said math was stupid, that they'd never use it in real life. She just wanted them to do their best.

There was still Jerry. He'd always gotten good grades. Maybe he'd be the one who'd move on up.

Okay, Lila, let's lose that image, Will and Jerry walking down the aisle in their caps and gowns, gold honor sashes around their necks.

Maybe this was why she wanted Will to move on. The mother in her hated the fact that she was sleeping with a child.

She shook her head. She could hate herself for cheating on Ray, but she had no right to condemn what she had with Will out of hand because of the difference in their ages. Maybe she just needed to live in the moment the way he did.

NINETEEN

Will hadn't gone home when Lila drove away. He went back into the hospital to look for Fred Dean. He wanted to ask Fred if what Lila had said was true. If he wanted to go to medical school, would he really be able to work while he was getting started? He'd always heard that medical students didn't have time for a job. He figured that was why most of them were such jerks. They'd never lived in the real world.

Nothing was going on in the OR, so he headed for the nurse's lounge. He'd cut though and catch the elevator to the upstairs surgeon's lounge.

He heard voices. He walked through the door and found Julie and Steve Dempsey sitting side by side on the only couch in the lounge. Her hand rested on his arm. She looked up and pulled the hand away.

"Will," she said, "What are you doing here?"

"I was looking for Fred," he said.

"Papa Bear?" Dempsey said.

"Who?" Will asked.

Dempsey grinned. "That's what we call Fred in the anesthesia department. I thought everybody knew."

"No," Will said. "I've never heard that."

"I suppose that makes sense. No one would say it around you because they figure you'd squeal to Fred," Dempsey said. He put an arm around Julie's shoulder. "What was it Fred said earlier? Oh yeah, that you and Lila are the best team in the OR. Funny, I didn't know there was a competition going on. Did you know there was one, Jules?"

"Some people seem to think there is," she said. She laid her hand back on Dempsey's arm. Will studied her face. He'd seen this look before, when they'd been assigned to Sheila Cole together. Maybe that was part of what attracted Julie and Dempsey to each other.

It's them against the big, bad A-team.

His jealousy faded.

"I'm sorry I bothered you," he said. "I'm going to check upstairs and see if Fred's asleep. Have a good night."

He walked into the hall. He heard the low rumble of Dempsey's voice and then Julie's high-pitched laugh. He stopped and thought of going back.

It would be nice to kick his pretty boy ass. At least to try.

He turned and headed for the elevator.

The doctor's lounge was supposed to be off limits to everyone but the doctors, but it really depended on who was in there. The door was propped open, which was the unofficial sign that regular people were welcome. Dempsey was a closed-door guy, while Fred had an open-door policy.

Fred was the only one in the room. He sat in a gigantic black leather lounge chair, reading a medical journal. Will knocked. Fred looked up.

"Will," he said, "Come in."

They were on the ninth floor of the hospital, the penthouse. One wall was floor-to-ceiling glass. There were blackout curtains, but Fred had left them open.

Will walked past Fred to the window. He looked out over the city that surrounded them.

"It's quite a view," Fred said.

Will thought of the Fourth of July.

"Why did you come down to watch the fireworks with me and Lila on the Fourth if you had this view?" He asked.

Fred shrugged. "Fireworks are sort of a family thing," he said. "It's no fun watching them alone."

Will nodded. It must get pretty lonely up here, sometimes. Still, wasn't that the idea? They didn't call this floor the penthouse for nothing.

But even the Greek gods came down from their mountaintop sometimes.

Will turned from the window and took the lounge chair beside Fred. He sank into the plush leather, groped for the wooden handle on the side, found it and pulled. The chair snapped back. He might as well be riding a mechanical bull. He struggled back into an upright position and surrendered to the soft leather.

There was a football game on the wide-screen television that filled the wall opposite the window. The players were nearly life sized. Fred had the sound turned down.

"So what's up?" Fred asked.

"Lila and I were talking tonight," Will said. "She said I should think about going to medical school."

Fred seemed surprised. "You've never thought about it before?"

"Not really. I never liked school and it seems like you guys have to go to school forever. I just wanted to get on with it, you know?"

"No," Fred said. "I don't." He seemed genuinely puzzled by the idea.

"You're right about having to go to school forever, though," he said. "It is a long haul."

"Lila said I'd be able to work part of the time. It might not be so bad if I could do that."

"Work?" Fred said. He grimaced. The word seemed sour to him. Will expected him to reach up and wipe his lips, trying to get rid of the residue it had left.

"You can't really work when you're in medical school," Fred said. "It's pretty much a full-time job."

On the big screen, a player burst from a pack of tacklers and into the open field. Will felt his heart quicken. He looked towards Fred who hadn't seemed to notice. Beyond the screen, the window was a black sheet.

"It'll be awhile before I could even apply to medical school," Will said. "I got an Associates degree in Tech school. I might have year of college credit, but most of my training was practical.

"You could work while you're pre-med," Fred said. "This job is ideal for that." He reached down without looking and cranked his chair from the lounge position. He stood. Will was amazed at how easily he extricated himself from the plush leather.

"One of the advantages of working in the OR," Fred said as he crossed to the window. "Is that you can work full-time and go to school. You could work the odd shifts or cover the weekends. You'd make a decent living and still have time on the job to study. If you work the night shift, you could even sleep while you're here. It's like working part-time but getting full-time pay."

Fred had left the journal he was reading in the chair opened to a photograph. It was a splash of red and white on the black leather. Will picked it up.

The bloody photograph was nothing new to him. The words were another story. They seemed like a foreign language.

"I worry about stuff like this," Will said. "It looks pretty deep."

Fred smiled. "It'll be awhile before you have to deal with anything like this. They let you walk before you run."

Will closed the journal and laid it back on the chair. "Won't I have to take some pretty heavy science courses right away, though? Won't I have to load up on biology and chemistry and math?"

"It's not like that any more," Fred said. "The powers-that-be aren't looking for Straight-A science majors. They're looking for 'well-rounded individuals'". He chuckled, as if those words were as senseless as 'working while in medical school'. At least they weren't sour.

"What about you?" Will asked. "Were you one of those 'well-rounded individuals' when you applied to medical school?"

"Hell no," Fred said. "I took molecular biology as an elective and I haven't worked a day since I started college. My old man was a pipe fitter. He always told me that he'd worked enough for the both of us."

Fred came back across the room and eased into the chair. He sat on the journal, fumbled for it beneath him. It slid down between the cushion and the arm of the chair. Fred reached down, but jerked his hand back out. "Shit," he said, "The damn thing bit me."

Will smiled. He knew that there were staples on the frame and some of them had come loose. Fred must have touched one of those. It was nice to know that there were some things even Fred couldn't do gracefully.

Fred pulled the journal out and laid it on the end table beside the chair.

"You'd only have to take the requirements," Fred said. "Some bio, organic chemistry. You could fill out your schedule with easy stuff: literature, history, poly-sci. I'm sure you'd be fine. Then it's all about how you do on your MCATS."

"What are those?"

"Those are the standardized tests everyone takes."

"Like SATS."

"Yeah," he said. "Just a little more intense. It also helps you that we have a med school here. They give preference to in-state students."

"I don't know. Med school still seems like a long haul."

"It is, but it's not like you're in a bubble the whole time. The first year is all book work. The second year you get out once a week. You talk to patients and work on histories and physicals. Third and fourth year is heavy on practical."

He tossed the journal to Will. "That's one of the things I love about medicine," he said. "The balance between books and life. I'm still learning every day."

"I learn new things every day," Will said as he tossed it back.

"Of course you do, but you're new to this," Fred said. He swung his arm back to toss the book again and it was obvious he expected Will to keep it this time. "Being a scrub tech is enough for you, now, but in a few years you'll know all the tricks. You'll be looking for more. It never hurts to push yourself, to explore. Think of going back to school this way: even if you don't end up in medical school, you might find something else that interests you."

"Thanks, Fred," Will said. He folded the magazine and stuck it in his back pocket. "That makes a lot of sense." He stood.

"Thanks again for your help tonight," Fred said. "You and Lila kept your cool when Dempsey dropped the ball. I appreciate that."

"No problem," Will said.

He stared at the wall as he waited by the elevator. No floor-to-ceiling windows here, just smooth, white plaster.

He thought about Fred and Lila. He appreciated their advice. He knew they were pushing him because they wanted to best for him.

Still, why was happiness always about moving on? He was happy now. Why did he need to imagine a time when he wouldn't be? Somehow, that seemed backwards. Shouldn't imagination be about hope? Shouldn't it make the rough times easier, by offering better times down the road? Why were we always looking down the road, anyway?

The elevator door slid open and Steve Dempsey strode out, eyes down. Will tried to sidestep, but Dempsey clipped his arm. Will bounced off like a defensive back trying to bring down a fullback.

"Hey, watch where you're going, will you?" Will said.

"What are you doing up here?" Dempsey asked.

"I told you I was looking for Fred."

"But you're not supposed to be up here."

"Fred didn't seem to mind."

Dempsey sneered. Once again his anger transformed him.

From GQ to mug shot in the blink of an eye.

"You and Fred," Dempsey said. "Papa Bear and his cub." He shoved past Will. At the door he faltered, then he threw his shoulders back.

"Dr. Dean," Dempsey said. His voice cracked. "Can we talk?" He plunged through the doorway.

When Will got to the ER entrance, Julie sat outside the door in the smoking area. When she saw Will, she hid the cigarette behind her back. She frowned, shook her head, pulled the cigarette back out and took a puff.

Will walked over to her. "I didn't know you smoked," he said.

"I quit a couple times a year," she said. "You just hit me at a good time. Don't worry. My starting back up doesn't have anything to do with us breaking up. I'm not stressing out or anything like that."

"Actually," Will said. "It looks like I did you a favor."

"How do you figure that?" she asked. She inhaled and let out a long plume of smoke.

"You're moving up. Anesthesiologists make the big bucks, don't they?"

Kathy's not the only one who's doctor material.

She tossed the cigarette down and crushed it under her heel.

"You have got to be kidding me," she said.

"What?"

"I'm pretty sure you dumped me, Will. I would have kept trying, but you seemed pretty determined to be rid of me."

He put a hand on her arm. "I'm not happy to rid of you," he said. "Things just didn't work out for us. You just took me by surprise before when I saw you with Dempsey. I know I don't have the right."

"You are such an asshole," she said. She glanced at her watch. "I have to get back upstairs."

"I guess I'll see you around," he said. He started towards his car.

"Wait," she said.

Will stopped and turned back to her.

"Would you ride back up to the OR with me?" she asked. "I need you to tell me what's going on between Steve and Fred."

"I'm not sure I'm the one who should do that," he said. "Steve isn't exactly my favorite person. I'm not sure I'd be fair to him."

"You really didn't like it when you saw us together, did you?"

He looked into her eyes. It was the same look she'd given him when they were together, as if nothing had changed.

"You're jealous?" she asked.

"I guess so."

"Good."

They went back in and waited in silence by the elevator.

When they got back to the OR, Chuck Segal sat behind the desk. He gave Will a funny look. "Don't ask," Julie said. Chuck shrugged and headed down the hall. He might wonder why Will was back, but not enough to let it interfere with his sleep.

"We can talk in the lounge," Julie said. "I'll meet you there." She disappeared into the OR. He went to the lounge. He sat down on the couch that Julie and Dempsey had been sitting on before.

What was he doing here? What point was there in telling her what had happened? Would she even believe him? Dempsey was her guy now. Whose version was she going to believe?

Julie returned with a blanket wrapped around her shoulders, She sat down beside him. He thought she'd take the chair across the aisle.

So why did I sit on the couch?

"What really happened between Fred and Steve?" she asked. "I know there was a problem with a patient. Everybody's talking about it, but no one will give me the details.

"Steve's been pissy all night," she said. "If he calls Fred, 'Papa Bear' one more time I'm going to scream." She put a hand on his knee. "What happened, Will?"

Will looked down at her hand, but when he looked back up and into her eyes, he knew that this was all about Steve. She might be his ex, but she was focused on her new guy.

"We had a strange case," he said. "They called us about a Triple A in the ER. The patient was stable, at first, so we started to get things set up, but the guy crashed on the way up. Steve thought the aneurysm had blown, but when we cut him open, it was intact. It turns out his heart had given out, so we just closed him back up."

"That must have been wild," she said. "You went from zero to sixty and back to zero in a matter of minutes."

"It was a trip."

"So what happened with Steve?"

"I told you that I don't want to tell you that part."

"Because you're jealous of me and him?"

"Yeah."

He looked down into his lap. He didn't trust himself to meet her gaze.

Suddenly, her head was in his lap. The warmth from the blanket radiated from her. She stared back up at him.

"So does this mean you want to get back together?" she asked.

He smiled. He ran his fingers through her hair.

"I just think that Dempsey's an asshole," he said. "I think you deserve better."

She reared up out of his lap. She stood and sat down across from him "Deserve better?" she said. "What the hell is that about? What are you, my father?"

"I didn't mean it that way," he said.

"How else could you mean it?" she asked. "You really are a piece of work, Will."

"That's why I don't want to tell you about what happened," he said. "I don't think I can be fair."

"Of course you can," she said. "You're too much of a fanatic about the OR to lie. You wouldn't lie to make him look bad or to spare my feelings. Just tell me, okay?"

"Okay," he said. He didn't want to look her in the eye. He focused on the lamp beside her.

"Steve was the one with the patient when he crashed," he said. "We were setting up and Steve burst through the door of the OR. He panicked. He shoved the stretcher at us like a hot potato. He didn't do a thing. We started CPR. Fred came in and threw Steve out."

"Steve shoved the stretcher away from him?" she asked. She shivered, pulled the blanket tighter around her neck.

"Like he couldn't get rid of the guy fast enough," Will said. "It would have slammed into the table if I hadn't caught it."

"Did he say anything?" she asked.

"Just that he was alone and that the guy had stopped breathing. He said it two or three times, 'I was alone.' He didn't do a thing for the guy, and he didn't snap out of it until Fred showed up."

"Papa Bear," she said. There was none of the sarcasm that Steve used when he said it. It was as if the words hurt her to say.

"Fred was a prick," Will said. "He could have let Steve stick around once things settled down. That might have helped, but it was like he wanted to punish him."

He looked back at Julie.

"I'm sorry," he said.

"Don't be sorry," she said. "I know I've got my work cut out for me with Steve."

Her smile showed real affection. Will felt another pang of jealousy.

"You and Fred would see that he's all right if you could just get past your natural dislike for pretty boys," she said.

"Pretty boys?"

"Of course," she said. "Steve's gorgeous. Guys don't care about that, though. All you care about are the size of another guy's balls."

Just what Lila said.

Will thought of Dempsey at the door of the call room, how he'd hesitated, but still gone in to talk Fred. That took balls.

Maybe he should give the guy a break. Maybe he should lighten up on everybody.

He'd been wrong about Julie tonight. He'd expected her to bond with Steve against Fred. He thought she'd rather tear everyone else down than grow herself. He'd been wrong.

Maybe people just needed a hand, sometimes. Julie reached across the aisle and put one of her hands on each of his knees.

"Hey," she said, "Where are you?"

"Sorry," he said. "Sometimes this stuff gets complicated."

"Tell me about it," she said. She reached out and touched his face, as if his thoughts could be passed to her through her fingertips.

"You should probably go," she said.

"I think you're right."

Maybe he'd been wrong about her. Maybe she'd grow past the stuff that had turned him off about her. He couldn't feel badly about that though, because that's what had given him a chance to be with Lila.

"I'll see you around," he said.

"Okay," she said. She leaned back in her chair. "When Steve gets back from his talk with Fred, I hope he'll be ready to tell me what happened."

"I think he will. It took guts for him to talk to Fred."

He put his hand on her shoulder, his fingers slipped between the warm cloth of the blanket and her skin. She put her hand over his.

"I hope so," she said. "Of course, he might try to tell me that he put Fred in his place. Either that or he'll still be whining. If either one of those happens, I might be calling you tomorrow."

"Okay,' he said.

He took the stairs down. He didn't want to take the chance of running into Steve. He was glad he'd had a chance to talk to Julie. Funny how much she'd changed in such a short time. Or maybe she'd always been like this, he was just too hard-core to see it.

He went out the door by the ER, scuffing his feet through the cigarette butts littered on the concrete. He headed towards the side entrance of the parking garage.

"Well, well," Lila's voice boomed out of the darkness. "I thought it was that skinny little patient I had to worry about, but I guess it's your ex-girlfriend, after all. I can't take my eye off you for a minute, can I?"

TWENTY

Lila had waited for Will in the shadows by the parking garage just as she'd done the night before. She hadn't seen him drive out. She knew he'd gone back to see that girl. She fumed for a half hour in the dark before he emerged from the ER entrance. He started for the garage, but then he turned and spoke to someone in the smoking area. At first, she thought it was an ER nurse. They came up with the patients to the OR sometimes, so he might have met one of them that way.

She finally recognized Julie. She wasn't worried, at first. It would have been rude for him not to stop and say hello. Then he followed her back in.

Her stomach heaved. She felt the taste of bile in her throat.

What the hell is going on? He knows the fickle little bitch has already moved on. Maybe that's it. He likes a challenge.

She glanced at her watch. It was already after one. This was crazy. Could she afford to stay out half the night, to make Ray suspicious, just to spy on Will? Of course, she couldn't.

But she couldn't leave.

She waited. Her mind went to another dark place, a dimly lit Room 12A. She saw Will and Julie on the OR table. She knew that it was crazy, but the image wouldn't go away.

She remembered the time she'd been with Will in Rm 12A. Now, Julie took her place in the vision. Will pumped Julie in her mind and she felt him inside of her. She squirmed and pressed herself against the seat. She got out of her truck and stood in the shadows as the minutes ticked by on her watch, as bodies roiled in the dark spaces of her mind.

I can't keep doing this. I have a life, a husband. What would Jerry say if he could see me now? I need to go home.

When he finally emerged from the ER door, she wanted to let him pass, didn't want him to know that she was even there, but her feet moved against her will and she ran towards him. The words flew from her throat. The edge in her voice frightened even her.

"Well, well. I thought it was that skinny little patient I had to worry about, but I guess it's your ex-girlfriend, after all. I can't take my eye off you for a minute, can I?"

He turned to face her. "Lila," he said. "What the hell are you doing here?"

"Waiting for you."

"Waiting? Don't you mean spying?"

"Damn right I'm spying," she said. "I guess it's a good thing. Is there anybody in this hospital you're not fucking?"

"What the hell is wrong with you? You're the only one I'm fucking. I thought you went home hours ago."

"I'd be there, now, if it wasn't for you," she said. "But you never seem to go home, anymore."

"I don't have to," he said. "I don't have anybody waiting for me."

Touche.

He reached for her and she slapped his hand away. He opened his arms and she jammed her hands into his chest. He staggered, but kept coming, took her in a bear hug and hung on. She struggled and they went down into the wet grass. They rolled around and she ended up on top. She drew her fist back. His eyes got big. He reared up and drove her to the ground.

She lay stunned, the breath knocked out of her.

"I'm sorry," he gasped. "What the hell is going on?"

She turned her face away as tears poured down her cheeks.

"If I let you up will you stop trying to kill me?" he asked.

She didn't answer. He waited.

"I'm all right," she whispered finally. He rolled off of her and sat in the grass, rubbing his chest.

"Why were you spying on me?" he asked.

"I saw you go back in last night to see your fashion model. Is that what you did tonight, before you hooked up with Julie?"

He put his arm around her. She didn't resist this time. They arranged themselves under the tree, her body between his legs and his arms around her.

"I did go back in to see Monique last night, but nothing happened. I just wanted to make sure she was okay. I went back in tonight to talk to Fred about medical school.

"When I came back out, Julie wanted to talk about what happened to Steve Dempsey tonight. You don't have anything to worry about, Lila."

"Maybe not tonight," she said, "But I know I'm living on borrowed time when it comes to you and me."

"Why do you keep saying that?"

"Because I'm old enough to be your mother," she said. "Because I am a mother. You're young and just finding yourself. Hell, now I've got you thinking about medical school. By the time you're practicing medicine I'll be sixty. Your life will be just starting and mine will be over."

"Would you listen to yourself?" he said. "If my life won't start for ten years, then what am I doing, now, just running in place?"

"Maybe," she said. "But you're supposed to be running towards something, building your future."

The way I built a life with Ray.

"Why do you always have to talk about the future?" he asked.

Because that's what grown-ups do.

"I don't care about the future," he said. "I love you now."

"Love?" she said. "How can you love me? We've only been doing this for six days. You're just confused. You've got me mixed up in the way you feel about the work. You're too young to even know what love is."

His arms tightened around her, more in anger than in reassurance. "So what are you confused about?" he asked. "Or maybe it's all pretty clear to you. Maybe I'm just someone who gets you off like you've never gotten off before.

"Maybe that's all I am to you, a boy toy that you keep around because sex with your husband has lost its kick."

She tried to get out of his arms so she could hit him again, but he'd anticipated that and held her tightly.

"Why are you so angry," he asked. "Because I mentioned your husband or because I'm right?"

"Neither one," she said. "If this was just about sex I wouldn't be hiding in the frigging bushes, hating the thought of you being with anybody else. I wouldn't care who else you screwed"

He sighed.

"I don't like what this is doing to us," he said. "Listen to the crap we accuse each other of. I can't keep doing this, Lila. You have to tell your husband."

She stiffened. "That would kill him."

"You're killing yourself," he said. He rubbed his chest. "You might kill me."

She tried to stop the laugh, but it still came.

"I never should have let this happen," she said.

"We can't change that, now."

Lights came around the corner of the garage, slid over them. She saw the blue lights on the roof of the hospital's security van.

"Oh Christ," she said. "Just what we need."

"Maybe they won't see us," he said.

The van slowed as it came parallel with them.

Will pulled his arms away and nudged her forward. He stood up. "I'll go talk to them," he said. "You slide around behind the tree."

She watched him as he walked over to the van. The window rolled down and a light flashed in his face. She heard the voices, serious, at first, but then the tone changed. Finally, she heard laughter.

How could he handle this so easily? Of course, this is like when the cops catch you parking and you have to talk your way out of it. That was another life for her, but it was only yesterday for him.

The van pulled away and Will waved for her to come over.

"It's okay," he said. "That was Mike Harland. He said he wouldn't fill out a report as long as we went home. He said that we should get a room."

"We?" Mike Harland and Ray had often been buddy-buddy at hospital Christmas parties.

"He didn't ask who you were, if that's what you're worried about. It's a guy thing. A gentleman never tells, you know."

"I thought guys always told," she said. "Besides, I never thought of Mike Harland as a gentleman."

"So you learned something new tonight. I told you that your life isn't over, yet." He reached out to touch her face, but she pulled away.

"You don't understand."

"No," he said. "I think you're the one who doesn't. Think about what's going on here. You talk about being old, but you admit that you feel like a school girl."

"That's not exactly a good thing," she said, "Hiding in the bushes, accusing you every time you go near another woman."

"But that's only because we have to hide what's between us," he said. "If we just stopped hiding, I think everything would be fine."

He waited for her answer. She didn't know where to begin. How could he be so naïve? Did he really think the world would let them be together, would pat them on the back and wish them all the best, that there would there be toasts and dancing and celebration?

More likely the world would look down on them, on her for destroying everything she'd built her life around, on him for selling himself short. Her oldest boys might break every bone in his body for messing up their lives. Jerry would break her heart with just a look.

"We'd better get going," she said. "Mike could be back any minute. I'll go first so he doesn't put two and two together." She looked into his eyes, then away, unable to face his disappointment.

"I can't keep doing this, Lila," he said. "Either we tell the truth or I'm done."

"You know I can't do that."

"Then I guess we're done."

He turned and walked away without looking back. She watched him as he went into the garage. She tracked his progress though the openings in the concrete. The other night, after Monique, she'd watched him take the steps two at a time, but tonight, he climbed deliberately, as if it was all he could do to keep moving, as if all he really wanted was to turn around.

She wanted to call him, to tell him to come back. Each step dug into her, but a little less each time. She knew this wouldn't be her last night watching from the shadows, but she finally believed that the last one would come. She was grateful he had the strength to walk away.

TWENTY-ONE

"Don't mess where you eat." Lila's words stuck in his mind as he took his seat at report the next afternoon. How many times had he heard her mouth those words? He could see the look on her face as she said them. She'd pinch her nose with two fingers as if to protect herself from the most foul odor imaginable, as if someone has just relieved themselves in the middle of the lounge.

She'd rolled her eyes in disgust the only time he'd asked her why dating your co-workers wouldn't work.

"Fucking is a transitory thing," she'd said "Work is the only thing that lasts."

So why hadn't she followed her own rule?

Will looked at Kathy and Murph in the corner, the only other people in the lounge. Kathy wrestled her hair into a bun. Murph thumbed through the sports page. When she'd finished with her hair, Kathy looked at Will. She smiled at him, ran her fingers quickly through Muph's thick, black curls. He swiped at her hand.

They seemed to be balancing their relationship with work just fine. Will wondered what their secret was.

No great secret. They're normal. I fell for Julie and then blew it because good looks and great sex weren't enough. Then I fell for a married woman twice my age. I keep blaming this on sex, but maybe I'm the messy one

He glanced at the clock. There were still a few minutes before report. He wondered if Lila would even show up. He remembered how he'd called in sick the day he'd decided to break up with Julie. Lila had called him a wimp back then. Maybe it was her turn to wimp out.

Why shouldn't she? This whole mess was her fault. If she'd just be honest, tell her husband what was going on then everything would be all right.

He heard the curtain jerk back in the locker room, plastic rings skittering across the metal rod. A locker door slammed. He jumped. He took a deep breath.

Get a hold of yourself, Will.

Julie came through the door. She smiled at him.

Maybe Lila *had* called in sick and done them both a favor. He felt the muscles in his legs relax. He stretched them across the aisle.

Julie sat in the chair next to him.

Just like old times.

"How's it going?" she asked as she pulled on her shoes. Her ankle socks were plain white. He touched them and made a face.

"Hey," she said. "I didn't have time to do laundry."

Or maybe she isn't worried about bait now that she's snagged a big fish.

"How's Steve?" he asked.

"He's okay," Julie said. "He and Fred worked things out. I think Fred just needed to see a change in attitude before he'd give him another chance."

"That's good. What are you doing here tonight?"

"Melanie called in sick."

"Melanie?" He drew his legs back and sat up straight.

Lila came through the door. Her face was flushed. She stared at the floor. She stepped over Murph. She didn't look in Will's direction.

"Lila," Kathy said. "You look awful? What's up? Is everything okay at home?"

"Everything's fine," Lila said. "I just didn't sleep much last night."

"Tell me about it," Julie said.

Everyone laughed but Lila. She tried but the laugh seemed to stick in her throat.

"Seriously," Kathy said. She moved into the seat beside Lila. "Is everything okay?"

"Everything's fine," Lila said. "I just had a bad night. I think it was something I ate." She smiled. "You know indigestion can be the end of the frigging world when you get to be my age."

Kathy nodded. Murph and Julie both seemed to relax, as well. Lila sounded like herself. That was enough for them.

"Okay, everybody," Martha said as she strode into the lounge from the door on the OR side. "Let's get going. Thanks for coming, Julie."

Martha arranged her notes in her lap. Will studied Lila's face. He wanted her to look at him, but she stared at the floor.

Martha outlined the cases but he wasn't listening. All he could think about was the pain on Lila's face. He remembered when report had been the high point of his day, when he'd approached each shift with joy and anticipation. He wanted that back.

So get it back. You're the one who pissed it away.

He hadn't meant to. He thought that by dating his co-workers he was being true to the work. He dated Julie because he thought she was just like him. When he doubted that, he'd gone for Lila, the surest thing when it came to the job.

So, here he sat in report, unable to focus on the work, trying to get Lila's attention, all the while knowing that he'd look away if he did. She'd been right all along. He felt like he was up to his neck in a giant pile of crap. He knew he was the only one who could dig his way back out.

When report was over, everyone slipped away but Julie. He tried to catch Lila's eye, but she stared at the floor as she brushed past him.

He wanted to throw his legs across the aisle to block her path, but he fought the urge.

"Are you ready?" Julie asked.

"Ready?"

"You and me," she said. "Doc Jamison, another fractured femur, Room 2."

"Oh, sure," he said, grateful that he wouldn't have to ask Martha about his assignment.

"Will," Martha said. "A minute?"

"I'll see you in the room," Julie said. She rolled her eyes and went out the door. Will wished that he could do the same.

"Have a seat," Martha said. She fiddled with her papers as he sat back down.

"Is everything all right?" she asked.

"Everything's fine. Why do you ask?"

"You seem distracted. I don't think you heard two words of my report. I'm used to a certain level of inattention from most of the crew, but not from you.

"Everybody who addresses a groups regularly has a face in the crowd," she said. "That's the one person you look to when you get tired of the boredom or the hostility on people's faces, the one person who makes you feel like you're getting through.

"You've been that person for me for the last few months, so you can understand my worry when you seem out in space somewhere. Have I lost my touch, or is something up with you?"

"It's not you," he said. "I do have some stuff going on. I didn't think it was messing things up until today. I guess I was wrong."

"Is there anything I can do?" she asked. " If you need to talk, you know my door is always open."

She smiled. The assurance that he was used to seeing in her face was gone. Her uncertainty more than anything brought home just how screwed things up for him.

"I know I've been distracted lately," he said. "I just don't know how to get my focus back."

"Of course you do," she said. "Focus is about limiting distractions. When you're in the OR, you focus on your part of the case, on getting the instruments set up, on getting them into the surgeon's hands. Life isn't so different, really."

"Thanks," he said.

"No need for thanks," she said. "I didn't do anything. I just reminded you of what you already know."

After his scrub, he stood with his arms up, the brown foam dripping down, and surveyed Jamison's room. He saw everything in the room as part of an equation, even the people. The fact that he wasn't sleeping with Julie, wasn't dealing with her anger, wasn't jealous of her anesthesiologist made the process much easier.

Okay, I am a little jealous, but it's nothing compared to everything else that's been going on here the last few months.

She saw him watching and came over. She pushed the door open and held it for him. "Ready partner?" she asked.

"Yeah," he said. "I'm ready."

The case was another external fixator, although it was a routine fracture. Jamison stood back and let his residents do most of the work. They sunk the pins one by one into the bone and arranged the crosspieces and rods. Will remembered the biker with the shattered femur, how Jamison had tinkered with the fragments until he had recreated a bone from shards of broken china.

"Good work, Gentlemen," Jamison said finally. He went out the door and left them to finish up.

Julie winked at Will as Jamison walked away. He was grateful that they were back to this. At least with Julie, he hadn't done any permanent damage. He wondered if he and Lila would ever be able to work together again.

He thought of Lila's eyes as she'd emerged from the shadows the other night. He remembered how he felt each night as he watched her walk away, knowing that she was going home to Ray. Maybe there were some things a person never got past.

Lila was doing a laparoscopic gall bladder in the room next door. He could sense her, almost feel her bristling through the wall. As long as they worked together, being here would be about being with her.

He found Martha after the shift sitting alone in the lounge.

"I thought about what you said earlier," he said. "You're right. I've really made a mess of things. I need to get my focus back. I think the best thing would be to start over."

"Start over?" she said. "I hope you're not talking about quitting."

"Of course not," he said.

"I wish I hadn't said anything, now," she said. She raked her fingers through her hair and dropped them to her lap.

"Don't say that," he said. "You did me a favor. I thought I had things under control. Before long everyone will be wondering what's going on with me. I don't think I could stand that."

She shook her head. "Personal issues can rip a team apart," she said.

"I was thinking I might work are different shift. Are there any openings in the morning?"

She laughed and shook her head.

"There are openings, but I can't see you on that shift," she said. "Most of the cases are elective surgery. You'll spend an entire shift of knees or tonsils or gallbladders, one right after the other. You'd probably be bored out of your mind."

"You might be right. Maybe I could work on the weekends. I know there are people who work just those hours."

"The weekend people are mostly going to school," she said.

"I might try school," he said.

She sighed.

"I'm not surprised," she said. "The good ones always do."

"But it isn't about school," he said. "I'm off my game. I need a change."

"So, your mind is made up?" she asked. She looked right at him, forcing him to meet her eyes.

"Yes," he said, "Everything is happening too fast. I need to focus on my work and slow things down."

"All right," she said. "I'll talk to Bev."

Bev was the morning supervisor. If his decision was made, it was obvious that Martha would help him get things done.

"Would you mind walking me to my car?" she asked. "I parked on the top floor of the garage. The lighting up there isn't exactly up to par."

That does have its advantages, sometimes.

"Sure," he said. "No problem."

They cut through the lounge on their way back to the locker room. She went through the door and he sat back down in his chair. His chair. He remembered when he'd come early every day and settled into this chair with a cup of coffee. Back when everything had been about the work, about what new challenges awaited him. He wanted that feeling back.

He was glad that Martha wanted him to walk out with her. He worried that Lila was waiting for him. He didn't want to see her. This whole stalking thing scared him. It wasn't like her.

He'd never understood when people talked about love as if it were madness. He'd been attracted to Lila because she was so real. This just didn't fit.

Maybe she wouldn't approach him if he was with Martha.

Or maybe she'll come out of the shadows with a gun and blow us both away.

He needed to get away from this drama.

Martha returned in a light-blue running suit. The zipper, pulled down between her breasts, revealed nothing but skin.

"Okay," she said. "I'm ready."

They walked in silence. He studied the darkness beneath the trees as they crossed the open space between the hospital and the garage. It saddened him to think of Lila in there, glaring out at them.

"I'll be sorry to lose you," Martha said. "Having someone around who's so versatile made my job a lot easier. Are you sure you can't work these personal things out?"

Will looked under the trees. He expected to see the fierce, red coals of Lila's eyes blazing there.

"I'm sure," he said.

They climbed the stairs and emerged on the top floor.

"That's me," she said, pointing to a silver BMW parked against the far wall.

It was hard to believe that he and Lila had been up here just the other night, putting the darkness to good use.

Martha pulled her keys out of her purse and clicked the alarm off. The lights flared in the darkness, then blinked back off.

"I'll talk to Bev tomorrow," she said. "We can probably make the switch in a few weeks. Thanks for walking me."

"You know," he said. "I've got some time off coming. I don't suppose I could take that?"

"I'll have to talk to Bev," she said. "It's a bit unusual. Your problems must be much worse than I thought. Are you sure we can't talk about it."

"No," he said.

"Okay," she said. "Come in tomorrow and we'll talk to Bev together. We'll work something out."

"Thanks for all your help," he said. "Thanks for understanding and all."

"Understanding?" she said. "I never said I understood." She unlocked the door, got behind the wheel and drove away.

Will waited with his back to the stairs, expecting Lila's voice, "So there's the latest notch in your belt, frigging Martha. I never knew that 'stick rammed up the ass' was your type."

But Lila didn't come. He felt relief but also sadness. He didn't want things to end this way. It was less than a week since the night he'd talked to her about Sheila and they'd ended up at his place. How had something that felt so right have gone so wrong so fast?

Because she was so much older than him? Because she had a husband? Because the only way it could work was as a fling and neither of them wanted that, at least not with each other.

He'd have to be more careful from now on. He wouldn't date his co-workers. He'd regain his focus on the job. He'd take some courses, look into med school.

Maybe that was why Lila had encouraged him to do this. She knew where they were headed. She'd known it couldn't last.

Always the savvy veteran. Always one step ahead.

TWENTY-TWO

Lila had watched as Will and Martha crossed from the hospital to the garage. She waited as they passed, but it wasn't control that held her back, it was exhaustion. She couldn't bring herself to speak to Will, but she finally accepted that she had to leave Ray.

She'd told Will from the start that that would never happen. He'd told her that he'd do whatever she wanted. It had seemed like a good plan.

Too bad we screwed things up by falling in love.

We? Maybe she should speak for herself.

She'd avoided Will all night, as if that would help her avoid the sure knowledge of what she had to do. It had done the opposite. Knowing he was there but not seeing him had been impossible. But even though she understood what she had to do, she couldn't handle it tonight. She let Will and Martha pass. She turned and walked to her truck.

The drive home was a battle just as it always was, but it was a different fight, this time. The familiar sights usually reminded her of what her life was really about as thoughts of Will clung to her mind. Odd that a police cruiser parked in the shadows with an alcoholic sheriff passed out behind the wheel usually comforted her.

Not tonight. She pushed it away, focused on Will, on the constant pull he exerted on her heart. She was tired of fighting it. She wanted to be happy.

She clung to Will as she navigated the curves of Route 9, as she slipped under the canopy of trees that lined their drive. She parked the truck besides Ray's and climbed the stairs. She checked on Jerry. That was the hardest thing, but she beat it this time. After that it wasn't so hard to crawl in beside Ray.

He woke and they visited for awhile. She made up a story about her night. He kissed the top of her head and fell back to sleep.

She got Jerry ready for school in the morning and lingered over coffee with Ray. She thought of Will. She took his strength and made it hers. They had a chance. They only had to take it.

As she drove back to the hospital, she was as sure of herself as she had been in months, since those first feelings back in July. She'd done that C-Section with Will and knew he was something special. She would have done something then, but Ray's heart attack put everything on hold. She'd hoped the months away would change the way she felt, but the first time she'd seen him, she'd been lost again. She still couldn't believe that he cared about her, too. She hoped she hadn't ruined everything with her anger and jealousy.

She wasn't kidding herself. She knew that the decision, itself, was all she could be sure of. Once it was made, all hell would break loose, but she knew she had to throw herself into the current and see where it took her.

In the locker room she pulled the curtain closed and dressed with care. She studied her face in the mirror on her locker door as she touched-up her make up. She pulled on her cap, slammed the locker door and pulled the curtain back. She stepped through the door into the lounge and into her new life.

She focused on Will's chair. He slouched there, as expected, the coffee cup balanced on his chest. He looked relaxed, at ease. She remembered his first months on the job, the joy he'd seemed to take in every day. They'd all made fun of him, at first, but that was where it all began for her.

She tried to get his attention, but he was focused on Martha as if it were his first report.

When Martha had finished, Lila realized that she hadn't given Will an assignment.

He glanced at Lila and smiled.

"Can I talk to you for a minute?" he asked.

"Of course," she said, but the look in his eyes threw her. She'd expected turmoil, but saw only peace. She understood. He wasn't focused on Martha because it was his first report, but because it was his last.

What have I done?

He slipped from the lounge and headed down the hallway to the roof. He climbed out the window and squatted down with his back to the wall. She expected him to play with the rocks, but he just stared out across the lawn, intent, it seemed, to take it all in.

"I wanted to say I'm sorry," he said. "I messed up. You told me right from the start that you couldn't leave your husband. I thought I could live with that, but I can't"

"But you don't have to, I—"

"Yes I do," he said. "You've been with the guy for thirty years. You've got kids and grandkids and a home you built together. It was insane for me to think that you could give that up."

"Why won't you let me talk?" she said. Tears of frustration poured down her face.

He reached out to brush them away.

She understood that she wasn't the only one who'd taken a journey in the last twenty-four hours. While she'd done everything she needed to prepare herself to be with him, he'd been steeling himself to move on without her.

She knew what it had taken for her to get to this point. There was life and there was she and Will. Life came naturally, the accumulated habit of fifty years. She and Will were the opposite of that. She'd wanted him for a long time, but they'd been only been together for six days. How could that compare to her life with Ray?

Six days? How can that even be possible?

With she and Will, there were no habits, no steps taken without thinking. Everything was hard and required a conscious decision. If she relaxed for just a minute she knew that she would slip back to her life.

He seemed so sure. She felt her resolve slipping away.

"I talked to Martha," he said. "I'm going to transfer to the morning shift, then work weekends when a slot opens up. I thought about what you and Fred said about med school. I'm going to take some courses and see how that goes."

Yesterday this news would have torn her in two different directions. She would have been happy that he was doing something good for himself even if it would take him away from her. Today it meant nothing except for the distance that it would put between them.

"When do you start?" she asked, measuring the time she had to show him that she'd changed.

"In two weeks," he said, "But I've got some vacation time coming. Martha said I could take it, now. I just stuck around to say good-bye."

"So this is it," she said. She took a breath. She exhaled. She fell back to her life.

"I think that's for the best," he said. "You know we've been crazy. We both need to get back to what counts."

"What are you going to do with your time off?" she asked.

"I haven't thought about it. Mostly, I just want to get away, you know?"

"Yeah," she said. "I know."

"I want you to know how much I appreciate everything you've done for me," he said. "I won't forget."

"Sure," she said. "I'm sorry that I got so crazy."

He held his arms open to her. She remembered the image that she'd fought just a few days ago: Will and Jerry marching together in cap and gown. Graduation Day.

She went to him. He pulled her close.

"I know it's for the best," he said. His grip tightened, as if he doubted his own words. She pulled away.

She watched him as he climbed back in the window, part of her in disbelief at how easily she'd stepped away from the person she'd been for the last twenty-four hours. Still, why shouldn't it be easy? That person was an illusion. The world she thought she'd left behind was all she'd ever had.

TWENTY-THREE

Will spent the two weeks after he left evenings with his old gang. He stayed drunk and high the entire time.

They never asked him why he was back. They left him in bed in the morning when they went off to work and when he was there in the afternoon, they cracked open a beer, fired up another joint and started in again.

The first Saturday night that he was with them, they went to their old hangout. At two a.m., when the rest of the customers had been thrown out, they waited with their friend Stu, the bartender, as he closed up and served them after hours. A woman with dark skin and blonde hair that didn't match approached him.

"You're new," she said as she draped an arm over his shoulder. "I thought only regulars got to hang around after two."

"That's Will," Stu said as he put another beer in front of Will and a shot of tequila by her hand. "He's one of those prodigal sons."

"Like in the bible?" she asked. She eyed Will suspiciously. She wore a dark blue halter top. Will studied the gold cross that hung down between her breasts.

This is not the time for us to remind her of her religious background considering how many potential sins she's anticipating at this very minute.

"Don't listen to Stu," Will said. He gripped the cross and pulled her closer to him. "I used to live on this stool. Stu's just pissed because I've been gone for awhile."

"But you're back now," she said. Her hands went to his face, latched onto his beard.

"I'm right here," Will said.

The next morning he sat with Stu in the kitchen nursing a beer.

"Hey man," Stu said. "You look like a piece of shit."

"You should talk," Will said, but he knew this was just bravado. Stu drank religiously every night. He was used to this. It had been a long time since Will had gotten this drunk. He'd avoided the mirrors in the apartment as he'd navigated his shaky path to the table.

"No man," Stu said. "I look like a hung-over piece of shit, but you've got something else going on."

Will shrugged. "Last night was just weird for me, you know?"

"Didn't the honeys meet with your approval?"

"It wasn't them. My head just wasn't in it," Will said. He sipped his beer. This swallow hurt as bad as the previous one, but he knew he needed to keep trying.

"No shit, man," Stu said. "You mean you had trouble getting it up? I hate it when that happens."

"No," Will said, "It was the opposite. I couldn't get off."

"Even with that blond Latina?"

"Even her. We went at if for hours."

Stu shook his head. "Jesus, man," he'd said. "If that's your idea of a problem, I don't even know you any more."

When the two weeks were over, Will headed back to work but the hospital seemed like someplace he'd never been before.

Things were different in the morning, coming in when the sky was still dark. The lobby bustled with patients coming in for their appointments.

He walked up to his locker and stared at the combination dial. He had no idea what the necessary numbers were. He dumped his knapsack in the corner and went to report.

He started in orthopedics, two total hips and a bilateral knee replacement. His trainer told him that working the day shift was all about the routine, about knocking the cases out, about getting things done. Timing was everything.

If Jamison was an artist, the total joint surgeons were robots. This was about cutting out arthritic bone, about slamming a new and improved metal joint into place. It was about sewing things up and moving on.

Still, he loved it that first day. After those last confusing days on evenings, after two weeks in a fog of booze and pot, it was great to focus. It was the perfect way to get his life back, by focusing on one step at a time, on which instrument to hand the surgeon next, which suture, which dressing, which drain.

It worked that way until about two p.m. and then it all started to come undone. The intercom sounded and it was Martha. Could the rest of his crew be far behind?

Every time the door opened, he looked up.

"Hey man," the surgeon said. "We're in the homestretch. You've done great all day. Don't blow it, now."

Martha was the first familiar face. Actually, he sensed her before he saw her. Her perfume filled his nostrils, a familiar fruity mist.

He turned and she stood beside a tall, slim kid that he'd never seen before. The guy looked like he was barely out of school.

"Welcome back," she said.

"Thanks."

"How was your time off?" she asked. "Did you do anything constructive?" One red hair slid down into her eyes. She tucked it back into her cap.

"Not really," he said.

"That's good," she said. "That's what vacations are for. How was your first day back?"

"It was fine. The day shift is different." The surgeon held his hand out for a needle driver and Will slapped it into his palm.

"I tried to warn you," she said.

"I know," Will said. "Don't get me wrong. It was just what I needed."

"I'm glad." She nodded towards the kid. "This is Bradley," she said.

Will pulled a gown from a side table and shook it open.

"It's good to meet you," he said. "I'm Will."

He held the gown out, but Bradley didn't move. Will stood holding the empty gown out before him.

"Will?" Bradley said. "Will Nathan?"

"That's right."

"The legend himself," Bradley said and slid his arms into the sleeves of the gown.

"What are you talking about?" Will asked.

Above the mask, Martha's eyes were playful. "I'm afraid Bradley is a bit tired of hearing about what big shoes he has to fill."

Will held out a glove and Bradley plunged his hand into it. He held out the second and they repeated the action. Will tied up the back of Bradley's gown.

"They're just trying to bug you," Will said as Bradley snapped his gloves tight. "They did the same thing to me. There was a guy before me named Miller. They acted as if they were going to have to shut the place down because he was gone."

"Thanks," Bradley said. He stepped up to the table and scanned the set-up.

"Have you done total knees before?" Will asked.

"A few."

"I wondered if you could stay over for a bit until Bradley feels comfortable?" Martha asked.

"Sure," Will said. He wasn't ready to go out into the hall, anyway. His nervousness since two o'clock had shown him he wasn't ready to see Lila.

This is as good a place as any to hide.

By the time Bradley told him it was okay for him to leave, the halls were empty. He went through the door of the lounge and there was only furniture, circles of lamplight on tables and chairs.

Martha was at the front desk.

"I have a feeling I have you to thank for my being in total joints today," he said.

"I asked Bev to give you something challenging on your first day back. No reason to bore you to tears on your first day."

They saved boring for the next day and the days thereafter. He got used to it, to the endless stream of gall bladders and tonsils she'd warned him about.

The one thing he never got used to was seeing Lila. It didn't happen very often. Martha still had Lila working with Melanie, so there were only accidental meetings in the hall and lounge. Each time he thought it would be better, but it never was.

He knew from the flush in her cheeks, from the way she wouldn't look into his eyes that it was torture for her, too.

He'd been working days for a week when he heard a familiar name in report: Sheila Cole, back for more skin grafts and revision of scar tissue.

He wasn't assigned to her case. There was a burn team on the morning shift. He just heard her name and listened to Bev's assessment of her progress. He wanted to see for himself, but part of him clung to those first few times he'd done her, to the feeling he'd had in the ICU that time they had to turn her. He knew it would never be the same.

Every week he heard her name, went through the same emotions, let them pass, until one Wednesday Bev met him in the hall. "You worked with Sheila Cole when you were on the evening shift, didn't you?"

"Yeah, I saw her a few times."

"A few times?" she said.

"Okay," he said. "I was in her room the first month."

Bev shook her head in admiration.

"I'm going to put you in with her today. Lindsey's been doing her and she has the day off."

"Okay."

He felt an unfamiliar feeling rise in him. Excitement. Things had become so routine he barely recognized it.

I've got to get off this foolish shift.

He was setting up his table when they wheeled her into the room. He turned, wanting to assess her progress. Images from the first surgeries flooded his mind: red seeping wounds, hands drawn up like claws.

She met his gaze. She smiled at him. He turned away.

Most would have been shocked by her appearance. Her face was scarred, the forehead the only smooth skin, just as he remembered. Her whole body was shriveled up, shrunken by the shock of her ordeal. Still, he had gotten used to that in those first weeks.

The shock for Will was her eyes. He'd never seen them without the morphine glaze. He'd never seen them alive.

He heard her voice, light, musical. She giggled. He heard Fred's voice, the low timber in sharp contrast to hers.

"Will," Fred called. "Come over here for a minute."

Will turned and went to the table.

"Sheila wants to get a look at you," Fred said.

"You're new," she said. "Lindsey is usually my scrub tech."

Will tried not to stare at her smile, so out of place in the ravaged face. He met the eyes once more, but had to look away from the life that shone there.

"Lindsey's off," he said.

"I'm surprised they put a rookie on me," she said. She brushed her cheek with her fingertips. "This must be quite a shock."

"Not really."

"Oh come on," she said. She reached for his arm but stopped, as if she'd just remembered that he wore a sterile gown. "You don't have to lie to spare my feelings," she said. "I saw the look in your eyes. I'm used to it."

"I'm not lying," he said. "I've worked on you before. I was with you from the start when I worked the evening shift. If I'm shocked it's because of how much progress you've made in the time I've been on the day shift."

"Ah," she said. Tears flowed from the corner of her eyes. "You worked on me at the beginning. I'm so sorry," she said. "I know that must have been terrible for you."

Terrible for me?

"Don't be sorry," he said.

"The nurse's in the ICU rotated the first few weeks I was with them because no one could stand it two days in a row," she said. "I'm sure it must have been the same down here."

"Actually," Fred said. "Will volunteered for your case every week for the first month. He got you through the worst and never said a word. He even broke up with his girlfriend because of you."

"Dr. Dean!" she said. She slapped Fred's arm. Will was surprised she didn't call him Papa Bear.

"What is he talking about?" Sheila said as she turned back to Will.

"He's making that up," Will said. "The girl and I broke up for other reasons."

Her eyes got big. More tears came but her smile grew.

"I hate to break this up," Fred said, "But we do have business we need to get done here."

"Of course," she said.

"Maybe Will can visit you later and tell you all about his love life," Fred said.

"That would be nice," she said.

The case went smoothly. They revised scar tissue on her legs and thighs. Will barely recognized her body, the image that had been burned in his mind those first few times had been transformed.

Fred did nerve blocks on her and even though she was heavily sedated, Will heard her voice several times during the case, shreds of conversation between her and Fred.

Fred was different with Sheila. He seemed to have lost his objectivity.

Why had he told her I'd visit her? Since when did scrub techs make house calls?

After the case, Will focused on his instruments as they got her back onto a stretcher. He turned as they adjusted her blankets. She motioned for him to come over.

"Thanks for everything, Will," she said. She rested her hand on his arm, knowing it was all right, because the case was over. "You really made my day."

"How did I do that?" he asked.

"When you told me how much progress I'd made," she said. "It's hard to remember that sometimes."

"It's true," he said. "It's great to see you smile."

"Come on, young lady" Fred said, "You know your mom is waiting for you in the room."

"Okay," she said. "Good bye, Will. Thanks again."

"Anytime."

He cleaned up his room and went on to his next case, a drainage of a rectal abscess.

He looked for Fred that afternoon before he went home. He found him on the roof.

Fred leaned against the wall, smoking a cigarette, looking out over the city. Both actions were totally out of character for Fred. He didn't smoke and the only time Will had seen him on the roof was the night they watched the fireworks.

Will eased himself through the window. Fred looked up and smiled, as if he'd been expecting him.

"Why did you tell Sheila Cole I might visit her?" Will asked.

"I was just playing with both of you," Fred said.

"Does she know that?"

"Of course she does," he took a long drag on the cigarette, blew out a long plume. "Sheila and I play all the time. It's part of our routine."

"What ever happened to keeping our objectivity?" Will asked.

Fred threw the cigarette down and ground it out on the crushed rock surface.

"You know how I feel about getting too involved with the patients," he said. "But Sheila has to be different. It isn't enough for us to fix her burns. With her injuries most people can't even look at her, and if they do, most of the time they stare. She needs people who can talk to her without wincing."

"So now we're social workers?"

Fred's glare withered Will.

Now I know how Steve Dempsey felt.

"We just have to be human," Fred said. "Most of the time we suppress that for the good of the patients. This time we get to remember. It's a win-win for a change. Enjoy it. Treat her like a human being when she comes to the OR. If we're not careful, by the time she gets back into the real world, she'll forget how to talk to people. It isn't just muscles that atrophy, you know."

"I hadn't thought of that."

"Of course you didn't. Talking isn't usually in your job description."

He had that right. Everyone had different roles in patient care. The lines seldom crossed. Will had always been happy being one of the guys behind a mask, but he could see how they might have to step out from behind it in this case. Still, it was only necessary to talk to Sheila Cole in the OR suites. Once the case was over, they'd send her back to her room and move on to the next procedure. It made perfect sense.

And yet, Will found himself outside her room once his shift was over. He didn't go in. The door was partially closed and he could see her through the crack between the door and the jamb. She shifted uneasily on the bed. She sat up and swung her legs over the side, but then she pulled them back in and lay back down. She pulled the sheets over her and kicked them off.

"Can I help you?" a voice said.

He turned and for a moment, he thought it was Lila. The woman was plain and stocky and angry. The hair puffed up around her face was the only feminine touch.

"A asked you a question," she said.

"Oh, hi," he said. "I was just checking on Sheila."

"Really," she said. She brushed her hair out of her face with her thick fingers. "What exactly can you check standing out here in the hall? What are you, a doctor or a peeping Tom?"

"Doctor?" He said. "I'm not—"

"Shh!" she said. She held a finger to her lips and waved for him to follow, not bothering to see if he came, sure, it seemed, he would.

She stormed down the hall. Nurses stood back, letting them pass. They studied Will, some suspiciously, some sympathetically.

Finally, the woman turned and went into a consultation room. She entered as if it was her private office. There was a small table and two chairs, one on each side. A window filled the far wall.

Will followed her inside and she closed the door.

"So," she said. "What's the story? Are you a resident, an intern, a med student?"

"I'm not any kind of doctor," he said.

"So, you're a nursing student. I guess this was bound to happen. The word has spread. Everyone has heard about the miracle burn patient. Everyone has to see the show."

"Look," he said. "I'm not a nurse. I'm not a student. I'm a scrub tech. I worked on Sheila this morning. I worked with her the first few months after her accident."

Why am I explaining myself to this woman? Who the hell is she?

"Look, Mam," he said. "I don't know what I did to upset you, but today was the first time I ever really talked to Sheila. Those first times I saw her she was always under. I just wanted to visit with her. Really, that's all it is."

"Of course," she said. "You wanted to visit. You were just out in the hall because you had to get your nerve up. Can't have the poor girl see the look on your face, the one that shows her she's a freak, the one that mirrors every scar, every shriveled up muscle, every missing finger."

"Mam, please," Will said. "Who the hell are you?"

"I'm her mother."

Of course.

No wonder he'd compared her to Lila. They were both matriarchs, both mother grizzlies, defined by mates and offspring. Ready to sacrifice everything for them.

Well, almost everything.

"I'm her mother," she repeated. She slumped into one of the chairs as if the weight of the words drove her down.

Will sat across the table from her. Sheila's first surgeries after the accident came back to him in a rush of images: red flesh, ravaged muscles, thin white strips of ligaments and tendons slicing through them. He saw her eyes, clouded by the morphine haze.

Those few hours once a week had drained him, had driven he and Julie apart. This woman had been there through it all, had seen them whittle her child away one piece at a time. They'd rebuilt Sheila as best they could, but how must that seem to this woman, who'd raised her from a child, who knew every inch of her flesh as if it were her own. Whatever anger had just slipped out, Will knew there must be more. He wished that he could take it all.

He stood up. The chair hit the wall behind him.

"This was a mistake," he said. "I didn't mean to upset you."

Mrs. Cole stared at the table. She dismissed him with a wave of her arm. Lila's arm. He paused.

"You're right about one thing," he said. "I was working up my nerve to go in, but it isn't what you think, it isn't how she looks. I'm a scrub tech. I don't talk to the patients much. I didn't know where to begin."

Mrs. Cole stirred.

"You said that you worked on her the first months after the accident?"

"Yes."

"You saw her at her worst."

"Yes. I told her today how much progress she's made. It made her happy. I thought it might make her happy if I visited."

She waved for him to sit back down. He hesitated.

"She's always happy when she goes to surgery," she said. "They've got her as high as a kite. It's different when she comes back down. She's in so much pain."

Will thought of the glimpse he'd had of Sheila through the crack in the door, the uneasy twists and turns, as if no position was comfortable. No morphine drips to save her now, no battle between dreams and pain.

And she's been living like this for months.

"Mornings are better," Mrs. Cole said.

"Excuse me?" Will asked.

"If you really want to visit it's best to come in the morning, just before she goes to therapy. They give her something to help her work through things. It's her best time," she said, smiling sadly.

Her best time. A few minutes between the drugs kicking in and the therapist kicking her butt. It doesn't seem like much.

"I'm sorry," he said. "I'm working tomorrow. I get my break at ten."

"That's too late," she said. "She'll be downstairs."

"I'm sorry," he said again. Not just because he couldn't visit, but for all of it. It didn't seem like much.

"It's not you're fault," she said. She didn't sound very sure. He wasn't either.

He thought of all the fights he'd had with Julie. Maybe she'd been right after all.

Why did we do this? Who was it really for?

He wanted to leave. He knew she must want the same. They stared out the window but neither of them moved.

TWENTY-FOUR

Goddamn fireworks. Frigging Fourth of July. Goddamn frigging Will.

The Weston Centennial Barbecue and Fourth of July Extravaganza was still the biggest thing in their little town. The year before, Lila had been working, incensed that Martha had stuck her with babysitting duty.

As if Will Nathan was anybody's baby.

That night she'd gotten her first real glimpse of Will in action. Before that he'd been fresh meat, a handsome stud she joked about with the girls in the locker room, a nine-point-five on their scale of ten. That night he'd shown her the substance behind the looks. He was something that she'd never seen before, the complete package.

But she wasn't the only one who got surprised that night. She still remembered the look on Will's face after she'd changed out of her scrubs. It was as if he'd never thought of her as a woman before.

I guess I showed him.

Of course, this was another anniversary. She'd driven home that night, confused, exhilarated, only to find Ray half-dead in their bed.

Talk about your frigging wake-up calls.

That should have been enough. Her whole time with Will should have been lived out in that day, the promise snuffed out by the image of her incapacitated husband. What more did she need to see to realize that nothing good could come of it? A day, a month, a year, it could only end badly. What did it say about her that she hadn't understood all of it that night?

It wasn't about understanding anything. I had to try. It lasted for six days and then I went nuts. Will walked away and I let him.

Lila shook her head as she sat on her throne, a wicker beach chair in the bed of her pickup truck. Her sons' trucks formed a circle around her. Years ago Ray had scouted out the best spot and each year one of the boys camped out early to reserve it. It stood on a rise in the eastern corner of the common, equidistant from the beer and barbecue tents. They'd have an unobstructed view of the fireworks when they began.

Lila glanced on her watch. Twenty minutes.

She surveyed her kingdom. Each of the boys had set up his own encampment around Ray's truck. Folks in town called it the Waznek Complex. There were grills and coolers, lawn chairs and volleyball nets.

Roland had set up a tarp over his area. This would be their refuge if the rain that had threatened earlier in the day materialized. They'd be packed in as tightly as they'd been a year ago, bursting the walls of the ICU waiting room.

Funny how little things take me back.

She studied the sky. The clouds had blown over. Her family was free to spread out. The grandchildren were scattered across the grass divided into age groups. Every now and then a younger child tried to barge in on a group of bigger kids, but they were quickly rebuked.

The youngest kids burrowed into a huge sand pile that had been trucked in for the latest improvement on the common, concrete footings for the picnic tables. Roland had included its proximity to their spot as an omen.

"God loves the Wazneks," he'd declared.

Ray clamored into the truck and handed her a foaming cup of beer, its white excess dripped down the side and into the bed of the truck.

"Thanks, babe," she said, as he settled into his chair on her right hand.

"Your wish is my command," he said.

"A cheeseburger would be nice," she said.

"Oh Jesus," he said. He groaned as he tried to stand. She put her hand on his arm.

"Don't be stupid," she said. "Hey, Wesley," she yelled to the nearest pack of grandkids. One head shot up above the crowd. The pack swarmed away as he turned to her.

"Yeah, Nana?"

"Could you get your old nana a cheese burger?"

His gaze followed his cousins as they moved away, then he jerked his head back in her direction. "Okay," he yelled and headed towards the barbecue tent.

"How did we ever get such sweet grandkids?" she asked.

"Just lucky, I guess," Ray said.

"Lucky, my ass," she said. "We worked our tails off to get our kids right and they did the same with theirs."

"I was just teasing," he said. "I know it doesn't have a damn thing to do with luck."

Ray took a sip from his diet soda. She winced. She knew how hard it had been for him to stop drinking. It must be especially hard today, since drinking was the main adult activity of the day.

She put her hand on his arm and squeezed.

"I shouldn't have sent you on a beer run," she said. "That was cruel."

"It's okay," he said. "You're not the one who ruined my heart. I made my own bed."

He took her hand and laid their interlaced fingers in his lap.

She didn't think about Will again until the fireworks splashed across the sky. She heard the oohs and ahs of her grandchildren, watched the bright tufts of red and green.

She fought the urge to look over her shoulder into the cab of the truck. She couldn't afford to remember the things she and Will had done to each other in there.

Voices echoed in her head, but which voices, her grandkids' or her and Will's?

How did a six days become reality while thirty years became a lie? Would it always feel this way? If it did, she knew that she'd go crazy.

She held on to the hope that some day she'd wake up and the things she loved would be enough again, not overshadowed by Will Nathan. It hadn't happened yet, even though it had been nine months. She'd just have to keep breathing until it did.

A new type of firework exploded then. It wasn't a tuft or a floating ribbon. This was like a weeping willow, bright green tendrils branching out, each one sprouting ten more until they hung over the common like a thousand drooping branches.

Something new. Last year gone for just an instant.

Wesley leapt onto the tailgate. Lila had forgotten this food run. She couldn't believe that he'd persevered even after the fireworks began.

Talk about your good kids.

He thrust the burger into her hands and turned away, already scouting out his cousins.

"Where's mine?" Ray asked.

The child froze, turned to Ray in disbelief.

"Aw, Gramps."

"Don't worry about it," Ray said. "I'm sure your Nana will share with me."

Wesley smiled.

"Like hell I will," Lila said.

Wesley sagged.

"You go on," she said. "Your Gramps isn't a cripple. He can get his own burger."

The child raced away before they had a chance to change their minds.

"I'm glad to hear you say that," Ray said. He squeezed her hand.

"You're happy that I won't give you a bite of my burger?" she asked.

"No," he wouldn't meet her eyes. He stared down into the bed of the truck. "You told Wesley that I'm not a cripple."

"I never thought that."

"That's what you say, now," he said, "But you did baby me, at first."

"Here," she said, 'Hold this."

She handed him her beer.

Once her hand was free, she swatted him. He tried to block her hand and beer splashed all over them.

I should have handed him the burger.

"I know things got weird for awhile," she said, "But I never thought you were a cripple. You abused your heart. You've always been a beer-guzzling workaholic and I was scared because I wasn't sure you could change."

He raised the beer as if in a toast, then handed it to her. "But I did change," he said.

"Yes," she said. "You did." She sipped her beer.

He kissed her, swirling his tongue around her mouth. He smiled when he pulled away.

"Can second-hand booze kill you?" he asked.

She threw herself at him, toppling her chair, bringing his down with the crush of their bodies. They sprawled in the bed of the truck, as the fireworks exploded over their heads. They tussled as they'd done when they were teenagers. She tugged at his belt.

"Jesus Christ, babe," Ray said, "This is a family event."

"I know," she said. "I guess I can wait until I get you home."

At home in bed, Lila lay awake listening to Ray's breathing. Two years ago his drunken snoring had kept her awake all night. Last year his shallow respirations had taken them to the ER.

This year his breath blew through his lips in the smooth and steady rhythm of a man spent and satisfied. She was grateful for such progress.

I've got to hold on to the little things.

Ray's breathing. Will's face. It hadn't been with her tonight when she'd made love to Ray.

Before. Now. Not during. Frigging baby steps.

TWENTY-FIVE

Will watched the fireworks at work alone out of the roof, missing Fred and Lila.

After six months on the day shift, he'd finally gotten a slot on the weekend crew, working sixteen-hour shifts on Saturday and Sunday, from seven a.m. to eleven p.m.. When the summer courses had begun at the University, he'd registered. The summer session was perfect for him. Each course was a four-week run. They met every day for four hours in the morning. The teachers piled on the work. It was a total immersion.

It had been a shock, at first, but he surprised himself by how quickly he adjusted. Still, working weekends was the only thing that kept him sane. Just about the time he felt like his brain would explode if he jammed in another fact, a trauma would come flying through the door and the flush of adrenaline would cleanse him.

On the weekends, all the cases were trauma of one kind or another. There were orthopedic cases from car accidents, some gunshot wounds and lots of neurosurgery. That was new to Will.

He didn't like neurosurgery. After the initial rush of getting set up and getting the patient under, the cases were boring for a tech. Only the surgeons knew exactly what they were looking at when they focused on the brain. Sometimes Will even wondered about that.

One thing that Will enjoyed is that he always worked with the same people on the weekends. His circulating nurse was Flo, who worked weekends so she could be with her kids during the week. She had three girls under the age of eight. She and her husband didn't believe in childcare.

She still worked because they couldn't afford to live on one income and because she knew she needed to spend some time out in the world with adults.

"Hey," she'd said. "I don't want to end up talking baby talk. I want to make sure my kids have a good life, but I don't want to forget who I am and relive my childhood through them."

Will wondered about her husband. He had to be quite a guy to work all week and then watch kids the entire weekend. When most guys were settling down with a sigh of relief to watch the game, he'd be organizing a field trip to the zoo. Better yet, he'd be cooking macaroni and cheese, changing diapers and breaking up hair-pulling fights.

T. J. Roberts was their orderly. She was also in school, though she was a business major. She came from a long line of self-made men and women who didn't believe in funding their children's education. She'd worked in the OR for two years out of high school until she figured out what she wanted to study. Now, she took a full load of courses and financed her life by working the weekend shift.

Best of all for Will, he wasn't attracted to either of them. A year ago, he would said they weren't his type, but if Lila had shown him anything, it was just how meaningless that phrase was.

Flo was pretty enough, but in spite of saying she needed to spend time with adults, she never talked about anything but her family.

T.J. was a tomboy with curly black hair and freckles. She reminded Will of Murph. She was a devoted student, but cared only about business and economics.

For both of them, the OR was just a job. They were good at it. Will meshed with them, but only like parts of a machine. There was no sexual feeling beyond that. It was perfect.

Still, he enjoyed the weekends most when Fred worked. They hung out together in the doctor's lounge. The others accepted that Will was with Fred and welcomed him as one of their own.

It wasn't all fun. Fred was strict about Will's studies, making sure he didn't waste time.

"You'll need discipline when you're in med school and during residency. You need to do your reading while you're at the hospital. It's the only way to stay on top of things, to stay sane."

Fred was off tonight, and Will had asked Flo and TJ if they wanted to watch the fireworks.

"I can't," Flo had said. "Ricks bringing in the girls and we're going to watch from the front lawn of the hospital."

"The view is better on the roof," he said.

"For grown-ups, maybe," she said. "Rick and I would spend the whole time trying to keep our girls from running off the edge and out into space."

"Of course," he said. "I'm not used to kids."

"You will be some day," she said.

"What about you?" He asked, turning to TJ.

"Can't," she said. "I've got a big economics test."

"I've got homework, too."

"See that's the difference between you and me," TJ said. She ran her fingers through her hair, pushing it back from her eyes. "It isn't homework to me, it's my real job. You need to learn the difference."

Thanks, Fred.

"I'll see you later," he said. "Have fun."

"You, too," she'd said.

****

Will watched the ribbons and tufts of color in the sky. One was like a weeping willow tree. Something new.

Something not last year.

Last year at this time he'd been on the cusp of so many things. Of course, he hadn't known that, then.

He'd always been the faithful type. He fell hard and didn't want to let go. His friends had always given him a hard time about it. That was one reason why his relationships in the OR had been so confusing. Everything came at him too fast. First Julie, than Lila, even Monique. Too much.

Too much, too fast, too real.

Isn't that how everything is supposed to be in the OR? Isn't that why I love it?

He heard voices through the window. Someone was in the office. He wondered if TJ had changed her mind and come to see the fireworks, after all.

One of the voices was a man. Then he recognized the woman's voice. It was Julie. The man must be Steve Dempsey. He hunkered down against the wall, hoping that they wouldn't see him. He pressed his butt into the stones of the roof.

What the hell am I doing?

He stood up. Dempsey sat in a chair with his feet up on the desk. Julie leaned against the desk. One hand rested on Dempsey's knee. He was in scrubs, but she wore civilian clothes, a white tube top and black spandex biker shorts. Her nipples pressed against the thin fabric of the shirt. Her face was red, as if she'd just come in from the sun.

Will cleared his throat. Dempsey's legs jerked, the chair toppled backward. Julie grabbed his arms to keep him from falling.

"Jesus Christ, Nathan," Dempsey said.

"You scared us half to death, Will," Julie said, but her smile showed that she was enjoying Dempsey's predicament as much as Will.

Will slid through the window.

"I'm sorry," he said. "I was watching the fireworks."

"You shouldn't spy on people," Dempsey said.

"I wasn't spying. I just had my back to the wall and you couldn't see me. I got up as soon as I heard voices."

Julie placed her hand on Dempsey's arm. "A lot of people take their breaks out on the roof," she said. "We should have checked."

"I suppose."

Will wanted to leave, but Dempsey propped his feet back on the desk, blocking his way.

"You're always underfoot, Nathan," he said. "I can't even get away from you up in our lounge."

"Maybe you should take that up with Fred," Will said.

He knew he shouldn't have said that. It would just make Dempsey angrier, but the guy had asked for it.

"Jesus," Julie said. "Why don't the two of you just piss on the leg of the desk and get it over with?"

Will smiled.

Dempsey just glared.

Julie placed a hand on each of his shoulders. She put her face inches from his.

"Will can't leave because you're in the way," she said. "You can't complain that he's underfoot and then block his exit."

Dempsey pulled his legs down.

"I'll catch you later," Will said as he headed for the door.

Dempsey moved his legs just enough to clip Will's knees. Will stopped, turned back, ready for whatever Dempsey had to offer. Then he thought of Julie's comment.

"Why don't you just piss on the leg of the desk and be done with it?"

He smiled and turned back towards the door.

"What is wrong with you?" he heard Julie whisper as he went into the hall.

"I never liked that kid," Dempsey muttered.

He knew what this was about with Dempsey. Part of it was that Will had seen him on his worst day in the OR. Part of it was that Fred favored Will. The last straw was that Will had been with Julie first.

So what's my problem?

He'd broken up with Julie, but he was still jealous. Maybe he was having second thoughts because things hadn't worked out for he and Lila. Maybe it was seeing Sheila Cole in the OR, her mom outside her room. Julie was right. He'd never looked down the road those first weeks that they'd worked on Sheila. He'd never wondered what her life would be like after everything they'd put her through. He'd lost respect for Julie because she had doubts. Maybe he was the one who should have asked those questions.

He headed back towards the front desk, knowing that he needed to check in with Flo. If TJ was taking a break from her schoolwork, they could all rag on Dempsey together. He wasn't the only one who disliked the guy, he just had more reasons.

His mind went back to Julie again. He smiled as he thought of her breasts pressed against the thin, white fabric of her tube top, her face flushed. He remembered when he'd put that color in her cheeks. Not the sun. Not Dempsey.

It didn't matter. He'd done the right thing when he broke up with Julie. There was no getting past the rift that Sheila Cole tore between them. Just as there had been no getting past the fact that Lila had a husband. Some things a just deal breakers. He'd known that once. He'd never forget it again.

TWENTY-SIX

The smell of coffee roused Lila. Once there would have been bacon, eggs and the smell of grease filling the house, but the heart attack had put an end to that. The heart attack had changed a lot of things.

She sat up, checked the clock: seven am. Ray would be leaving for work in a half hour. Something new.

When he was drinking, he always took off the day after the Fourth. Even if he'd been scheduled, he called in sick. Too much fun at the festival.

It's a good thing Ray was the best worker there, or they'd have fired his sorry ass years ago.

How had Ray managed all those years? He worked six days a week. He got drunk every Saturday night. He slept until noon on Sunday, then got up and worked around the house the rest of the day. It was a miracle his heart hadn't given out sooner.

Maybe it had, he was just too frigging stubborn to lie down like that old guy in the OR with the aneurysm.

She brushed her teeth and took a quick shower. She knew she didn't have much time before he left, but she didn't want him to see her until she looked her best. They'd taken each other for granted too long. Look where that had gotten them.

Ray on his deathbed. Me in Will's bed.

Ray sat at the kitchen table, sipping coffee. She knew the bowl before him was for instant oatmeal

Take that cholesterol!

He looked up from the newspaper and smiled.

"Good Morning," he said, "Happy July Fifth."

She leaned over and kissed his forehead, ran her fingers through his curls.

"Did you think about it, too?" she asked. "Not just last year, but all the years before?"

He nodded. "I used to have some rough ones," he said. "If they had printed up T-shirts that said, "I survived the Weston Fourth of July Barbeque", I'd never have worn one July Fifth. The jury would still be out. You should have seen the look on Jack's face when I said I'd be in today."

"You were killing yourself," she said. And then it was there. She fought it, but it came, a tiny voice, alien, unyielding.

Things would have been so much simpler.

Nausea tore her stomach. She turned away from him. Somehow, her letting Will go didn't seem like much of a deal for Ray.

"Are you okay, Babe?" he asked.

"Yeah," she said. She felt his hand on her arm. He tried to turn her towards him, but she resisted.

"I think I'm coming down with something," she said. "You'd better keep your distance."

He wrapped his arms around her and rested his head on her shoulder.

"Come on," he said. "We've been swapping colds since Junior High. It hasn't killed me yet."

She shuddered.

"Whoa," he said. He felt her forehead. "You're shaking. Have you got a fever? Maybe you've got the flu."

Sobs racked her body. He turned her to face him. She buried her face in is chest.

"Lila," he said. "What is it? Tell me. What's wrong?"

"I cheated on you," she said.

"What are you saying?"

"I fucked one of my co-workers, you frigging moron. What do you think I'm saying?"

He jerked away from her. "Who?" He said. "When?"

"Last fall. It was with Will."

"Will? That kid? You've got to be kidding me. We always joked about the kids at work, the fresh meat."

"I never joked about Will."

He stopped, stunned, as if he realized the truth of this and the implications.

"Is it over?" he asked.

"Yes. No."

"Which is it, Lila? What the hell is going on?"

"He broke it off, but I still have feelings."

"Feelings? How can you have feelings for him?" he said. "He's not much older than Jerry, for Christ's sake. Tell me you're horny. Tell me he's a great lay. Don't tell me you have feelings for him."

"But I do."

He turned, kicked a chair out of his path. He smashed his hand into the wall and went into the hall. She heard him as he made his way down the narrow corridor. Finally, she heard his voice on the phone.

"Jack, this is Ray. I'm sorry to jerk you around like this, man, but I need to be off today, after all." He paused.

"No, I didn't tie one on. Something just came up.

"Lila? I guess you could say that.

"Look, I might need a couple days. Will that mess you up too bad? No. Good. Thanks, man. You're the best."

She heard the phone slam down. She waited. Maybe Ray was right. They needed to deal with this. Her mistake all along had been trying to deal with this on her own. Ray was her best friend, after all. If he couldn't help her through this, who could?

She heard the back door slam.

She ran into the kitchen, but he was gone. She looked out the window and saw him getting into his truck. She wanted to rip open the door and call to him, but the look on his face froze her. He might be her best friend, but he was also a man who'd just found out his wife was in love with another man.

She let him drive away.

TWENTY-SEVEN

He'd been working weekends for about a month when Flo told him that Kathy and Murph were coming in to do an emergency heart. He helped her set up the room and then went out to wait for them.

TJ sat behind the desk. She drew one hand through her wild, black curls as she shoved her hair out of her face. She closed the economics text that lay opened before her.

"I don't know how these people expect me to get an education if they book heart surgeries on the weekends," she said. "During the week they've got a half dozen people to run their tests to the lab and fetch blood. Since it's only me, I'll be running like crazy the rest of the night."

"I'll help you," Will said. "The heart team will be doing the real work. I'll be free."

She drew her hair back into a ponytail and tucked it into her cap. "I thought surely you'd be hanging out with your old pals Murph and Miss Kathy," she said.

"It'll be good to see them," he said, "But you're my crew, now."

"Thanks," she said.

The buzzer sounded. They looked up and Kathy and Murph were at the door. Murph waved. Will went to meet them.

"My man," Murph said. He nearly crushed Will with a hug. Kathy leaned in and brushed her lips against his cheek.

"It's been too long, Will," she said.

They stood back from each other. Murph looked different. His hair was cut in the latest style. Without the unruly curls, TJ looked more like him than he did himself.

He wore tan slacks, a dark sport jacket and button down shirt.

"When did you become such a sharp dresser, man," Will asked.

"We went out to dinner," Murph said. "The place had a dress code."

Will had never seen Murph take this much care with his appearance. Maybe this meant he was in it with Kathy for the long run.

She looked as good as she always had, tanned and elegant, in a black, sleeveless top and white jeans.

Will went with Murph into the locker room.

"How have you been, man?" Murph asked.

"Good," Will leaned back against his locker.

"How's school?" Murph asked.

"It's okay. I've been taking some summer courses. Getting a taste of it, you know."

"That's wild man. I don't know how you do it." He took off his sport coat and hung it on the rack where the doctors hung theirs. He took off his shirt, folded it neatly and laid it in his locker.

"You could do it, too," Will said, "If you wanted to."

"No, I don't think so. I'm happy where I am."

Why not? He got a woman who's doctor material without becoming a doctor.

"So, how is everybody?" Will asked. "Martha, Melanie, Lila?"

He slipped that last name in and hoped Murph wouldn't hear the catch in his voice.

"They're good. Pretty much the same." Murph pulled off his slacks, made a perfect crease in them and hung them on a hanger in the locker.

Who is this guy?

"Actually," Murph said. "Martha's the only one who's the same. Everyone else is different. Remember that look Melanie used to have on her face all the time, like she'd just stepped into a pile of shit?"

"Yeah," Will said. "A face only a mother could love."

"That's the one. She isn't like that anymore. Her work is better, too. I think it started when Martha teamed her up with Lila. You know Lila always was a great teacher."

Will pulled open the door of his own locker so Murph couldn't see his face.

"She taught me a lot," Will said.

Murph pulled on his OR cap. For the first time, Will felt like he was looking at his old friend.

"So how is Lila?" Will asked.

Murph's smile disappeared. "She's not so good," he said.

"What do you mean?" Will asked, rummaging around in the junk in the bottom of his locker, keeping his face turned away.

"She's not the same old Lila," Murph said. "Don't get me wrong, she's still a great nurse and a great teacher, but she doesn't seem to have her heart in things the way she used to. She's kind of subdued, you know?"

"No," Will said. "That's hard to imagine. She was always a pistol."

He slammed his locker, tried to compose his face, turned back to Murph.

They went into the hall and headed towards the heart room.

"The new people don't really notice the change," Murph said, "And Melanie probably never paid much attention before they worked together, but Kathy and I know the old Lila. We miss her."

"Miss who?" a voice said behind them. They turned. It was Kathy.

"Lila," Murph said. "Will asked how everybody was and I was telling him how Lila seems different."

"Is she?" Will asked, directing his attention to Kathy.

"It's subtle," she said, "But she's not the same. You know how she used to be a pain in the ass, sometimes, used to skewer everybody with a word?"

"Yeah."

"She doesn't do that anymore."

They reached the room. Beyond the window of the scrub room, Flo waited in the corner. She waved at them, but held her hand up when Kathy moved towards the door.

"I guess everything's set," Kathy said. "We've got a few minutes."

"Fred and TJ just went upstairs for the patient," Will said.

Murph turned on the water. "Why don't you scrub in for awhile," he said to Will.

"Sure." Will moved in beside him and hit the control with his knee. They stood side by side before the metal sink.

"What do you think happened with Lila?" Will asked.

"It's got to be something at home," Kathy said. "At first I thought her husband was still having problems with his health, but I talked to Mixter and he said everything was fine."

"It could be something else besides his heart," Murph said. "Wouldn't that be a bitch? Survive open heart surgery and get taken out by cancer or some such shit."

"Don't even say that," Kathy said.

"Yeah," Will said. He shut off the water and turned towards the door.

Kathy leaned on the window ledge with her elbows spread wide, the same pose that Lila used to take. Everything about her was different, her narrow hips, her tall slim frame, her hat weighed down by the burden of her hair, but it still made him think of Lila. His stomach lurched.

When will this ever end?

"You okay, man," Murph said. "You don't look so hot."

"I'm okay. These double shifts get to me sometimes."

"Maybe Lila has a problem with one of her kids," Kathy said.

"Aren't they all grown?" Murph asked.

"Her youngest is still in high school," Kathy said. "Maybe he got into drugs or got his girlfriend pregnant."

"Yeah," Murph said. "You figure it has to be something like that."

Will didn't like the way Kathy and Murph just assumed the problem was with Lila's family. That was the way the world defined her, as if she didn't exist outside those boundaries. One more example of how hard it would have been for her if she had chosen to be with him. The world wouldn't just have judged her harshly, she would have ceased to exist in its eyes.

Fred and T.J. wheeled the patient into the room.

"We're on," Kathy said.

Will worked with Murph for the first hour. After that he broke scrub and helped T.J. run tests to the lab and pick up blood.

After the case, he watched in the locker room as Murph transformed himself back into his new self.

"What I can't figure out is how you stand being here every weekend," Murph said. "Don't you miss hanging out, having fun?"

" I'm off Friday night's," Will said. "I get all the excitement I need then."

Murph pulled his shirt from his locker. He looked at it as if he couldn't believe he was about to put it on, as if this had to be a mistake.

"Sometimes I wish I'd gone to college," he said. "Don't get me wrong, I love my job and I'm glad I skipped classes and papers and all that bullshit, but every time I hear someone talk about college, I feel like I missed out."

Will nodded. Maybe he should tell Murph the truth. His life was quiet, mostly study and work.

"There's one thing that I know I missed out on," Murph said.

"What's that?"

"The honeys."

"Ah," Will said. He nodded. The campus was the finest collection of female flesh that he had ever seen.

"Don't get me wrong," Murph said. "Kathy is the best thing that ever happened to me. I just never thought I'd settle down so young. I don't know if I'm ready."

He walked over to the coat rack and pulled off his sport jacket. He slipped into it, as if that would reinforce the path he was on.

"I don't know, man," Will said. "I think you've got it made. You know how everyone always had Kathy pegged to snag a doctor, and she chose you. Don't blow it because you didn't get to screw a bunch of girls who aren't even in her league."

"Don't you think I know that?" Murph said. "But there's another side to that. Sometimes I wonder how long it'll be before she stops slumming and leaves me high and dry. You don't know what it's like man, living every day waiting for the other shoe to drop."

"So what are you complaining about?" Will said, "You're with a gorgeous woman and if she dumps you, you'll get your chance to screw around. You can't lose."

Murph smiled. "That's why I miss you, man," he said. "You got your own way of looking at the world. It's easy for you to talk, though. You're still in the screwing around phase. Wait until you find the woman of your dreams, then you'll see how it feels to worry about losing her."

One more thing Will couldn't tell him. One more bubble that he couldn't burst.

They walked back out to the front desk where Kathy waited for them. Murph hugged him again. Even Kathy opened her arms to him this time. He went to her and she hugged him. She held on tightly.

"Hey," Murph said, "Break it up."

She pressed her lips to his ear.

"Call Lila," she whispered.

Will pulled away.

"Any closer and you guys would have had to get a room," Murph said. He poked Will's arm just hard enough to take it past a joke.

"Calm down, stud," Kathy said. "We're all friends here."

"Sure, sure," Murph said. "Will knows I'm playing."

"Of course," Will said.

After they walked away, he went back down to the heart room. One glance told Will that Flo had everything back in place. He sat down on the OR table.

Why had Kathy told him to call Lila? Had Lila told her about them? He couldn't imagine Lila taking that chance.

Maybe Kathy did see Lila as a person, not just somebody's wife and mother. She knew that the changes in Lila had happened since Will left. Maybe all her talk about Lila having family problems was a smokescreen.

But why had she told him to call? She couldn't understand how complicated this was. She might think she knew about going against the world, but this wasn't like her and Murph, just a matter of her lowering her expectations and Murph improving his wardrobe.

For he and Lila, it had to be all or nothing. He hated nothing, but each day he understood more clearly that having everything with Lila might have been harder still.

TWENTY-EIGHT

Ray didn't come home for three days. Lila waited silently under Jerry's angry glare. What could she tell him?

I fucked somebody not much older than you.

Finally, on the morning of the fourth day, Ray's truck pulled into the driveway. She watched him from the bay window in the living room as the truck swerved from side to side, kissing the ropes that lined the gravel, somehow missing the posts they swayed from.

When he eased into his space next to her truck, she waited for him to get out, but the doors never opened. She finally went down and found him slumped over the steering wheel, asleep. She leaned in close to him but the stench of alcohol on his breath drove her back.

"Oh, Jesus, Ray," she said. "What the hell is wrong with you? You know the doctor said you shouldn't drink any more."

He didn't stir.

She wanted to help him into the house, but she knew he was too heavy for her. She'd have to wait until Jerry got home from school.

Won't that be a pleasant scene?

She leaned him down onto the seat and arranged his legs. She covered him with his jacket. He'd just have to sleep it off. She prayed he'd snap out of it before Jerry got home.

She went back to the house and lay down on their bed. She laid her head on her pillow and hugged Ray's pillow to her chest. She fiddled with the fringe of the pillow sham, remembering how much he'd grumbled when she'd first put it on. She caressed the tiny, balls of yellow yarn and soon she was asleep.

She slept fitfully, her dreams glimpses of Ray and Will. Ray's face when she told him, Will's the last time she'd seen him. She saw herself as she made love to both of them. Finally, she saw Ray's face pressed against the back window of her truck as she made love to Will.

She sat up in bed, her heart racing from her memories of Will, from the image of Ray's anguished face in her mind. She heard the back door.

"Ray," she called and ran into the kitchen, where Jerry wrestled his father, still passed out, through the door.

"Did you know he was out there?" Jerry asked.

"Of course I did. I'm not strong enough to get him in by myself."

"He's drunk," he said. "He knows he's not supposed to drink anymore. What did you do to him, anyway?"

She fought back tears. It was either cry or fight back. Three days of frustration welled up in her.

"That's between your father and I," she said. "Just get him into bed and go to your room."

Jerry looked as if she'd slapped him.

It's all so easy for him. Everything is black and white.

Or maybe that was the problem. Before Will she'd been satisfied with gray.

She moved to help him, but he shrugged her away.

"Leave us alone," he said.

She followed him into the bedroom. He tumbled on to the bed. His father's body pinned his arm. He struggled but didn't ask for help. When he finally jerked his arm free, she spoke.

"I'll take care of him, now," she said.

"I can—"

Enough.

"I've got him, now," she said gently. "You're a lifesaver, but we have to take it from here."

"But—"

"Just go."

He hesitated.

"Please?"

"Okay," he said. "I'll be in my room."

"Thanks," she said. She wanted to touch him, but she knew she wouldn't be able to bear it if he pulled away.

She undressed her husband. She lay down beside him. She fingered the hair on his chest as she'd done the fringe of the pillow sham.

She awoke to the sound of the shower. She wondered how he'd slipped away without waking her. It was no mystery, really. She'd barely slept for three days. Once she'd known that he was safe, she'd finally let down her guard.

Safe? That's a good one. Safe from everything but me.

The water stopped running. He came back in, rubbing his hair dry with a towel, wearing just his boxer shorts. The red hair on his chest glistened with moisture.

He seemed surprised when he saw her, as if she had no right to be here. He covered his chest with the towel.

"Where have you been?" she asked. "I've been worried sick."

"I'm not sure," he said. "Different places." He crossed the room to his bureau and pulled open the top drawer. He dropped the towel on the floor.

"You could have called me," she said. "Let me know that you were okay."

"I wasn't sure you'd care," he said. He searched the drawer, pulled out a pair of jeans and a t-shirt. He tugged them on. She wondered when she'd ever see his chest again.

"How can you say that?" She said. "Of course I care."

"You have a funny way of showing it," he said. "Fucking a kid half our age."

She knew she deserved that. She waited.

Ray leaned over to pick up the towel. He folded it and dropped it on the bed. He ran his fingers over the footboard, the footboard that he'd picked up at the Weston flea market and stained for their tenth anniversary.

He watched his fingers on the wood, but her eyes went to the bed, to the quilt his mother had hand-stitched for them, a forest of pine trees. At least it wasn't the one that she'd done for their wedding.

"Look," he said. "I know a lot of people cheat. Hell, the guys down on the site are always bragging about stuff like that. I thought we were different."

"I thought we were, too."

He paused, as if those were the last words he'd expected to hear.

"You thought we were too?" He spat the words back at her. "Then how the hell did this happen?"

"I can't explain it," she said. "I've replayed it a thousand times in my head, but it doesn't make any sense. I wish I could take it back, but…"

"But you can't," he said. "Any more than I can pretend it never happened."

He still watched his fingers, as if he needed to look at anything but her. She looked around the room, taking in every piece, each one chosen by them and fit into the puzzle over the years. All gone.

"So what are you going to do?" She asked.

His fingers stopped moving. "Don't you mean what are we are going to do?"

"No," she said. She took the towel from the bed and headed towards the bathroom. "I know what I have to do. I just need to pack a few things."

He grabbed her arm. She tried to twist away, but he squeezed down hard. She shoved the towel into his face, but he pinned her against the bed.

"Don't I have any say in how this goes?" he asked.

"Of course you do," she said. "As long as you understand that staying together isn't an option. Things have gone too far for that."

How could she make him understand without telling him the one thing that had made it clear to her?

I wished you dead.

She'd loved him for thirty-five years. She still loved him. It just hadn't mattered once Will told her that he wanted her. For her, Will had been everything, but she hadn't allowed herself to see the truth. If there was one thing she should have learned in the OR, it was never ignore the truth. Wishing that aneurysms never burst wasn't much help when one was elbow deep in a bloody abdomen.

"What are you saying?" Ray asked. "You're going to leave me for this kid?" He eased up and she squirmed away. She rubbed the spot on her back that had been pinned against the bed.

"You're willing to give up everything we've built for a kid who's still wet behind the ears?" he asked.

"Don't call him a kid," she said.

"Why not? That's what he is. Can't you handle the truth?"

He sneered at her. She hated herself for what she'd brought him to.

Him. There it was again. When did I stop thinking in terms of us?

She was going to have to get used to that. She was going to have to get used to saying "I".

"I don't want to mess things up with Jerry any more than they already are," she said, "So, I'll be the one to move out. You didn't do anything wrong. You don't need to be living in the bars."

"You're going to move in with him?"

She looked down at the towel in her hand. It seemed like a hundred years since she'd started across the room. She finished the trip.

The hamper was wicker. She'd waited for years to upgrade from plastic to wicker. Now, she'd probably have to go all the way back to a cardboard box, maybe to a pile in the corner of the bedroom.

"I asked you a question," Ray said.

"I've already told you that it's over between me and Will," she said. "It has been for months. I don't even see him anymore. He's back in school and only works on the weekends. He's moved on."

"Then why are you doing this?" he asked. "Don't you at least want to try to work things out?"

She turned from the hamper to the medicine chest. She pulled out her prescriptions. She sat on the toilet. The seat was padded. The cover was fluffy green. The walls were white, gleaming like the porcelain of the commode. The green trim at the corners matched the seat.

Ray stood in the doorway.

"Did you want to work things out?" she asked.

"I don't know," he said. "But it seems like we should try."

"Seems like? That's not much of a reason," she said.

Still, she weakened. Thirty years is a long time. What would they tell the kids?

What will I tell them?

She grabbed her toothpaste and toothbrush, shampoo and deodorant and stood with her hands full. She knew that she should pack a bag, but she didn't have one. She and Ray never traveled. The road between Weston and the hospital was it for her.

She thought of every cartoon kid who'd ever run away from home with his belongings tied up in a bandana hanging from a stick.

She'd probably get as far as those kids did. Ray would find her at the end of their road, huddled by the mailbox with "Wazneck" printed in black letters on the silver metal.

Ray still blocked the door, but the spirit that had pinned her to the bed earlier was gone from his eyes. He simply waited. She pushed past Ray and tossed her shampoo, toothbrush and deodorant on the bed.

"I don't want anything," she said. "Just my personal stuff and my truck. I know you can hurt me in the courts, since I'm the one who screwed around, but I hope it doesn't get messy. For Jerry's sake."

"You know I wouldn't do that," he said.

"Thanks," she said. "We should set up a schedule for me and Jerry as soon as we can. If he wants to see me, that is."

"Of course he'll want to see you," he said.

"I don't know. They say this kind of thing is hardest on teenagers."

She opened her dresser and piled her clothes on the bed. Nothing fancy, just socks and underwear, a few tops and jeans. Enough to get her through the next few days.

She remembered that she still had a laundry bag somewhere in the back of the closet. That would do.

She felt Ray's hand on her shoulder. "I can't believe you're doing this," he said.

"I have to. I can't be a wife to you this way. I've been doing a half-ass job of it for a long time."

"You could have fooled me."

"I did."

He pulled his hand away.

She went to the closet. She dug down behind a pile of her shoes and Ray's work boots and found the bag.

She went back to the bed and stuffed everything inside.

She'd forgotten her hairbrush and gel, so she went back into the bathroom. She studied her face in the mirror, the spikes and blonde streaks in her hair.

Why do I still have it this way? I only did it for Will.

Back in the bedroom, Ray lay on the bed with his arm over his eyes. His three-day binge had finally caught up with him.

"Call me when you figure out where you're staying," he said without uncovering his eyes. "I'll worry about you until I know."

"Okay," she said. She stuffed her brush and gel into the bag and pulled the string tight around the top. She threw it over her shoulder like a seaman's bag.

She looked at Ray. She wanted him to look at her, but she was relieved he didn't. She wanted to touch him but knew she couldn't. She walked out into the hall.

She paused by Jerry's door and knocked. "Come in," he said.

He lay on the bed with his arm over his eyes. It was as if she'd never left the room next door. She sat down on the bed and ran her fingers through his hair. He pushed her hand away.

"How's Dad?" he asked.

"He'll be okay."

"Where was he the last few days?"

"It doesn't matter," she said. "He's home. Now it's my turn to go."

He jerked his arm away.

"Where are you going?" he asked. "Why are you going?"

She ran her fingers through his hair again. This time he let her.

"You know that something's going on with me and your dad," she said. "He and I need some time apart."

"Are you getting a divorce?" he asked.

"I don't know," she said.

"You're too old to get a divorce," he said.

She smiled.

Out of the mouths of babes.

"Nobody said anything about a divorce," she said. She gripped his hair and tugged. "We just need some time to think. I'll call you and we can set a time to get together this weekend if you want."

He pulled away from her. He slid off the bed and stood on the other side, keeping it between them.

"I don't know," he said. "It's up to dad.'

Her heart sank. He was already taking sides, as if he sensed that she was to blame.

Why not, I'm oozing guilt from every frigging pore.

"I'll talk to your dad, then," she said. "We'll see."

She went around the bed, cornered him and hugged him. He let her, but it was his only response.

"I'll see you soon," she said.

She walked out the door and headed down the stairs as tears blinded her. She grabbed the banister so she could find her way.

At her truck, she tossed the bag into the passenger seat and leaned on the door. She looked back towards the house.

She wanted to take it all in, to impress it on her memory as if it was still hers. Then she saw Jerry in the window of his room.

He was like something from the cover of a horror novel, where a child is visible in a hole that forms a window in the attic of a somber mansion. The child's twisted face is framed in red. When the cover is pulled back, the child is engulfed in flames.

Jerry's face was angry, unforgiving, but he wasn't the only one who was in hell.

TWENTY-NINE

Will sat on the roof with his back against the wall, the window just over his shoulder. He was hiding from Fred, who knew he had a huge test on Monday and was monitoring his study time.

If only it was as easy to hide from the junk inside my head.

He stood up and walked to the edge of the roof. He leaned over to pick up a stone to throw, but thought better of it. There weren't enough stones to fix the way he felt.

Will had had early classes for the first session of summer school. The second time around he decided to try afternoon courses. His weekend hours had turned him into a night owl. He did his best studying late at night.

Most mornings he slept until his class at noon, but this morning he'd woken up early. He thought about Sheila Cole. He knew that she was back in the hospital for more surgery and PT.

Her mother had said that mornings were the best time to visit. He knew there wouldn't be many days when he was up in time to see her. He thought he'd take the chance.

When he'd gotten to her room, he'd remembered his last visit, how angry her mother had been when he'd waited outside the door. He knocked gently on the door and went in.

He was surprised to see the chair beside the bed empty. He'd thought her mother never left her side.

Sheila had her face to the wall. She shifted uneasily in the bed. He remembered when he'd watched her through the crack in the door. He took a step back.

Is she still in pain? Her surgery was the day before yesterday. She should be okay.

Suddenly, she turned completely over, flipping like a gaffed fish. Her covers flew away. The IV line snagged on the bedpost. Will lunged to keep her from pulling it out. He brushed against her arm.

She jerked her arm away. Her eyes shot open. They were full of pain, but also something else. Anger. No, rage.

"Who the hell are you?" she gasped. She clutched for the sheet that she had tossed away, trying to cover up. She couldn't reach it. Will could almost hear her muscles tear as she tried to push them past their limits. Her eyes filled with tears. Will grabbed the sheet and put it in her hands. She shoved it back at him.

"Who are you?" she screamed.

"My name is Will," he said. "I'm a scrub tech. I worked on your case. We talked. You told me to come visit."

"Are you shitting me?" she asked. "You're a fucking scrub tech and we talked once in the OR and you think I'd remember you? You think I want you here? It's bad enough I have to see you people down there. Every time I start to heal, every time I get a minute's rest, you whisk me down to tear me up again and you think I want to you to come to my room and shoot the shit"

"I'm sorry," he said. "I'm so sorry."

"Sorry?" she said. "Sorry. A lot of good that does me. Why are you here? Why would you want to talk to me? What do you think I'm going to do, give you a big kiss and thank you for saving my life? Is that what you came for? Here, come close, I'll lay one on you."

She sat up in bed and opened her arms. She puckered her lips and closed her eyes.

Her arms looked better than they ever had, though they were still ravaged with scars, but her face was still pinched and red, her lips almost non-existent. She pursed the thin white lines that once might have been plush red.

"Come on," she said, "Slap one on me. My hero!"

Will turned and walked into the hall.

"Wait," she called behind him. "Wait. I want to thank you. Thank you for my life. Thank you for these lips."

Mrs. Cole was running down the hall. She saw him and she stopped. He steeled himself for the assault.

"You're Will," she said. "You're the scrub tech."

"That's right."

"What are you doing here?"

"I came to visit. You said mornings were best, before PT. I knew she was back in the hospital. I've been busy, taking classes. I had a chance to come, so I did."

His voice died. He couldn't keep it up.

"They cancelled PT today," she said. "This last round of surgeries has been really tough. She's in so much pain. Didn't you see her in the OR the other day?"

"No," he said. "I only work on the weekend, now. I take classes. I have the mornings off, but most of the time I've been up late studying and I sleep in."

"Come on," Mrs. Cole said. She led him back into the consultation room.

Will remembered the first time she'd led him here, how she'd acted as if this were her office.

Of course she had.

How many times had doctors led her into a closet just like this? How many times had she listened to them as they'd clicked off what they'd done that day? How many times had they adjusted their prognosis, sometimes for the better, more often for the worse? How many hours had she spent in here, alone, absorbing everything they'd told her, trying to work up the courage to face Sheila once again?

This wasn't just her office. It was, her refuge, her sanctuary, and her own private hell.

She sat in the chair on the left side of the table.

Her chair.

He took the one across from her. He looked out the long window that stretched from floor to ceiling. He realized that this was almost the same view that they had from the roof outside the OR. He saw the wide lawn, the huge grey stone. He expected to see fireworks materialize above the trees. Instead, he felt her hand on his wrist.

"I'm sorry you had to see her this way," she said. "She's really been doing much better. She hasn't been this angry in a long time. I think the setbacks bother her, more, now. She doesn't want to go backwards. She even threw me out this morning."

"I didn't know," he said. "Back then when we were working on her. I didn't know."

"You couldn't have known," she said.

"I should have."

"No," she'd said. She had tightened her grip on his wrist. He'd tried to pull away but she'd clamped down harder. "You couldn't. If you had, you might have given up."

* * * * *

Back on the roof, Will picked up a stone, after all. He strode across the roof, ready to let fly. He thought of Mrs. Cole without stones, seeing this same target, the large grey rock on the lawn, blocked by floor-to- ceiling glass. He opened his hand and the stone slid out of his palm and back onto the roof.

"There you are," Fred said. "Didn't you tell me you had a huge test tomorrow? You said it was going to be a bear and here you are goofing off again."

"I went to visit Sheila Cole this morning," Will said.

"Why in hell did you do that?" Fred asked. He eased himself through the window. "We talked about this. I told you to be human when you saw her in the OR again, but going to her room is crazy, especially after what we did to her on Thursday. How bad was it?"

"Bad," Will said. "I don't understand it. She seemed fine that last time we did her."

"That's the drugs, Will. I keep her pretty mellow in the OR. Once they wear off though... "Fred shook his head. What did she say?"

"She went crazy. She cussed me out. "It made me wonder, you know?"

"What do you mean?"

"This is what Julie and I used to fight about. She said we weren't really thinking about Sheila, that we did all this for ourselves. Today made me think that she was right. I loved the way Sheila's cases made me feel. I never thought of how it was for her."

"You're a kid," Fred said. "Everybody feels like that, at first. You have to keep some of it even after you've been around awhile. Without it you couldn't do your job."

There was that word again. Couldn't. Fred understood. So did Mrs. Cole. Did Sheila?

"I'm not surprised she cussed you out," Fred said. "I'm sure she hates us all some days. We always knew she'd have to go through hell, but what was the alternative? We couldn't let her die. She wasn't brain dead. She's still one hundred per cent in there. We didn't have a choice. Sometimes this job sucks. It's not all emergency C-Sections and Triple A's, you know."

Fred chuckled and shook his head. Will wanted to hit him.

"Remember that old grey guy who crashed on Dempsey in the elevator?" Fred said. "Dempsey freaked out, but the rest of us were ready to move heaven and earth to save the old coot. He was already dead, but did that stop us? Hell no."

Will bent down to pick up a stone. He threw it and hit the grey boulder dead center.

"Nice shot," Fred said.

Will held out a stone to Fred, but he shook his head.

Will threw three times. Hit, miss, hit.

"It doesn't seem that simple when it comes to Sheila," Will said. He walked back over to the wall and slumped down against it. He felt Fred's hand on his shoulder.

"I'm sorry you had to see her that way," Fred said. "But maybe it's for the best. A guy gets spoiled working as a scrub tech. You guys pretty much get all the fun. Think of this as a glimpse into your future. This kind of stuff is rough, but it's part of being a doctor. It really is worth it."

"I hope so," Will said.

"Hey," Fred said, "Have I ever steered you wrong?"

"No."

"Good. Come on. You've got work to do." Fred turned back towards the window. "That's one thing you really have to work on," he said. "Focusing on your studies."

"I guess you're right," Will said, as he got to his feet. He brushed bits of crushed rock from the seat of his scrubs.

They crawled back through the window and headed towards the OR. Fred paused at the elevator for the doctor's lounge.

"Are you coming up?" he asked

"I left my books out by the front desk," Will said. "I was reading with TJ."

"She's still out there," Fred said. "You could learn a thing or two from that girl."

Maybe she's the one who should go to medical school.

"I'm sure I could," Will said. "I'll be up in a minute."

The elevator came and Fred stepped in. He punched the button for the penthouse but held the door open with his hand. "You're not going to sneak back out on the roof, are you?" he asked.

"No, I've had enough of a break. I'm ready to go."

What he was really ready for was some action. He'd had enough of organic chemistry, but anything was better than going around in circles in his head about Sheila Cole.

"Okay," Fred said as he pulled his hands away.

"Doctor Dean," Flo called, but the doors had closed. Will turned to her. He expected to see her surrounded by her family, but she was alone. Her only family was the OR Open Heart tray that she held cradled to her chest as if it were a baby.

"They need us in the ICU," she said. "The heart patient is going bad."

"Don't they have time to bring him over here?"

"Not until they get him stabilized," she said. "They've already reopened his chest."

Will glanced at the elevator doors. "Should I get Fred?"

"There isn't time. Dempsey and TJ are already over there. We'll have to page him."

She held the Open Heart kit out to him. "Carry this, will you," she said. "It's heavy."

He took the tray. They sprinted the hundred yards to the ICU. Two housekeepers eyed them suspiciously as they ran by.

The patient's cubicle was much too small for the number of people who'd crowded into it. Will remembered being here with Sheila. He could smell her. He felt the weight of her body on his arms. He shook his head, trying to push these away.

"How many times have I asked you people to clear the fucking garbage off this tray?" Mixter railed and Will was back in this moment.

"All I need is a fucking needle driver and a goddamn set of pick-ups," Mixter said. "By the time I dig through the rest of this crap, this guy is going to bleed out on me."

He pulled a rack of instruments from the ICU's tray. He threw them against the wall, just missing one of the nurses.

Will dropped the tray that he'd brought from the OR on the patient's over-bed table. He tore the tape on the tray and pulled the corners back. He pulled on a pair of gloves, found the needle driver and pickups and waved them in Mixter's face.

"It's about fucking time," Mixter said. He grabbed the instruments and dipped back down into the chest. He threw several stitches and poked at his work with his finger. Finally, he leaned back.

"Okay," he said. "I got the bleeder. We can take him to the OR. Is that okay with you, Steve?"

Will noticed Dempsey for the first time. He stood calmly at the head of the bed, feeding drugs into the IV tubes, checking the patient's vital signs on the monitors.

"Give me a minute, will you?" he said.

"As long as it's just one," Mixter said, but his voice was easy, relaxed.

They transported the patient with his chest open and Mixter riding shotgun on the bed. The two housekeepers hadn't moved. They stared, open-mouthed.

Now they know why we ran.

Fred met them at the front door.

"Nice of you to join us, Fred," Mixter said, but there was still the same easy tone in his voice.

"I knew Steve had you covered," Fred said.

Will looked at Dempsey, but he hadn't heard them. He was intent on his monitors.

Will remembered the day when he shoved the old, grey guy away from him like a hot potato.

He's come a long way.

Later, Will sat with Fred in the doctor's lounge. They'd just settled down to their studies, but Will was still enjoying the buzz he'd gotten from their run to ICU.

Will looked down at his organic chemistry textbook. Symbols danced on the page. The box of plastic beads and rods that he used to configure various molecules and compounds sat on the table by his chair.

The red and blue dots and the clear plastic rods that held them together reminded him of the external fixators that

Jamison used to reconstruct smashed femurs. The difference was that once Will had finished with the molecules, the only thing that he could do was smash them and start over.

Why do I spend my days cramming my brain full of facts when the only time I feel alive is the few hours every weekend that I'm doing cases? Why did I put my life on hold? Why am I trying to be something that I'm not?

Because I needed to change my hours. Because I had to get away from Lila.

Oh Jesus.

He glanced to his right, where Fred still read his journal. Perhaps he felt Will's eyes on him, because he looked up and nodded towards Will's book with his best schoolmarm imitation.

Will nodded, looked back down, but his mind was on everything but organic chemistry. He understood what he'd done. He'd gone to school to hide from Lila, and there was only one way to fix it.

He smiled. A weight was lifted from him. For the first time in months, he felt like himself. He knew what he needed to do. He needed to get back behind the surgical drapes, and there was only one reason to come out from behind them. He'd visit Sheila Cole again, but otherwise he'd get back where he belonged.

THIRTY

Lila tossed her underwear into the pile at the foot of the bed. It landed on top and slid down the side and on to the floor. She looked at the clock. Ray would be dropping Jerry off in twenty minutes for a visit. It would only be for a few hours, but it was a start.

I really need to shove this crap into the closet. Why didn't I just spring for that hamper when I was in Super Giant last week? The frigging Chinese make a nice, cheap hamper.

She walked into the living room. Except for the piled laundry the apartment was immaculate. It was easy to keep up with one person and two rooms. She had a lot of time on her hands. Time. Something that she'd never had before. Even the last few years with all the boys but Jerry gone, she found things around the house to keep busy. A house can be just as needy as a family.

Found. Maybe that was her problem. She'd always found things to do, anything to keep from asking what her life was really about.

What it was about? What kind of shit is this? My life was always right there smacking me in the face: Ray and the boys, work and the house. This isn't about my life, it's about me.

Something had always been missing. She knew that, now. She wasn't the first woman to fall for an inappropriate man. She wasn't the first to have an affair. Lots of people did. She was probably one of the few, though, who'd walked away from her life after the affair was over.

Was that all it was with Will, some little voice inside me screaming for its freedom?

She went into the kitchen and checked the refrigerator. She'd stocked up with all of Jerry's favorite foods.

There was a liter of Red Splash Cola, macaroni and cheese and a bag of baby carrots. He was the only child she'd ever had who'd eat a vegetable without having his arm twisted off.

She checked the freezer. It held the real stockpile, the frozen pizzas. There were thin crust and deep dish, on French bread and in pockets. Those were calzones. She suspected the company that produced them knew this but feared that such an exotic name might scare off their target group.

She closed the door. Jerry probably wouldn't eat much, anyway. He was still too angry with her to do more than show up. She told herself that was all she could expect.

He was old enough that he could have just refused to come. No judge would have forced him. She knew she'd have to be patient.

She made one more circuit of the apartment. She looked at the clock. Ten minutes.

Ten more minutes to ask myself what in frigging hell I'm doing here. One of these days Jerry's bound to ask. It would be nice if I had an answer. Of course, it would be nice to have the answer for myself.

Not that it was so complicated. She'd gone from her father's house to Ray's with only a short stint working for Uncle Sam in between. She'd defined her life by those three men for 52 years. Then Will came along and he was number four.

This wouldn't be much help when she talked to Jerry. What else would he think except that he was just another man who'd taken over her life?

She looked at the clock. She decided to wait for them on the street. She wanted to see Ray. She hoped that he'd come up when he dropped Jerry off, but she suspected that he wouldn't. She missed him. Not the "check your make-up in the mirror, what am I wearing?" kind of missing, but missing still. He was her best friend, after all.

On the front porch, she sat in one of the wicker chairs her landlady, Peggy, provided. The chair matched the house.

The only thing that would have been a better match is a goddamn porch swing.

She knew that she'd been lucky to find this place. Just across the street was a row of the chicken coops that passed for apartments these days. The only place to sit outside of these was on the concrete steps. She could see a few stray beer cans and paper wrappers from the burger joint on the next block. She knew the cans were filled with cigarette butts. She'd seen her neighbors smoke and drink and litter out on the steps. She'd heard their music at night.

Peggy's was an older building that had once been a house and had only been broken up into apartments after the fact. Lila had had her doubts when she'd climbed the narrow stairs that first day. As soon as she'd pushed the door opened and felt the sunlight from the huge bay window that filled the front wall of the living room, though, she'd known this was perfect for her. She hadn't felt so light since the first few weeks when she'd realized that she was falling for Will.

Ray's truck pulled around the corner. Jerry's face clouded when he saw her sitting outside, but Ray just smiled.

She knew they'd have to work things out, at least make it so Jerry didn't feel the need to protect Ray. She remembered how Jerry had been there for her when Ray was sick. This was different. A kid shouldn't have to protect his parents from each other.

Jerry climbed out of the truck.

"You should have waited upstairs," he said. "It isn't fair to dad."

She reached out and smoothed a wild spike of hair on the top of his head. "Why don't we let him decide that?" she said gently.

Jerry looked towards his father, as if he hadn't dared to before this. He saw the smile.

Ray nodded.

"I guess it'll be all right," Jerry said. "Be nice."

Lila smiled in spite of herself.

Be nice.

She walked to Ray's side of the truck.

"How have you been?" she asked.

"I'm okay," he said. "You?"

"I've been better," she said.

He wouldn't meet her eyes. He looked at her house, at the apartments across the street, as if the neighborhood was much more important than her face.

"House looks nice," he said, finally.

"It's okay," she said. "Better than that mess over there." She nodded across the street.

"Be better if you were still in Weston," he said.

"Come on, Ray," she said. "Don't do this."

"I'm sorry. What do you expect me to say?"

She wondered what he'd be saying if she hadn't walked away, if she'd told him about Will and begged forgiveness. He was a good man, but would he have been able to do that? Would he have wanted to but ended up punishing her, instead? Maybe he still would if they tried to work things out.

"I miss you," she said.

He frowned, as if he understood that she meant it as a friend.

"Have you seen that kid?" he asked.

She put a hand on his arm. "I told you that that's over," she said.

Ray pulled his hand away and tapped his fist on the steering wheel.

"That's what I don't understand," he said.

"I need time," she said. He kept tapping. She regretted the words as soon as she said them. She knew it wasn't time that she needed. She just needed to be on her own. She'd just given him the easy answer.

Someday I'll get past this shit.

"It's good to see you," she said.

The tapping on the wheel sped up and stopped.

"Have a good time with Jerry," he said. "He'll come around. I guess we all need time."

"Thanks."

She climbed the stairs, angry at herself for giving Ray false hope, worried about her time with Jerry.

She remembered the day she'd left home, how Jerry had stood in his window, caught in his own private hell. She imagined him in the front window of her new living room, now. Had he watched she and Ray down in the street, trying to figure out how things were going between them? She hated herself for giving him false hope, too.

Every time she'd seen him since she'd moved out, she'd seen the same look in his eyes. She knew it wouldn't change unless she went back home. She knew she couldn't.

As she approached the apartment, the smell of pizza filled the hall. She took a deep breath. She allowed herself the chance to hope.

She opened the door and Jerry was in the kitchen watching the microwave as the timer ran down. He looked up when she came in. He blushed as if she'd caught him doing something wrong.

Maybe he's just mad at himself for deserting his post.

"I didn't eat much lunch today," he said. "You should have seen the crap they served in the cafeteria. It really blew."

"Watch her mouth, young man," she said, but her heart wasn't in it. She couldn't hide her smile. "Do they still serve mystery meat every Monday?"

"More like Monday, Wednesday and Friday," he said. The microwave rang off and he pulled his snack out. He'd decided on the pizza pocket, the calzone.

He raised it to his mouth, but she stopped him.

"Slow down," she said. "You know those things cook from the inside out. You'll burn your mouth."

"Okay," he said and laid it back down on the plate. He eyed it eagerly.

I need something to distract him. Not school. Something important.

"Hey Ma," he asked. "Why do you work in the afternoon, not during the day like most folks?"

So who's distracting who?

She shrugged. "I always have," she said.

"But why did you start?"

"Because of you and your brothers," she said.

She smiled as she remembered the years when they were young. Her days had been spent trying to corral the lot of them. She'd headed off to work each afternoon exhausted, but grateful for a chance to move beyond the chaos.

She'd listen to her co-workers, most of whom had just crawled out of bed, complain about how tired they were, how life in general was too hard. She'd drawn a sigh of relief and headed off to spar with Jamison. Compared to dealing with a houseful of screaming boys, it had all seemed like child's play.

"I know you had a good reason when we were kids," Jerry said. "But why did you keep it up once we were all in school?"

"Well," she said. "There was still a lot I needed to do for you. There were always activities during the school year and once summer came around we were all right back together. We had a lot of fun, didn't we?"

"Sure," he said, "But didn't you miss Dad? Maybe that's why things got messed up with you guys. You never saw each other."

He picked up the calzone and broke it in two. Steam poured out from the center. Bits of cheese and meat fell onto the plate. He picked one up and popped it into his mouth. His eyes got big and he breathed quickly in and out.

"I told you," she said. "You have to be patient."

"I know," he said. He waited.

Both for the calzone and the answer to his question.

"Things are different when you're married," she said. "Sometimes you make sacrifices. We couldn't just think about ourselves, we had to think about the family. We were a team."

"But didn't you miss him?" He pressed.

She cursed his choice of snack foods. Why hadn't he gone for thin crust, New York Style? If he had, he'd already be eating, maybe he'd have shreds of burnt skin on the roof of his mouth, but he wouldn't be staring at her, waiting for an answer.

"You might be right," she said. "Sometimes you end up making more sacrifices than you intended. Why are you asking this, now?"

"Because I know how he might have felt. I never see you anymore, Ma."

Funny, I thought that was the way you wanted it.

"Maybe you could change your hours," he said. "If you worked in the mornings, I could come over most days after you got off work. You could come to my games and stuff."

He didn't look at her, as if he was afraid of her answer, as if she hadn't just left his father, but him, as well.

He looked down at the calzone. He didn't seem as interested as he'd been before. The steam had dissipated. Soon, it would need another round in the microwave. He waited.

"Well," she said. "I've never really thought about it. I will, now though. I've got to tell you, kiddo, it would be hard. Your body gets used to a certain routine and I've been doing this forever.

"My job would be different, too," she said. "They do different types of surgeries in the morning and sometimes it gets kind of boring."

He looked at her and she saw the resignation in is eyes, as if she had already made up her mind and was just making her excuses.

"Hey," she said. "I'm being straight with you. I just never thought about it before. Give me time. It's actually a pretty good idea."

"Really?" he said.

"Really."

He picked up the calzone and took a bite.

"I'll bet it's cold," she said.

"No," he said, "It's just right."

Later, she sat on the front porch and watched Jerry and Ray drive away. She wrestled with the realization that Jerry had brought with his question, that Will wasn't such a leap for her after all. She'd carved out a life away from her family long before he ever came along.

She'd started working evenings for the kids, but somewhere along the line it had become for her.

She considered Jerry's proposal. She didn't want to work days. She hated the routine, the types of cases. Martha might be a bitch, but she knew her people and she put them where their talents lay. Bev on days did the best she could, but there were just too many people to juggle. Who knew what kinds of cases she'd be stuck with?

Still, she had to think about it. This would be for Jerry. She felt like she'd lost him, and now he was offering her a way back in.

She knew that he probably harbored plans to get she and Ray back together, but she couldn't do anything about that. All she could do was be there for him.

She looked across the street at her neighbors, their nightly card table set up by the steps. A boom box rasped beside them. Dominoes flashed in the streetlights.

One of the players, a kid not much older than Jerry, saw her and raised his bottle, nestled in a brown paper sack to her. She nodded, but stood and went inside. She'd thought she'd been invisible. She wasn't entirely unhappy to find that she'd been wrong.

THIRTY-ONE

Will thought it a good omen when he found Martha in her office. He'd been nervous about having to track her down in the OR, afraid that he'd run into Lila. He planned on talking to Lila, but he wanted it to be on his own terms, not with everyone around.

First, though, there was Martha.

"Hello, Martha," he said.

She looked annoyed at being interrupted, but once she recognized him she smiled.

"Will," she said. She held her hand out to him.

"It's good to see you," she said.

"You, too."

He wasn't lying. She looked as good as she always did.

Does this woman ever age?

Her hair had grown out just a bit. He knew she'd probably be getting it cut within a day or two. She wore gold, hoop earrings. Those would go before she went into the OR. She wore ankle socks, a shocking red that matched her hair. That was one fashion statement he never thought she'd be a part of.

"I've been getting good reports about you from Flo," she said. She smoothed her skirt down. "She's happy to have you. How's school going?" she asked.

"That's kind of what I wanted to talk to you about," he said.

"No problems, I hope?"

'No," he said. "I'm doing fine. I'm just not sure school's the right thing for me. I miss the work too much. I'm going a bit stir crazy."

She glanced down at the notes on her desk. He knew that she was in the final preparations for report. He stood.

"I should let you finish," he said. "I'll get a cup of coffee or something. I'll come back in after you talk to everybody."

She put her hand on his arm and pushed him back down.

"I'll be fine," she said. "I can always wing it if I have to. It won't be the first time."

Somehow, "winging it" was not a phrase he would have ever applied to Martha.

"So," she said. "What you're trying to tell me is that you want to change your hours again."

"That's right."

"You want to go back to the day shift?"

"No," he said. "I want to work evenings again."

"I see." She turned to the wall beside her desk and pulled down the schedules for all three shifts. She spread them out on her desk.

"When you left," she said without looking up, "You hinted that there were personal problems. Has the time away helped you to get past those problems?"

"I think so. I know that coming back is the only way to know for sure."

She shook her head. "That's not good enough, Will," she said. "You can't keep bouncing around like this."

She looked up from the schedules, challenging him with her eyes. This was the Martha he knew.

"I'll make it work this time," he said.

"Good."

She studied the schedules again.

"You know I'd love to have you back," she said. "How soon would this be?"

He glanced at the calendar. "I have two more weeks of classes this session. Anytime after that."

"It might take a little while," she said. "Coming back to evenings is no problem, we're pretty depleted. We'll need to find some one who could work for you on the weekends, though."

"That's fine," he said. "I don't have a problem with working weekends. I mean I'm looking for a little steadier action, but I know I have to wait my turn. I know I've bounced around on a lot the last year."

"I'm sure everyone on the shift will be glad to have you back," she said.

He wasn't so sure, but he was ready to find out.

"Is Lila working tonight?" he asked.

"Of course." She glanced at the clock. "She's probably in by now. She's adopted your old habit. She comes in early every day. "I'll bet she's in the lounge."

He found her in the lounge sitting in his chair. There wasn't a cup of coffee balanced on her stomach, which was just as well. She would have scalded herself the way she jumped when she heard his voice.

She scrambled to her feet.

"Will," she said, "What the hell are you doing here?"

"I came to talk to Martha. I'm sorry I scared you."

"Martha?" She said. She eyed him suspiciously. "Why Martha?"

"I came to see if I could get my old hours back."

He studied her face. He wasn't sure what he expected from her. Not that the color would drain from her face the way it did, that she would grab her stomach as if he'd punched her.

"Lila," he said. "Are you okay?"

He took a step towards her. She held up a hand.

"I'm sorry, Will," she said. "You scared the life out of me when you came in. Then you tell me that you're coming back. Let's start over. It's good to see you."

She smiled shyly. She put her hand on his shoulder. There was nothing flirtatious in this. She seemed as anxious to hold him at a distance as she was to make contact.

"It's good to see you, too," he said. "You look good. How's everything going? How's the family?"

"Everybody's fine."

"And Ray, his heart, I mean?"

She blushed. He knew it wasn't right for him to ask about Ray, but he wanted her to see that he was ready to move on. He'd have to if they were going to work together.

"Did you want to sit down?" he asked. He motioned towards his chair.

"After you," she said. "I was just keeping it warm for you."

He wondered if that meant she'd always expected him to come back, that she wanted him back.

Maybe this isn't such a good idea, after all.

She must have read his face.

"It's just a figure of speech, Will," she said. "You always were too damn serious."

He sat down. She took the seat across from him. They could have laid their legs on each other's laps like they used to do in the truck.

"You want to come back to evenings?" she asked. "Are you going to take morning classes? When will you have time to study?"

"I don't think school is right for me. I'm doing fine," he said, anticipating the question. "I just miss the work, you know?"

She shook her head. "I don't buy this, Will," she said. She stood and walked to the end of the lounge. She came back and stood over him.

"It has to be something more. You're scared or you're lazy. You miss the work? Come on, Will, you can do better than that."

He shrugged. She was doing it again, trying to be his mother when he needed something else from her.

"Look," he said. "I appreciate what you're trying to do, but you've got it all wrong. I'd never even thought of going to school until you and Fred started talking about it. I was happy as a tech. I thought I could work while I went to school and have the best of both worlds, but that isn't happening. I can't do things half-ass and right now that's exactly what I'm doing in both work and school.

"I was hoping that you'd understand, but if you don't that doesn't change a thing. I'm coming back, Lila. If you don't want to team with me, that's fine. We'll tell Martha and she'll make sure it never happens."

He stood, but she blocked his way.

"I'm sorry,' she said. "I'm trying to be your mother again."

"How can you still think that way?" he said, "After everything that's happened. After…"

"I know," she said. "Maybe that's why things got so crazy between us. I tried to deny who I am. Maybe that's what you did when you went to school. No good ever comes of doing that."

"So what do we do, now?" he asked.

"We work together," she said. "That's where everything started for us, both good and bad. We always were a hell of a team."

"You're right," he said. He stood back up and opened his arms to her.

"We'd better not go there," she said.

"I'm sorry," he said.

"Don't apologize. It's just best not to blur the lines."

They stood without speaking. Neither seemed to know what to say.

"So when's this going to happen?" she asked, finally.

"A few weeks at the earliest," he said. "I've got two more weeks of classes and then it's just a question of when we find somebody to work my weekend hours."

He looked up at the clock.

"I'd better go," he said, "It's almost time for report."

"Why don't you stay?" she asked. "Everybody will be glad to see you."

"That's okay," he said. "I've had enough excitement for today. Could you tell everybody?"

"I'm sure Martha will take care of that," she said.

"I'll see you soon," he said as he fought the urge to take her in his arms.

Maybe I can make this work.

"I'll see you in a few weeks."

He was awakened by pounding on his door. He sat up in bed and grabbed his alarm clock from the side table. It was six am. He got out of bed, pulled on a pair of scrub bottoms and went to the front door.

"I'm coming," he yelled as the pounding continued. He jerked the door open. Murph stumbled into his arms.

"Murph? What the hell are you doing here, man? Do you know what time it is?"

Murph grinned sheepishly and waved his arm at Will.

"No watch," he said, slurring his words.

Murph shoved past Will and threw himself on the couch, covering his eyes with his arm.

"What the hell is going on, man?" Will asked.

"Kathy dumped me," Murph said. His chest shuddered

"Dumped you?" Will said. "You're kidding."

Will still couldn't see Murph's eyes, but a thin line of mucous dripped from his nose. He sobbed and a bubble formed in one nostril and burst. Will grabbed a dishtowel from the rack by the sink.

"Wipe your nose, man," he said. He shoved the towel into Murph's hands

"I'm sorry, man," Murph said as he grabbed the towel. "I know I'm a mess. I should have been ready for this. I always knew I was living on borrowed time. She moved on."

"Moved on with who?"

"With fucking Mixter, that's who."

"Mixter? I thought the guy was married."

"He is married. He didn't care any more about his wife than Kathy cared about me. I didn't have a chance. It's all about the bucks." He rubbed his fingers together.

"Come on, Murph. Kathy's not like that."

"We thought she wasn't. In the end, I guess they all are. It's all about the houses, the cars, the prestige."

"Jesus, can you hear yourself? If she dumped you she dumped you. It's rough but it happens. You have to pull yourself together."

"I'm telling you man. It's not just me and Kathy. Things have gone to hell since you left the shift. They've all gone crazy. It's more like a whorehouse than an OR. Kathy and Mixter. Julie and Dempsey. Even Lila left her old man, for Christ's sake."

"Lila?" Will said, "Lila, left…" He couldn't finish the sentence. All the air went out of his lungs, as surely as if Murph had stiff-armed him.

"Can you believe it, man?" Murph said. "She's been with the guy for thirty years and she dumps him the same year he has a goddamn bypass.

"I'm telling you, Will. These women have all gone insane and I'm up to my neck in it every day. What am I going to do, man?"

He threw his arm back over his eyes. He moaned.

Will knew that he should say something, but he couldn't. Lila had left her husband.

Why didn't she tell me? We broke up because she said she couldn't do it.

"I'm so screwed," Murph said.

Will knew he needed to help his friend. He could worry about his own problems later.

But Lila left Ray, for Christ's sake.

"What are you going to do, Murph?"

"I don't know, man. Do you know what it's like to work every day with your ex-girlfriend and the guy who stole her from you?

"I was clueless, man. Here I was getting my hair cut, upgrading my fucking wardrobe and the two of them were laughing their asses off at me the whole time."

"You don't know that, man," Will said. "They probably felt bad about doing that to you. Sometimes people can't help themselves, you know?"

Murph uncovered his eyes. He sat up and stared at Will. Most of the mucous had dried up in his nose. He wiped away what was left with the back of his hand.

"You sound like you're talking from experience," he said. "I didn't think you were like that, man."

Will shook his head. "I didn't think I was either."

He stood and went back into the kitchen. "You should eat something, man," he said. "You want some cereal." He pulled open the cupboard and pulled out a box of corn flakes and another of instant oatmeal. He shook the oatmeal. When he opened the box, he saw that there was only one package left.

"Eat? Are you kidding me," Murph said. "My stomach is a mess. I can't eat."

Will flipped on the front burner of the stove. The pilot light clicked three times and then the flame popped on. He put on the teapot.

"At least have some coffee," Will said.

"Okay, okay, I'll have coffee. Stop trying to change the subject, man. Who was it? Who did you cheat on? Or who cheated on somebody because of you?"

Will turned back to Murph. He couldn't tell Murph about he and Lila. Time for another lie. He'd hoped that he was done with lies.

"When I was still going out with Julie, I met Monique, this patient who came down for a scope. We knew something was there the minute we met. She was with somebody, too, but it didn't matter, you know?"

"No," Murph said, "I don't know, but I'm starting to see that the rest of the world does. Is that why you broke up with Julie? I thought you said it was stuff about the work."

"It was," Will said. "She never found out about Monique."

"So what happened to her?"

"She's gone. Nothing good can come when you start off like that."

"Tell me about it," Murph said. "I guess that's one good thing. Who knows how long Mixter will stick with Kathy before he starts looking around again."

The teapot whistled and Will poured two cups of coffee. He tore open the oatmeal packet and poured it into a bowl, then added water.

"You want anything in your coffee?" he asked Murph.

"Just some whiskey," Murph said.

"Not a chance," Will said.

He got the milk from the refrigerator. He poured it into his cup and held the carton up to Murph. He shook his head.

"So, you're saying you know how Kathy felt," Murph said. "You still don't know what it feels like to be in my shoes. I can't keep working with these two. I'll go out of my mind. They don't have a problem with it. Kathy keeps telling me that I need to compartmentalize. What kind of shit is that?"

Damn good shit.

"I don't want to quit, man," Murph said. "I don't think I could stand working at any of these crummy little hospitals or surgery centers around here. I'll go out of my mind doing that. Either way I'm screwed."

"Maybe you could work the weekends," Will said.

"Weekends? I thought they had a full crew."

"They're going to need a scrub tech," Will said. "I'm going back to regular hours. You could take my place."

Will kept his eyes aimed down at his oatmeal. He waited for the questions, but they didn't come.

"Haven't you been listening to me, man?" Murph asked. "You can't go back to evenings. They've all gone crazy."

"I learned my lesson with Julie," Will said. "You really can't mess where you eat, man."

"Kathy and Mixter can," Murph said. "The didn't let it mess with their jobs. They're goddamn robots"

"Some people are," Will said. "I just know that I'm not one of them."

Murph signed. He finally sipped his coffee. Will took that as a sign that he could eat his oatmeal.

"I guess I'm like you, man," Murph said. "I have to get out of this shit. Maybe I'll take you up on that weekend thing."

He put his coffee down and lay back on the coach. He seemed to relax for the first time since he'd burst in. His breathing grew steady and soon, he was asleep.

Will stood over him for a few minutes, then got a blanket and covered him. He went back into the bedroom. He sighed.

So, he'd solved Murph's problem, the immediate one, that is. They could switch hours. Murph could hide out on the weekends until he got his bearings back.

Will had his own problems to deal with. Lila had broken up with her husband.

And how is that my problem? She didn't even tell me. She doesn't want me to know. She wouldn't do it for me. Why did she do it now?

Will sat up so quickly that he spilled coffee on the legs of his scrub bottoms. The hot liquid seeped through the thin material.

She met somebody else. That must be it. Someone who's the real thing, not just a kid.

The coffee reached his skin and he jerked the drawstring on the pants and let them fall. He stood with the pants around his ankles. He knew he looked ridiculous and yet, that seemed appropriate. He felt like a fool.

He thought about Lila with somebody else. He thought of her leaving Ray because of that person but not for him. She'd acted as if their time together was agonizing for her and now this.

Maybe that's why she hadn't told him. She'd moved on. Wasn't that for the best? He was going back to evenings and he was supposed to be learning to keep things compartmentalized. If Lila wanted to lie to him, wouldn't that make it easier? Shouldn't he just go along with her and pretend that that nothing had ever happened between them?

Hell no.

One way or the other, they needed to have this out. If Lila was with somebody else, he 'd learn to live with it, but he wasn't going to let her pretend that she'd gone back to her old life. Whatever was going on, he needed to know just what he'd been to her.

Maybe I was just her first step out the door.

Until he got some answers, he'd never be able to move on. He'd never be able to get back into his work. He'd never be able to get his life back the way that it should be. He'd never plug the hole burning in his gut.

THIRTY-TWO

Lila prowled the aisles of the Super Giant department store waiting for a hamper to call her name. Piles of merchandise rose up on either side of her, vying for her attention. Back in the day when home furnishing had mattered to her, she would have savored every minute. Today she just wanted to find something to hold the pile of clothes at the foot of her bed so Jerry wouldn't take it as a sign that she was falling apart.

In the past, she would have probably been in ReceptaCity, the store that specialized in storage and containers. They had thirty thousand ways to organize and all of them fantastic. It had always been one of her favorite places. She'd whiled away many an afternoon in that store. Today she just wanted to get what she needed and get out. Easy enough.

If only it were that easy to figure out what I'm going to do when Will comes back to work.

She found the hampers. Not thirty thousand, but a good selection, everything from plastic for ten dollars, all the way up to wicker at a thirty-two-fifty.

Once, she would have lingered, looking for the perfect color to match her décor. Now, she didn't have a décor, just four white walls and thrift shop furniture. She could try to match the bedspread. Ray had let her keep the one from their bedroom, but there were no pine trees on these hampers, not stenciled on the plastic, not woven into the wicker slats.

She went with white, matching the décor, after all.

Better watch it, this could be a slippery slope.

She knew that Will would be an even slipperier one.

She liked her life these days. She was alone and she liked it that way. She wanted a chance to explore, to find out what this really meant. She feared that if Will said the word she'd give it up in heartbeat.

She'd tell herself she had no choice, that this wasn't just needing a man to fill her life, but the real thing. Would she just be fooling herself?

She walked to the cash registers and took her place in the shortest line, waiting behind a half-dozen other women with their carts piled high.

Where's a frigging express lane when you need one?

Perhaps stores like this couldn't afford to encourage such concepts as ten items or less. She wondered how they'd feel about fifty-year-old women falling in love with twenty-year-old kids.

She asked herself for the hundredth time if she'd really loved Will, or if it was just that she'd been with Ray so long that she didn't want to believe she'd destroyed their marriage for a fling?

She finally reached the cash register. The girl behind it stared in disbelief when she saw Lila only had one item. Lila glared back at her.

The girl looked down and dragged the hamper across the scanner. It beeped expectantly and seemed as surprised as its human counterpart when nothing followed.

The girl rang up the sale. "Debit or credit?" she asked cheerfully, finally back on familiar ground.

Lila waved the ten-dollar bill that she'd been holding the whole time in the girl's face.

The girl seemed confused as she studied the panel of the register. Lila wondered if she'd gotten into the wrong line. Maybe cash wasn't an option. She searched for a sign that said this. The girl's face brightened as she found the right button and tapped it with her finger.

"Nine Ninety-nine," she said.

"Keep the change," Lila said as she handed her the bill, enjoying one last burst of confusion on the girl's face as she walked away.

As she walked to her truck, Lila ran over everything about Will in her head. When she'd first broken up with Ray, she'd asked herself what she really felt for Will. Was it real, or was she just kidding herself? Was she trying to make up for lost time, relive her youth, find something that she'd given up when she settled down with Ray? She still wasn't sure.

It didn't matter why she'd been with Will. What she did know was that she was alone for the first time in her life and that she liked it. That was part of why she hadn't said anything to Will, even though a part of her wanted to scream the words at him.

She wasn't ready to be with someone again. She needed time.

She laughed.

Sure, wait until I'm sixty and he's thirty. We'll have a hell of lot more in common, then.

She reached her truck. She tossed the hamper in the back and got behind the wheel.

She wondered if she could ever really be with Will. As wild as she'd once been about him, she didn't want to go back. She hated the person she'd been back then, the way she'd felt, her jealously and anger.

Best to let the feeling die, instead. Best to be alone. She couldn't trust herself.

She turned the key, started the truck and headed for the exit of the parking lot. It seemed to be a mile away. There were almost as many types of cars in the lot as there were hampers in Receptacity.

She reached the exit and pulled out into traffic, heading home.

She knew that she'd only bought herself a little time by not telling Will the truth today.

Somebody's bound to spill the beans.

She'd tried to keep her situation secret. She'd given Martha her new phone number, of course, but she knew she'd never talk. Martha might be a bitch, but she was a professional.

Kathy was the only person who knew. She'd always known that Lila had feelings for Will and noticed the changes in her when he'd left. Once Kathy found out that Will was coming back, she 'd probably want to let him know.

I'll just tell her I want to keep it between us.

She parked in front of her apartment. She wished it was one of Jerry's days to visit. She pulled the hamper from the back of her truck. She hugged it to her chest as she climbed the stairs.

THIRTY-THREE

Will took his last exam on a Friday morning. When he'd finished, he stood at the top of the stairs of Aiken Hall, the flagship of the campus core, atop a grey cascade of concrete steps.

A line of students flowed up and down the grey concrete. The co-eds exhibited every style imaginable: preppie and hippie and business class. Their uniforms were polo shirts, khakis and flip-flops, flowing skirts and peasant blouses, jackets and slacks. One girl wore a tie, the finishing touch on her business suit. Another wore one loosely around her neck, over a tank top and between the folds of a loosely fitting vest.

There were backpacks and briefcases, books pressed to breasts. The books and a thin t-shirt were often the only thing keeping those breasts in check.

He thought of Murph. This is what he said he'd missed about not going to college.

Murph had been staying with him. Even as Will tried to finish up his classes and study for exams, they'd gone out drinking every night. Will crawled out of bed at noon every day to hit the books or go to class while Murph had slept until it was time to do it all again.

Last night Will had begged off because of his exam and Murph still hadn't been home when he'd left that morning. Will wasn't worried. He knew Stu and the boys would watch out for Murph.

It would all seem pretty lame if I hadn't done the same thing to get over Lila.

The only difference was that while Murph drank and smoked at levels Will had never even approached, he hadn't even tried to be with a woman.

Will had tried to fix him up with women from the bar, but Murph was having none of it.

"What's with him?" Stu had asked. "Doesn't he know there's only one way to get a woman out of your head? You have to screw so many that you finally remember they're all the same in the dark."

"I guess he's not ready to be rid of the last one," Will said. "I guess he wants to hold on to her face a little longer."

Stu shook his head.

"Guy needs to stop beating himself up."

"He will," Will had said.

Maybe tonight would be the night. They'd celebrate their newfound freedom, his from school and Murph's from monogamy. Will glanced at his watch. There would be plenty of time for that later.

He pulled out his cell phone. Mrs. Cole had given him her number. He dialed.

"Hello," she said, her voice wary.

"Mrs. Cole," he said. "This is Will Nathan."

"Will Nathan? Oh yes, of course, the scrub tech."

"I was wondering how Sheila was doing this morning. I just got out of class and thought I might drop by. It's not a bad time, is it?"

"No," she said. "She just got back from PT, but she's feeling fine. I'm sure she'd love to see you, but let me check."

Will waited, heard muffled voices. Mrs. Cole must have placed the phone against the fabric of her blouse. He tried to gage the timbre of Sheila's voice. Was it the sweet lilt he'd heard in the OR or the anger that she'd shown him that last time in her room?

"She said today would be fine," Mrs. Cole said, as her voice came back clear and strong. "How soon will you be here?"

"I'm just across campus. Give me five minutes."

He paused when he got to the door of her room, torn between waiting and rushing in.

It's not as if either one worked for me before.

He knocked.

"Come in," a voice called.

He hesitated. It wasn't Mrs. Cole. He'd expected her to be on guard, only this time as much for him as for Sheila.

He pushed into the room. Sheila sat in a chair by the window.

"Hello," she said.

He walked towards her, making eye contact immediately, knowing that he couldn't flinch, be evasive, or look away. She seemed to feel the same way. Her eyes were on him, too, as if this were a grade school staring contest, as if neither of them could blink.

"Will?" she asked.

She doesn't recognize me.

"Yes."

"Scrub tech Will?"

"Yes."

"My angel and tormenter?"

Oh yes.

"I'm afraid you have me at a disadvantage," she said. "This is the first time I've seen you when I wasn't full of narcotics. A lot of things are fuzzy to me. Have a seat."

She gestured to the chair a few feet away from hers. He sat and could have inched his foot out and easily touched her blue, hospital-issue slippers. Instead, the blue toes snaked out and touched him.

He looked at her. Her eyes were bright, affectionate.

"There," she said. "That's taken care of."

"You really don't recognize me," he said.

""If I don't recognize your face it's because the first few times you saw me I was unconscious in my morphine prison. After that I was high as a kite.

"Still, I remember you telling me that you'd worked on me right at the start and that I was making great strides. I remember Dr. Dean saying that you'd broken up with your girlfriend because of me."

She batted her eyelashes at him.

"I never thought I'd get to be a heartbreaker again," she said.

Her smile faded as if a bad memory clouded her eyes.

"I remember that you showed up in my room on my worst day and got your ass chewed big time. Welcome to the freak show."

She shook her head as if this would drive the memory away. Will wanted to speak, but he had no words.

"I remember that," she said, "I don't recognize your face, but I know it was you. I remember your eyes, the pain that I saw there."

They sat for a moment, as their shared history passed over them. The room pressed in around him as it had those first few times they'd been in the OR, that time in the ICU. He knew that he had missed it.

"So, tell me about the girl," she said. "Dr. Dean said I was the cause, but you said there were other reasons."

"It happened about that time, but we had other problems," he said.

"Now you've hurt my feelings," she said. "You could have lied."

She pouted. At least he thought she did. Expressions were difficult on her face, frozen by the scars. Everything was in her voice, enough to let him see her feelings: joy, disappointment, even pique. He thought of what Fred had said, "She's 100% in there." Fighting to get out.

She's a spirit with a damaged shell.

He looked out the window. The view from here was different than her mother's office, from the OR roof. All Sheila had was a grove of trees behind the hospital. Maybe that was better. There would be birds, animals, maybe a family of raccoons whose antics might distract her. For now she needed his antics.

"Julie and I met on the job," he said. "We just clicked.

"But then you worked on me."

"I worked with you every week, but when she got assigned, she freaked out."

He hesitated.

"It's okay," she said. "I'm used to it."

"Julie couldn't handle it," he said. "It was the first sign of trouble for us, but things might have worked out if I hadn't met somebody else. Julie and I stayed friends. She's a good nurse."

"And this other nurse?"

"She and I were the perfect team in the OR," he said. "We felt the same way about the job."

"Even about me?"

"Yes."

"So she passed your toughest test?"

"I suppose."

"It sounds like work is more important to you than sex."

"Not exactly," he said. "The sex was great with both of them."

She slapped his arm.

"Why Will Nathan," she said, "You make me blush."

This time the voice was a Southern Belle, ("I do declare.") and even though her mask stayed frozen, her complexion pale, the blush was in her voice.

"So how are things with woman #2?" she asked.

"That's over, too," he said. "She's married. She's much older than me."

"I'm sorry," she said.

"It's okay," he said.

"No," she said. "I don't think it is."

"All right," he said. "It hurts like hell."

"That's better."

Her claw skittered down his arm and settled on his hand. Afraid to look at her, he focused on those eight digits, her stiff three covering his five, the space between his thumb and fourth finger empty. He glanced at her and she was focused on the same thing.

"Aren't we a pair," she said, finally. "I got burnt to a crisp in a frigging car accident and I'm feeling sorry for you."

Her body shuddered. For a moment he panicked.

Oh Jesus, I've done it again. I've upset her. Mrs. Cole is going to kill me.

"Yes sir," she said. "We take the frigging cake."

Her voice shook, but then her tone registered.

She's trying not to laugh at me.

She tried to hold back the laughter, but she failed. It tore from her body in a shriek that took her breath away, that took both their breaths away, until they were gasping for breath, tears rolling down their cheeks.

They heard footsteps in the hallway. Mrs. Cole burst in, frightened by the ruckus, murder in her eyes for that foolish man who kept upsetting her girl, angry at herself for giving him another chance.

"What in God's name is wrong with you?" she said. "Why can't you—"

But Sheila held up a hand.

"It's all right," she said.

Mrs. Cole paused, reading the words, unsure, knowing that she'd heard this in her daughter's voice before, but it had been so long ago. Finally, it registered: laughter, silliness and fun.

Her eyes filled with tears.

"It's all right, mom," Sheila said. "It's more than all right. Will and I have been discussing his pitiful love life.

"Why don't you go down to the cafeteria and get a cup of coffee?" Sheila said. "I think this might take awhile."

Mrs. Cole hesitated in the doorway. She grilled Will with her eyes.

"We're fine, Mrs. Cole," he said. "Actually, I'm pitiful, but Sheila's fine."

"Stop," Sheila said, pressing a hand to her side. "Enough. You're killing me."

"All right," Mrs. Cole said. "I'll be in the cafeteria,"

"Good," Sheila said, and Will understood that this was a big step. Before, Mrs. Cole had been just down the hall in her consultation room, within ear shot, ready to come running. She turned and walked back out.

"So," Sheila said. "Tell me about Girl #1. What did she say about me? I want details."

When Will got back to his apartment at three p.m., Murph was still asleep on the sofa. That was no surprise. His hair was disheveled, back to pre-Kathy days. A string of drool hung from the side of his mouth.

Maybe tonight he'll do something besides drink himself silly. Everything takes time.

"Hey," Will said as he poked Murph in the ribs. "Get your sorry ass up. It's time to party."

That night they went to "Pappy's", a dance club that he'd often gone to with Julie.

Murph might not want to get with the honeys, but at least we can look at some.

Pappy's was the place to do that. Will thought that he was back on the stairs of Aiken Hall watching the co-ed waterfall, although here hippy maidens were in short supply, their flowing skirts and scarves replaced by sequined sheaths hugging hard bodies. Short skirts showed long legs. Jewelry reflected churning lights. Gold chains and huge, dangling hoops bounced up and down. Only breasts had more freedom as low cut tops barely kept them in check.

In the VIP booths things were less frantic but just as intense. These creatures sat around tables, smiling and talking as if the dance floor was another world, separated by a protective bubble. Will knew this was a line he'd never cross and then he recognized Monique.

She sat at one of the tables, intent in conversation with a guy who was obviously the top dog at her table. His black hair was clipped short, his black, silk shirt fit perfectly. The silver watch at his wrist and diamond stud in his ear were the only glitter to offset the black.

Monique also wore black. White skin was the contrast to her black: pale cheeks and white neck glowing like other people's jewelry. The guy was focused on Monique and she on him, while all the others at the table glanced their way nervously. One woman spoke to him. The guy glanced at her, annoyed.

Released for just a moment, Monique looked out over the dance floor. Her eyes met Will's. She smiled, held up two fingers in a quick salute.

When the top dog turned back to her again, she placed a white hand on his black sleeve and whispered in his ear. He frowned, glanced out over the crowd and found Will. He nodded. Will nodded, but the smile of Top Dog's face made him realize that the nod had only been in response to Monique's whisper.

She stood and moved through the crowd. It parted for her as if she were royalty, the maneuver complicated by the height of her platform heels.

My angel patient complete with fuck-me heels.

As she came closer, he saw her suit was sleeveless with white pin stripes. The top three buttons were undone to show a generous view of white skin. Her hair was shorter than it had been before, a deeper black, as well, offsetting her pale cheeks.

"Murph," he said.

"What?"

"You're on your own. See that woman coming towards us?"

Murph saw Monique and his eyes got big.

"We've got history," Will said. "I'm going to talk to her."

"Go for it, man," Murph said.

Will walked to her.

"Hello," she said when she reached him. "It's great to see you."

She took his hand, hesitated and then hugged him.

He leaned in close and spoke directly into her ear.

"Is that your idiot boyfriend?" he asked.

"Of course not," she said as she pulled back, blood exploding into her cheeks. "I told you that I dumped that guy the day of my surgery. If I was back with that jerk, I certainly wouldn't be running over here to see you. I'd be sneaking off in the opposite direction. I'd be too ashamed."

"It's not my business," he said.

"Of course it is," she said. She took his hand.

"Come on," she said. "It's too loud in here. Let's go out to the lobby."

She led him to the door. The music died as it slid shut. His eyes squinted in the normal light. She led him to a couch across the room and sat. She didn't let go of his hand.

He took advantage of the light to really look at her. She was like the woman she'd shown him in the fashion magazines that day in the ER. Her eyes, accentuated by blue shadow, seemed twice as big as they'd been before, though he wouldn't have imagined that possible. Still, he couldn't help but think that she'd been more beautiful the first time he'd seen her.

"Hey," she said. "Where are you?"

"Back in the ER," he said.

"Then we both are," she said. She squeezed his hand.

"Things like that don't happen very often," he said.

"I would have thought they happened to you all the time," she said.

"No," he said.

"How many other times?" she asked.

He thought about the patients who had really touched him. Sheila Cole was the only one who was in the same class as this girl but for very different reasons.

"You're the only one," he said.

"I'm glad," she said.

His eyes fell to her breasts, the smooth, white skin between those three buttons. He imagined what it would be like to finish the job, to take her breasts in his hands and caress then.

It could have been real, not just imagination, but I walked away.

She chuckled. He met her gaze.

"Well," she said. "I don't need to ask you where you are, now."

"I'm sorry," he said. "You look incredible."

"Better than the last time you saw me, I'm sure."

"Not really," he said. "Just different."

"Oh come on," she said. "I'd been puking for three days. I didn't have any makeup and I was wearing a hospital gown. I'm sure I looked like hell."

"You still put most of those women in there to shame," Will said, nodding in the direction of the dance floor.

"But you still left me," she said.

"I had to."

"And now?"

"That's over."

"I'm sorry."

"What about your new guy?"

"Ah," she said. "Robert. He's great."

"How did you meet?"

"He's an editor for a magazine that I freelance for."

"You're a writer?"

She looked surprised, but then she nodded.

"Of course," she said. "You don't even know what I do for a living. It's odd. I feel so close to you but the truth is we don't know each other at all."

"That's true," he said. "A writer. That's great. Would I have seen anything that you've written?" he asked.

She shook her head.

"My stuff isn't exactly mainstream. I write for business journals. I do a lot of in-house publications for corporations."

"That's too bad," he said. "I mean for me. It would be fun to know what you do."

"Like I know you," she said.

"It doesn't really matter, though," he said. "All that matters is if this guy is a jerk, too."

She blushed, but it was different this time. He knew the flush in her cheeks before had been embarrassment. The old boyfriend was a bad memory, one she didn't want to relive. This time her cheeks told him that she didn't mind answering questions about this new guy.

Just my luck.

"Robert's great," she said. "He's the first guy I've ever known who really sees me."

She ran her fingers through her hair, pushing the black strands to attention. She paused, and then she ran her fingers through his hair, as well.

"Well," she said, "Maybe there was one other."

He caught her fingers and pulled them into his lap.

"And I really was the only one for you?" she asked.

"Of course," he said. "Most of the time I hide behind the surgical drapes. I do my job but I never really see the people. If I'd been your scrub tech and not your transport person, I wouldn't have even seen your face.

"Okay," he said, "One of the other guys might have said, 'Wow, get a load of this one,' and I'd have checked you out but I wouldn't have really seen you."

Her face would have been no more real to me than her breasts in my fantasy.

"And you wouldn't have gotten caught in the cross fire between those two doctors," she said. "That crazy old guy and the Ice Queen."

"Noley Baines and Jill Ackerman," he said. "Not their finest moment. Not mine either"

"Don't be ridiculous," she said. "I'll never forget how kind you were to me that day. When I never heard from you I started to wonder if you were just doing your job."

"No," he said. "It was more than that."

She smiled. The color in her cheeks was pride, now. Then she glanced at her watch. She stood quickly, unsteady for the first time on the too-tall heels.

"I should get back to Robert," she said.

"Of course," he said. He reached into his pocket. He pulled out a pen and a slip of paper from an earlier ATM transaction. He wrote his phone number on it.

"Here," he said. "Take my number. If things change for you, I mean."

"Ah," she said. "Déjà vu."

He shrugged.

"You never know," he said.

"It's nice to think so, isn't it?" she said.

"Yes, it is."

Top Dog appeared in the door across the lobby.

"Come on," she said. "I'll introduce you."

She took his arm this time.

"Robert," she said. "This is Will Nathan. I had surgery last fall and he was the one who brought me down to the OR. He took such good care of me."

Will held out his hand and Top Dog took it and shook it firmly. Will expected him to crush it, but there was just the right amount of pressure. Will thought of Steve Dempsey's reaction every time Will came around Julie. How she'd teased them about marking their territory. There was none of that with this guy.

Top Dog, my ass.

"That's cool," Robert said. "Working in the OR, that must be something."

"It's all right," Will said.

He felt Monique's arm slide out of his. She moved over beside Robert and slipped her arm under his.

"It was great to see you, Will," she said.

"You, too."

Robert took her hand and led her back towards the door. Will waited. She didn't look back. He went back to sit on the couch. Her scent lingered in the fabric.

He looked down at the pen in his hand. He opened his wallet and found the neatly folded scrap of paper that she'd given him on their night. Her number was faded, but he could still make it out.

He went back across the lobby and pushed into the dark madness of the main room. He scanned the crowd, hoping to see Murph on the dance floor with one of the countless beautiful women in the room. Murph stood by the wall, nursing a beer. He looked so pitiful. Will pushed through the crowd to rescue him.

THIRTY-FOUR

Lila waited in the lounge on Will's first day back on the evening shift. She glanced up at the clock. It was two-thirty. She wondered why he hadn't made it in yet. He had always been the first one to arrive.

Maybe things will be different this time. He won't come in early, won't savor every minute. Things change. After all, they changed for me.

She was the one who came in early, now. She wanted to be with people. She wanted to see her crew. Not that she really had a crew, anymore, not the way that it had been before.

It had started when Julie went back to nights. Then Will had left. His replacement, Bradley, was a jerk, all attitude with no talent to back it up. Martha had replaced Julie with a string of temps.

Melanie had gotten her act together and become a decent tech, but the change wasn't reflected in her face.

I still want to slap that sullen smirk off her face at least once a day.

Kathy and Murph's break-up had been the final straw. It affected everyone.

Murph had been so pitiful that Lila was happy when he decided to go to weekends, even though she'd miss him, even if it meant that Will was coming back.

She wanted to see Will. That was one thing she couldn't deny. She just didn't know if it was for the right reasons.

One good thing about the break-up of the crew was that it might help her to keep Will from finding out about she and Ray. Murph was the most likely one to talk, so it was good that he was gone. Lila knew Kathy would keep quiet if she asked her.

Kathy came through the door. Lila almost didn't recognize her because she'd cut her hair. It was as short as all the regulars. She'd finally adhered to the dress code.

She sat down in the chair across from Lila. She had her shoes in one hand. The other hand automatically grasped for the hair that wasn't there, still programmed for her pre-game ritual of wrestling it into her cap.

"Jesus," Lila said. "What happened to your head?"

Kathy laughed and ran her fingers over the sparse curls.

"I'm just ready for a change," she said. "It's a whole new ballgame, now."

Lila nodded. "Murph's gone," she said. "You must be relieved."

"I think it's best for everybody," Kathy said. "I hate that he took it as hard as he did."

She pulled on her shoes, adjusted the fringe of her baby-blue ankle socks. She slipped her hat on. Her fingers fell to her lap. She played with the hem of her skirt, as if she wasn't sure what to do with the extra free time.

"We're early," she said.

"Yes, we are."

"You must be anxious to see Will."

Lila blushed.

"I think it's great," Kathy said. She reached across the aisle and touched Lila's knee.

"I always knew you had feelings for the guy," she said. "Now that you're free, you can do something about it."

Lila looked up at the clock.

Where is he?

"I'm glad you mentioned this, Kathy," Lila said as she leaned towards Kathy. "I don't want Will to know that I split up with Ray."

"Why not?" Kathy asked. "I thought that was probably why it happened."

"Not really. Will and I split up even before Ray and I did."

"Whoa," Kathy said, holding her hand out in front of her. She jerked forward in her seat. Lila jerked back so they wouldn't bump heads.

"You and Will got together?" Kathy whispered.

"Yes," Lila said, "But it was only for a short time."

"And this was before you left your husband?"

"I know it was wrong," Lila said, "But I couldn't help myself. I just went crazy for awhile."

Kathy leaned back in her chair. She shook her head. "I can't believe it," she said. "I didn't have a clue."

"Was anyone suspicious? Lila asked.

"Not that I know of," Kathy said. "Everyone knew that you were sweet on Will, but we figured it was just a crush. Nobody ever thought you guys would get together."

I'm sure they were laughing their asses off at me. The old broad mooning over the young stud. I almost wish they had found out.

Melanie came into the lounge and dropped into the chair beside Lila. Her disposition, as usual, suited the poorly lit room.

My little ray of sunshine.

Bradley was next. He sat across from Kathy. Martha had picked him as Murph's replacement on the heart team.

Kathy squirmed in her seat. Lila smiled. It was obvious that Kathy had a lot more questions about Lila and Will, but was holding her tongue because of Melanie and Bradley.

"Good afternoon everyone," Martha said as she came through the door. Will was right behind her.

Martha took her seat in the green chair. Will sat beside her. This chair was usually left vacant.

Too close to the goddamn fire. Guess Will's not worried about getting burned.

Martha spread out her notes in her lap. Lila glanced down at her ankle socks. They were shocking pink.

Lila did a quick survey. Kathy wore her baby blue socks. Melanie wore aquamarine with dolphins. Her own were green with red chili peppers. She winced. They had been Will's favorites.

"As most of you know," Martha said. "Murph has gone to weekends. As much as I hate to lose Murph, Will, our prodigal son, has returned. I know you're all as happy to see him as I am."

"Hello, everybody," Will said.

Oh great, the old blanket hello.

But as he said the words, Will looked around the room. He made eye contact with each person. Lila wanted to crawl under her chair. Their eyes met.

"It's great to be back," he said. His eyes cut through her. She felt the blood rising in her face. She fought the urge to run into the locker room.

"Okay," Martha said, "I wish we had time for a reunion, but we have a full board tonight, so let's get started."

"Bradley and Kathy, you're the heart. Mitral valve and bypass with two jumps." She turned towards Bradley. "Do you think you're ready to fly solo?" she asked.

"I'm ready," he said. "Besides, I know that Kathy will take care of me."

"Lila, you and Melanie are with Jamison. He's got two hips."

"Will, I've got something new for you: an anterior cervical fusion with Dr. Bowen."

"Neurosurgery," Will said.

"That's right," she said. "A new service and a new partner." She gestured towards a tall, slim black woman in the corner. Her short curls were metallic gold.

"You're with Adel," she said.

The pairings set, they all stood and moved towards their partners.

"One more thing," Martha said. They waited.

"I hope these new teams work out," she said. "Things have been a merry-go-round the last few months. Let's settle down, okay?"

Sounds good to me.

Melanie stood.

"I have to pee," she said. She went back into the lounge. Bradley and Kathy walked out into the hall. Will talked quietly with Adel at the other end of the lounge. "I guess we'd better go," Adel said. He gestured for her to go first. When they passed, Will's hand brushed Lila's shoulder although he didn't look at her.

This time she felt the warmth between her legs. She prayed that he wouldn't turn around, that he'd just keep going.

I guess I don't have to wonder who'll spill the beans about me and Ray. It's probably going to be me.

She didn't get to talk to Will until almost ten. He and Adel were on break in the lounge.

"I'm going to ICU to get some coffee," Adel said. "I can't take the crud our machine turns out. Did you want to come?"

"No thanks," Will said

"I can bring you a cup," she said.

"Thanks, that would be great."

"How do you like it?" she asked.

"Black," he said.

"Coming right up," she said. As soon as she was out the door, Will turned to Lila.

"It's good to see you," he said.

"Likewise."

"You look great," he said. His hands moved restlessly in his lap. She wondered if he was fighting an urge to touch her.

Of course he is. It's all he can do not to throw you down right here on the floor of the lounge.

"How have you been?" he asked.

"Good."

"How's Ray?"

"He's fine," she said, forcing herself to smile. "Mixter did a great job and Ray's taking care of himself, now. He sticks to his diet. He quit drinking."

"That's great," Will said. "So many people just start right back in with the same bad habits after a bypass. I know you'd straighten him out if he did that, though."

"Of course," she said.

Will's face clouded at her reply. He looked away, as if he needed to look at anything but her.

"This dump never changes," she said, trying to change the subject. She took in the dim lights, the rummage sale furniture with a sweep of her arm.

"It's even more depressing on the weekends," he said. "Without the people, I mean."

Without the sardines, it's just a can.

"It's not like you're coming back to work with your old gang, though," she said. "Things have changed. Julie is back on nights. Murph's gone. You're doing neurosurgery with Adel."

"She's cool," he said. "But it's not like working with you. Do you suppose Martha will put us back together?"

"Wouldn't it be too weird?" she asked.

"I think I can handle it, now."

"Oh really?" she said. She stood and headed for the locker room. He grabbed her arm.

"What's wrong?" he said.

"'I think I can handle it,'" she said, her voice mimicking his. "You're over us. We're just co-workers, partners, pals."

"I never said I was over you," he said. "I doubt I ever will be."

She slumped back into a chair by the door.

"I just accept the way things are," he said. "I never said I liked it. We have to move on, don't we?"

The tone of his voice jarred her. He seemed to be asking if there was still a chance.

Does he know about me and Ray? How could he? Maybe Kathy was wrong. Maybe the others figured it out. Maybe they spilled the beans.

He waited. He seemed sad, indecisive. He wasn't her Will.

"Yes," she said. "We have to move on."

He sighed. "I know it's for the best," he said. "I can't keep screwing up my job by letting my feelings get the best of me. It's like you always said, 'Don't mess where you eat.'"

Now he's quoting me. I'm his mother after all.

"It is better when you keep things separate," she said. "We're living proof of that. Murph and Kathy are, too."

"It's best to be with someone who isn't a part of the job," he said. "I guess that's how it is with you and Ray."

Why does he keep asking about Ray? What's he fishing for?

"It works for us," she said.

Adel came back in with two cups of coffee. She handed one to Will.

"I'm sorry, Lila," she said. "I've only got two hands."

"That's okay," Lila said. "You have to watch out for your partner, anyway."

"That's right," Adel said. She turned to Will. "Want to go see what Martha has in store for us, partner?'

"Sure. I'll see you later, Lila."

"You bet your ass you will."

He smiled at her, as if her vulgarity pleased him.

Good old Lila.

They left the lounge and Lila gasped, as if she'd been holding her breath since Adel went for coffee.

He still cares. He's moved on, but not because he doesn't care. How the hell can he still care? How the hell can I?

Not that it made a difference. They were wrong for each other. She'd ruined her marriage. He'd compromised his work, the thing he loved the most.

She knew she loved him. She always had. Still, it didn't change a thing. She'd never be able to look at him without thinking about what a coward she'd been, about what she'd done to Ray. She'd think of Jerry the day that she'd moved out. She knew that she'd never hate Will, but she'd always hate herself.

She knew she needed to let him go. He needed to be with someone his age, someone who wasn't a part of the job. He wanted to be her partner again. She wasn't sure if she could even do that, but she knew that she should try.

She found him in the scrub room. He stood over the sink, working the brown soap into his arms. He turned to her and she saw the good surprise in his eyes.

"Doc Jamison has a wrist fracture," he said. "Do you think he'll be happy to see me?"

"Don't get your hopes up," she said. "He bitched when you went to weekends, but he's okay, now that he knows Melanie and I can take care of him. He's as fickle as a frigging school girl."

"You're probably right," Will said. He tossed the scrub brush into the trash and slid his arms under the water, rinsing away the thick, brown suds.

"I'm surprised Martha didn't give this one to me and Melanie," Lila said.

"She was going to," Will said, "But I begged." He kicked the foot pedal for the water and it slowed to a trickle and stopped.

"Well," he said, "Duty calls."

"Hold on a second," she said. She pulled his mask down. She reached out to scratch his nose. He jerked away.

What the hell is wrong with him? You'd think I grabbed his dick.

"Settle down," she said. "I'm just trying to act like a good partner. I miss that, too, you know."

"You just took me by surprise," he said. "I'm okay, now."

He leaned forward. She ran her finger down the bridge of his nose. Her hand shook. He shuddered. Their eyes met.

"Too soon?" she asked.

"I guess."

"We'll get there," she said.

"Do you really think so?" he asked.

THIRTY-FIVE

Jamison frowned when he saw Will.

"Is it already the weekend?" he asked.

"No," Will said, "I'm back working during the week like the regular folks."

"I don't need you during the week," Jamison said. "Who's taking your place on the weekends?"

"Murph," Will said. He held a gown up for Jamison who walked into it. He turned around and Adel tied him in the back.

"Murph?" Jamison said. "He's a heart man."

"Yes," Will said. He held out a glove and Jamison plunged a hand into it.

"What good will he do me?" Jamison asked. He shook his head in disgust.

"He's a goddamn plumber.

"I can't believe you did this to me, William," he said as he slid his hand into the second glove and snapped them both tight around the cuff of his gown. "We had things set up perfectly: Lila and Melanie during the week, you and Flo on the weekend. I'll have to speak to Martha about this. I wish you folks would get your lives together and stop messing up my OR."

He sat on a stool and rolled to the table, nudging the resident out of the way. He sized up the fracture with a quick glance.

"Hand me the depth gage and a 2.5 drill bit," he said.

Will handed him the tools and settled in. He wanted everything available as soon as Jamison needed it. He hoped he'd be able to produce them before he asked.

He smiled. Jamison hadn't asked why he'd come back. Of course, he hadn't. He'd never asked why he'd gone to weekends. For him, Will was just a cog in a machine.

I'm home.

When they had the bone in place, they waited for the X-ray tech. Will's mind wandered.

Why won't Lila tell me that she's broken up with Ray? She lied to my face. I guess she's really over me. No wonder she wants to scratch my nose, I'm one of her kids, again.

But she reacted when she touched me, too. I saw it...

"William? Earth to William..."

His head jerked up. Jamison stared at Will. Every other eye in the room was on him, too.

Probably can't wait to see Jamison rip me a new asshole.

Jamison disappointed them all. He chuckled.

"I know you're not used to working the entire shift, William," he said, "Being a weekend guy, and all, but I need for you to keep up."

"I'm sorry Doctor Jamison," Will said.

"Doctor Jamison?" he said. "Why so formal? Just refer to me as 'that pompous lunatic' the way everyone else does."

Will smiled. He looked at the protruding ulna, loaded a tap into its handle and slapped it into Jamison's palm.

"That's better," Jamison said.

After the case, Will sat in the lounge, cursing himself for slipping the way he had. He remembered Jamison's eyes above his mask.

Today he was all fun and games, but that won't last. Next time he'll chew me apart and I'll deserve it. I can't do this again. I came back to face things, to face Lila. Whatever's going on, I have to know the truth.

He waited for Lila by the truck on the top level of the garage. He ran his fingers over the cool metal of the tailgate. He glanced into the cab, remembering the times they'd been together in there, the things they'd done to each other.

He turned away from the truck. He walked to the wall that lined the edge of the roof. He leaned on the concrete and took a deep breath. He closed his eyes, but the images came again. He saw Lila's face in the dim light of the garage, her eyes closed, her mouth gaping. Stu always said that in the dark all women's faces were the same, but he'd been wrong.

Will opened his eyes and looked out across the lawn between the garage and the hospital. He saw the roof where they'd first watched the fireworks. He turned away from it and saw the large gray stone that they'd used for target practice.

"Will?"

He turned. Lila stood beyond the tailgate. Her hand rested where his had been a few minutes before.

But I'm sure her mind isn't in the same place mine just was.

She glanced at the cab of the truck.

Then again...

"What are you doing here?" she asked. "You know I can't--"

Can't? More like won't. Why is she lying to me?

"I just want to talk," he said.

"I don't have time," she said. "You know I have to get home. Ray—"

"Ray's not waiting for you," he said.

"How dare you—"

"Murph told me," he said. "You and Ray split up. Can we just stop with the lies?"

She slumped against the truck as if her lie had been the only thing propping her up.

"I'm sorry," she said.

"What's going on, Lila?" he asked. "When we were together, you told me that you couldn't leave your husband. I guess you just couldn't do it for me. Is there somebody else, somebody you met after we split?"

Anger stood her up straight. "Are you frigging kidding me?" she asked. She slammed her fist into the side of the truck. Tears rolled down her cheek.

"You think I replaced you that quickly?" she said. "You can't be serious. In my whole life there's been Ray and there's been you and that's it."

"But now you've left him," he said. "You couldn't do it for me, for us. Why would you wait until after we broke up?" he asked.

"Why did I wait?" she said. She shook her head.

"Do you remember the night you broke it off with me?" she asked. "The night you told me that you were going to change your hours and go back to school? I came here that night to tell you that I was leaving Ray."

"But you never said that," he said.

"I tried," she said. "You wouldn't listen."

He backed away from her. He leaned against the concrete ledge of the garage.

"Oh Jesus," he said. "You tried—"

"Yes," she said. "I tried, but you'd made up your mind."

"Why didn't you argue?" he asked. "Why didn't you fight?"

"Because I knew you were right," she said. "We were bad for each other. I hated what you brought me to. I hated who I was when I was with you. I was crazy and jealous and insecure. I didn't care about anything but you and me. My work and my family didn't matter.

"And it wasn't any better for you. You loved the job and I turned it into a frigging soap opera for you."

"But that was only because we had to sneak around," he said. "It would have been fine if we'd just been able to tell the truth."

"You really think so?" she asked.

"Of course, I do," he said. "I always believed in what we had. You're the one who wouldn't even try." He shook his head. "You said you'd decided to give us a shot that night, but you just gave up. I said I was done and you just let me go."

"That's what I'm trying to tell you," she said. "I didn't believe. I thought what had happened between us was a dream, that I had to wake up and get on with my life. For Christ's sake, Will, it was only a week, but if felt like forever. I felt like I was holding my breath the whole time. When you walked away I could finally breath again.

She leaned against the wall.

"You see," she said. "We've been standing here for less than five minutes and I can't catch my breath. I just don't have the nerve for this."

"The nerve?"

"You think it would have been easy for us?" she asked. "I'm 55 years old, Will. You're younger than all of my sons but Jerry. I've got grandchildren, for Christ's sake. It would have been a battle for us every day, us against the world. I'm not cut out for that."

"How can you say that? How can you know?"

"Because I let you walk away that night."

She pulled her car keys from her pocket and dug into the ledge, working at the cement around the edges of a small stone imbedded in the surface. It came free and fell to the floor of the garage. She kicked it under her truck.

"I still don't understand," he said. "If our breaking up was such a relief, why did you leave Ray? Why did you lie to me when you did?"

He put his hand on her shoulder and tried to turn her face towards his. He wanted to see her eyes, but she wouldn't look at him.

"I didn't do it for you," she said. "I did it for Ray. He deserved better. I did it for myself. I hated who I'd become: a crazy woman who compromised everything that mattered to her, a coward who stayed in her marriage out of guilt."

"But what does that matter, now?" he said. "You're free. We both are."

"I know we are," she said. "I'm just not sure that changes anything."

She turned around and leaned against the wall, her elbows resting on the rough concrete.

"We're different people, Will," she said. "You say I give you a hard time for being so young, but the truth is you know your feelings a lot better than I do mine. You follow them, too. You don't let anybody tell you what to think or feel. You broke up with Julie without a second thought. No fooling around. No holding back. I was crazy about you but I couldn't bring myself to leave Ray."

"But that's in the past," he said.

"Some things are never in the past," she said. "The first time I slept with you and went home to Ray, I ruined things for you and me forever."

"You were just trying to do the right thing."

"Trying to do the right thing," she said. "You remember that girl you brought down from the ER for a laparoscopy, the one Noley and Ackerman fought over?"

"Of course," he said. "I'm surprised you remember her."

"You mean because I'm not the one who fell in love with her at first sight?"

"Come on, Lila. That's crazy," he said.

Lila took his chin and turned his face to hers.

"It's not crazy," she said. "I mention her and you're trying not to smile. You know it's true as much as I do, but that's not the point. You fell for her, but you stayed with me. Did you ever blame me for that?"

"No," he said, and he knew that it was true. Even the other night, seeing Monique with The Top Dog, he'd never blamed Lila, never said "What if?"

"You made your choice," she said. "You never looked back. I didn't stay with Ray because it was the right thing but because it was easy. I thought you and I were the same, but we're not."

"We could be," he said. "You know what happened. You can do things differently this time."

"No," she said. "I can only do them differently next time."

With someone else.

She let his hand slip from hers. She slipped her car key into the lock.

"I need to get home," she said. "I won't make any jokes about being an old broad and needing my beauty sleep. I just need to go home. Nobody's waiting for me. The truth is I like it that way."

"Okay," he said.

She pulled the door open and turned back to him. They stood two feet apart. They waited. It was as if they remembered every embrace they'd ever shared. There was friendship and loyalty, lust and love.

She tapped his arm and got into the cab. She backed away and drove off without looking back. He leaned on the ledge again. He waited until he saw the truck pull out the front entrance. He watched her until she was out of sight.

THIRTY-SIX

Lila didn't go home. Instead, she took the road to Weston. Her apartment was five minutes from the hospital, but she needed time to clear her head. She rolled down the window and let the air rush in as she pushed down on the accelerator.

She thought of the look on Will's face when she'd left him. She knew that she needed to remember it. All the pain she'd caused in the last year came because she hadn't seen things as they really were.

She'd been in love with Will. It was the real thing, but she hadn't been able to admit that. She'd been so afraid of hurting Ray that she'd waited too long and lost Will. Once that happened, she had to hurt Ray, as well.

That's what happens when you look away.

She pictured Will's face again when she mentioned Monique. She remembered his face the day they'd done her surgery.

I wasn't just a crazy, jealous bitch that day. There was something there.

She remembered how'd he snuck back to see Monique that first night. How she'd watched and waited, seen him take the steps in the garage two at a time.

He'd felt something for that girl, but he'd stayed with her. Out of loyalty. Out of love. He saw things the way they were.

One more reason to love the kid. Twenty years old and already a stand-up guy.

He hadn't stayed out of guilt the way she had with Ray. He'd made a choice and lived with it.

Some might say Monique would have been the safe choice. She was his age. She was beautiful and intelligent. She was even a civilian. She wouldn't bring the complications he'd had with Julie and Lila. It made so much sense.

But Lila knew Will. He couldn't take the safe choice. He'd stuck with her.

The girls in the lounge were right all along. He's the real deal. Too bad I wasn't.

At the Weston green, Sheriff Chip Landers stood beside his patrol car, smoking. He saluted her with the red spark of his cigarette.

She knew that he'd tell Ray that he'd seen her, so she pulled up beside him.

"How's it going, Lila?" he said.

"Pretty good, Chip."

"Surprised to see you out this way," he said. "You headed out to the manor?"

"No," she said. "I'm still living in town. I just missed the old stomping ground, I guess. I'd appreciate it if you didn't say anything to Ray."

"I wouldn't dream of it," he said. "That old boy's pretty torn up about all this. Wouldn't want to rub salt in the wounds."

At least not in Ray's.

"Thanks, Chip," she said and put her truck in gear. She felt his hand on her arm.

"Any chance of you two working things out?" Chip asked. "The whole town misses you." He took the last drag from his cigarette and crushed it under his heal.

Pile it on Chip, why don't you? Now I've broken the hearts of an entire town.

"I miss them, too," she said. "But that doesn't change the way things are."

Chip pulled his hand away and stood back from the truck.

"You take care, Lila," he said.

"Thanks."

As Lila drove away, she thought of all the times she'd driven by this spot without Chip stirring from his sleep. Why did he have to be awake this night?

Actually, I'm glad he was. The old gasbag did me a favor.

She saw all the disapproving faces of her neighbors. She pictured the Weston Fourth of July Barbecue, but this time the theme was "What the hell is wrong with Lila Waznek?"

She studied each face. She didn't look away. It was good practice.

She circled back to Will's face. She wondered if he'd ever understand why they couldn't be together.

Of course, he will. The boy's a keeper. It just might take some time.

She knew that now she could move on, too. She even knew how.

She would transfer to mornings. She'd spend time with Jerry after school. She'd reclaim the parts of her life that could be reclaimed.

And the next time life decides to bite me on the ass, I'll be ready.

THIRTY-SEVEN

After Lila drove away, Will leaned against the wall of the garage wondering where to go.

Home? Where Murph waited to drag him out for another night of heavy drinking and ignoring the ladies in the clubs.

Should he go the doctor's lounge? Not really. Fred was off and Steve Dempsey would be more than happy to remind him that he didn't belong there.

This night was a reflection of his life the last year: from sky's the limit to dead end, from level ten to game over.

Sheila's nurses waved him through, even though it was long past visiting hours. Since he'd visited her on the last day of classes, he'd been back a half-dozen times. They assured him the she was still awake. She never did sleep much.

She sat in the chair by the window looking out over her private forest. He walked up behind her. She didn't see him, so he watched what she was watching for a moment. A thin, white stripe skulked along the edge of the trees, then undulated across the parking lot towards a dumpster. In the lights of the lot, a body formed around the line, a skunk's.

Will thought of skeleton Halloween costumes, white bones glowing in a black sheath.

"Will," she said as she looked up. "What are you doing here?"

He sat down in the chair across from her.

"Why am I always here?" he said, looking down. "I need some help from Doctor Love."

He waited for her foot to touch his, blue slippers on running shoes, but they didn't bridge the gap.

He looked up and her face was grim, unwelcoming.

She shook her head.

"Sorry," she said, "The doctor is definitely not in tonight."

"Okay," he said.

I guess it's my turn.

"Tell me about it," he said.

She folded her arms across her chest.

"Forget it," she said.

He prodded her foot with his. She pulled away.

"Talk, talk, talk," she said. "All any of you ever do is talk. Tell me to keep my chin up and keep fighting. You tell me there's gonna be a better day!"

Her hand shot into the air, three fingers tightened into half a fist.

"I want that day now," she said. "Tonight."

"So what can I do?"

"Get me out of here."

She stood, shoving her chair back, and went to her closet. She studied the one outfit that hung on a hanger, the one she'd worn in and would wear the day she left.

"Oh well," she said, "At least I don't have to agonize over my wardrobe."

She draped the blue top and black shorts over her arm and disappeared into the bathroom.

Will walked over and spoke to her through the door.

"What are you doing?" He asked.

"I'm changing. You can't break me out of this place if I'm wearing a hospital gown."

"Break you out? Come on, Sheila," he said. "I can't take you out of the hospital. I'll lose my job."

"Are you here on official hospital business?"

"No."

The door flew open. He threw his hand up to keep from getting hit in the face. Sheila didn't seem to notice.

She elbowed past him and walked to the corner, where a red baseball cap hung from an IV pole. She grabbed the hat and pulled it on. She flipped it around backwards and down to her eyes. She turned.

In the dim light from the bathroom she was a different person. Of course, he'd never seen her in street clothes before. He remembered the first time he'd seen Lila without her scrubs. That was the first time he'd thought of her as a woman. Now, he could see that Sheila was a teen-age girl.

The top was royal blue, long sleeved and turtle necked. Her shorts were tight and very short. In this light her scars were still visible. For the first time, he saw her future.

"So where did you want to go?" he asked.

"A bar would be nice," she said. "A real kick-ass dive."

"You're underage."

"A movie?"

"It's two am."

"A burger at Mickey D's."

"I'm not taking you out of the hospital. Let's go down to the cafeteria."

"Big spender," she said. "You really know how to make a girl feel special."

In the cafeteria she complained about the late-night menu.

"You said you wanted a burger," he reminded her.

"A Mickey D's burger," she corrected him.

She settled on a cafeteria burger and fries with an extra-large soda. He got coffee.

She made a complete circuit of the cafeteria as if there were a crucial difference between each table and chair, as if the view would improve the taste of her burger.

Maybe it will.

They settled in the corner, but the room was empty. Will knew that the next big influx of people wouldn't be until three am.

"It's sure dead in here," she said.

"It's between break times. There'll be a bunch of people here at three," he said. "We've got time."

"The hell we do," she said as she sprayed vinegar on her fries and doused the burger in ketchup. "Places to go. Things to see," she said.

"Excuse me?" He asked. "Have you heard a word I've said? We're not leaving the hospital. You're going to eat your burger and then I'm taking you back to your room."

She bit into the burger. Ketchup ran down the side of her mouth. When she spoke, huge hunks of meat were visible.

"Who said anything about leaving the hospital," she said. "Since you're too chicken to bust me out, I have another idea. I want to go on the Will Nathan Hospital Tour."

"The what?"

"The Will Nathan Hospital Tour."

She grabbed a napkin and wiped the ketchup on the side of her mouth. She balled up the paper and tossed it towards a trashcan in the corner, missing badly. She shrugged and took another bite of her burger.

"I want you to take me to all your hot spots," she said. "If I have to listen to tales of your miserable love life at least I should be able to see a few crime scenes."

"You're crazy," he said as he reached for a French fry. She slapped his hand away.

"I told you to get your own," she said.

"When did you tell me that?"

"When we were in line. You got just coffee and I said, 'Aren't you hungry?'"

"You never said anything about getting my own. I just want one."

"Damn you're cheap," she said, shielding the plate of fries with her hand. "You use your hospital discount to buy me dinner and then you try to eat my food."

"All right, all right," he said. He stood and headed back to the serving line.

"See if they put out any new kinds of pie," she called behind him.

After they'd eaten, they went to the OR.

"How can you want to come back here?" he asked. "You've been here a dozen times in the last few months."

While we put you back together piece by piece.

He scanned his badge and pulled the door open.

"This time I'm looking at things from your point of view," she said. 'Oh, is that Julie?"

Julie emerged from the lounge. She smiled when she saw Will but then she saw Sheila and the smile disappeared.

"What are you doing here, Will?" she asked. "And who's this? You know you shouldn't bring civilians here at this hour."

"This is Sheila," he said, withholding the last name, wondering if Julie would recognize her. She'd probably never seen Sheila's face.

But the scars have to be a dead giveaway. How could she forget?

"Julie," Sheila said. "It's so nice to meet you. Will's told me so much about you."

Sheila took her hand. Julie glanced down, saw the missing fingers and looked quickly back up into Sheila's face. For a moment Will thought that she would touch her cheek, would trace the mottled patches where new skin had replaced old. Instead, she placed her hand over Sheila's.

"Sheila Cole?" she whispered.

"The one and only."

Julie looked back and forth between Will and Sheila and then her face clouded.

"How much did Will tell you about me?"

"Just that you were part of my crew the first few months that I came down here. I feel like I know all of you: Lila, Lindsey, Doctor Dean."

She leaned in close to Julie and spoke in a stage whisper.

"He also told me that you were an item once. If you ask me, he really blew that one."

Julie smiled and shook her head. She nodded her gratitude to Will.

"So what are you two doing here, tonight?" she asked.

"I asked Will to take me on a tour of the OR. I've never been down here when I wasn't as high as a kite. He said that you're the boss and we have to clear it with you. Do you think it would be all right?"

Julie looked at the clock.

"It will have to be fast," she said. "We're doing a case in thirty-five minutes. You two will have to be out of here before then."

"Of course," Sheila said. She whipped off her ball cap. Her hair spiked out in all directions.

"I guess I need scrubs and one of those paper shower caps."

"That's right," Julie said. "I'll help you suit up."

"I'll meet you in Room 2," Will said.

"Okay," Julie said. She put an arm on Sheila's shoulder and guided her towards the women's locker room.

"Hey," Sheila said, "The locker room. That can be the next stop on the tour."

Will went down to Room 2. He flipped on the lights and sat on the OR table.

An OR tour. What exactly is there to see without cases?

He looked around. There were monitors and mayo trays and cabinets of supplies. Behind the glass were rows of suture in multicolored boxes.

He flipped on a monitor and one red line slid across the screen. Green zeros lined up in rows.

If the tour was for a group of kids, he could strap one of them up to the monitor to show them their vital signs. They could see their heart beating and listen to the sound of their blood pressure.

He remembered Sheila's vitals the first few times that she'd come down. He turned the monitors off.

Julie and Sheila burst through the door. Their bodies were so different, Julie the Botticelli woman and Sheila so frail. Julie moved with ease, as if she knew all eyes were on her. Sheila was hesitant for the same reason.

"If you get busted for this I'm washing my hands of you," Julie said, but her eyes were happy, contradicting every word.

"That's fair," Sheila said. "We'll just blame it all on Will."

"Thanks a lot," he said.

"I'll be out front," Julie said.

"Thanks, Jules," he said.

"Don't mention it," she said. She squeezed his hand.

"Hello?" Sheila said as she jabbed him in the ribs. "My Tour?"

She winked at him, a maneuver that involved the entire right side of her face.

"Take it away," she said.

"Okay," he said, "But there isn't really much to see this time of night."

"I don't really want to see," she said. "Mostly, I just want to feel."

"Okay," he said. "Just follow me."

They went from room to room, flipping lights on and off. Sheila remarked on the different set-ups and equipment for the different kinds of surgery: orthopedics, neurosurgery, open hearts. She loved the heart-lung machine.

"It's looks so simple," she said, "But it keeps the patient going while they work on them."

"The heart is pretty simple," Will said. "It's really just a pump. The brain, now there's the wonder. The neurosurgeons are always flying by the seat of their pants."

"So, I guess I was pretty lucky," she said. "My brain is the only part they never had to work on."

"That's right," he said.

Though we were flying by the seat of our pants pretty much the first few weeks with you.

He led her back into the hall. She caught his arm and turned him around. She stood on her tiptoes and pressed her lips to his ear.

"So, where's the fuck room?" she asked.

He pulled away, hoping that the dim lights in the hall would hide the rush of blood to his cheeks.

"What are you talking about?" he asked.

"Come on," she said. "I've read my share of hospital novels. I watch TV. Doctors do it in the on-call rooms, but the nurses and scrub techs sneak down to a room that never gets used at night."

She twirled on her heels, scanning the rooms as she did a three-hundred-sixty degree turn. She pointed towards 12A.

"That must be it," she said.

He tried to hold back the smile, but he couldn't

"You dog!" she said and poked him in the arm, but this time the blood rushed to her cheeks.

He glanced at his watch.

"Come on," he said, "We're almost out of time."

Julie was waiting for them by the front desk.

"You cut it pretty close," she said.

"I'll change back into my street clothes," Sheila said.

"That's okay," Julie said. She handed Sheila her clothes. "You can keep the scrubs. If anyone has earned them, you have."

Sheila smiled.

Is that a tear?

Sheila pulled off her blue paper hat and put her ball cap in its place.

"Thanks," she said. She held out her hand. "It was nice to meet you, I mean really meet you."

"Likewise," Julie said. She pushed the hand aside and hugged her. He looked over their shoulders and saw Chuck Segal pushing a patient on a stretcher towards them. Will took Sheila's arm.

"Let's go," he said. "We'll go out the back."

They cut through the lounge, knifing past the empty chairs and dull pools of lamplight.

"This is your lounge?" she asked.

"Yes."

"What a dump."

They walked into the hall and he wanted to tell her that he didn't mind the darkness in the lounge because the bright lights of the hall reminded him that he was crossing over into a new world, but she had already pushed through the back door of the OR.

"Where do these go?" she heard her call.

He pushed through the doors. She waited by the elevator that led upstairs to the doctor's lounge.

"That goes to the Penthouse," he said.

"The Penthouse?"

"That's what we call the doctor's lounge."

"Ooh," she said and punched the call button. "I'll bet their lounge isn't a dump."

"No, it's pretty nice."

"Show me," she said.

"We're not allowed."

She formed her half-fist and tapped him on the side of his head.

"Hello," she said. "We're not allowed anywhere we've been tonight."

"Julie is my friend," he said. "That's why we got away with sneaking into the OR."

"Dr. Dean is my friend." She jabbed the button again.

"He's not on call tonight."

"All the docs are in the OR doing that case."

"Maybe, maybe not."

The doors opened and she slipped inside.

"You owe me," she said.

"I owe you?"

After all this time she finally says it. I owe her for the pain, for a lifetime of scars and stares.

"Haven't I always listened to your problems in your love life? The least you can do is take a chance so I can see how the other half lives."

The doors started to close and he jumped between them. He hit the back of the elevator and she hugged him and held him up.

"I am so dead," he said.

"Oh come on," she said. "Live a little."

The elevator rose towards the penthouse.

"Okay," Will said. "We can only go in if the door is open. That's how the doctor's let us know. If the door is closed, we'll have to turn around. That means whoever's in there doesn't want to be disturbed."

"Is that because they're fucking?"

"No," he said. "It's a lounge, not an on-call room."

"So they do fuck in the on-call rooms."

The doors slid open.

"Just be quiet," he whispered.

He walked out of the elevator. He thought he was moving normally, but when he turned, Sheila was doing an elaborate pantomime, lifting her legs in slow motion, waving her arms, drawing her fingers to her lips with a sharp hiss.

The door was closed. He shrugged and turned back towards the elevator. He motioned for her to follow him. She nodded, but as soon as he reached her side, she darted towards the door, jerked it open and strode through.

Will wished the elevator doors were still open so he could dive out of sight.

"All clear," she called.

He went in and she stood in the center of the room, smiling.

"You're pretty proud of yourself, aren't you," he asked.

"Yes."

She circled the room as if she'd decided to buy the place and was pondering the redecoration. She ran her hands over the leather recliners, stood back to check out the big-screen TV. Finally, she settled by the window.

"This must be quite a view when the lights are off in here," she said. The lights in the room made the windows a mirror, giving her only her reflection.

"It's not so bad right now," he said.

"No," she said, "But I've been looking at myself in the mirror and thinking about nothing else for the past few months. I need a break, you know?"

Will killed the lights and she looked out across the town as is cascaded down the hill, at the mountains across the lake.

I wish that there were fireworks.

"This is nice," she said. "The docs have it pretty good."

"They figure they've earned it," he said.

"I guess I'm proof of that."

He had no answer for that. He stood beside her.

"We'd better go," he said, finally.

"Okay."

She was quiet on the elevator, as if she knew the tour was over, as if she didn't want it to be.

So make sure it isn't.

The doors opened.

"One more stop," he said.

"Really?"

"Yes."

"What more can there be?"

"The beginning."

"The beginning?" she said. She shuddered, as if he meant to bring her back to her first days in the OR.

"Not your beginnings," he said. "Mine."

He slipped through the window out onto the roof and held out his hand to her. It wasn't easy going, just beyond her range of motion, but she made it.

He leaned against the wall and dropped into a sitting position. She stood beside him. He reached up, took her hand and tried to pull her down beside him. She pulled her hand away but smiled down at him.

"This is nice," she said. "You done good."

He looked out across the lawn. Off to the right side of the roof was the wooded area that Sheila could see from her window. She looked in that direction and smiled.

"My enchanted forest," she said. "If you think raccoons and skunks looting dumpsters is enchanted."

They'd stopped at the vending machines on their way down from the penthouse. Each popped open a soda, tore the wrapper on a fried pie. She took a bite from her cherry pie and passed it to him.

"Want a taste?" She asked.

"Will I have to give you a bite of mine?"

"Of course."

He took a bite of hers and held his out. It was lemon. She took a bite. Her lips puckered at the sour taste. He offered her another bite. She shook her head. They ate in silence.

He stood and walked to the edge of the roof. He picked up a stone, found the huge rock on the edge of the lawn and threw. The stone hit dead-center and bounced away.

"Bull's eye,' she said.

He felt her beside him. She picked up another stone. She shook it in her hand and then threw, her arm stiff, her range-of-motion limited.

"Fore," she called, as the stone barely cleared the edge of the roof.

She turned back to Will.

"Gravity," she said, "It's a bitch."

She bent down again and picked up another stone. She rolled it in her alien claw and popped it into her mouth. She swished it back and forth from one cheek to the other. Her lips parted and she held it clenched between her teeth. She took his hand and walked to the edge of the roof. She pulled the stone back into her mouth and spit. They watched it fall. They stood without speaking.

"Okay," she said after a few minutes, wiping cherry from the corner of her lips. "You did your part. Now, I'll do mine. What did you need to talk about? What's so bad you had to come to me at two am."

He shook his head.

"I don't need to talk anymore," he said. "I'm okay."

"Don't be so sure," she said. "You still look pretty hopeless from where I'm standing."

He swiped at her. She ducked and her hat fell off. A gust of wind pushed it towards the right edge of the roof. They both scrambled to get it, but it toppled over before they reached it. They watched as it floated down and disappeared into the tangle of trees and bushes below.

"Now you've done it," she said. "But this is good. I didn't really want the tour to end."

She waved her free arm over the woods. She turned and dragged him towards the window with the other.

"On to my enchanted forest, sir," she crowed.

Later that morning, Will slept and dreamed of her.

In this dream, drops of medication landed on her chest, and though her wounds, hot, swirling rings of tissue, should have sent them hissing from their surface in white mist, the liquid turned to ice, instead, spreading out across her body in a layer of thin white, each drop feeding the advance.

It seemed as if they formed ripples in a pool, driven out in concentric circles even as they solidified, replacing the skin that she had lost with a sheath of diamonds.

Also by Ron Roy

Passing Time, a work place novel

Gene Wheeler has always wanted to be an engineer, but after failing math, he drops out of college and takes a job in his hometown paper mill. He hopes this dead-end job will allow him to be a robot - to go through the motions as he considers his options for the future. From his first day on the job, however, he finds himself caught between two groups of men, each devoted to the job in their own way and determined to include him in their ranks. The job is not the smooth ride he envisioned and he soon realizes there are no time-outs in life.

The story takes place at a time when the company is in decline. The question of making concessions to The Company or standing strong with the Union divides the men. *Passing Time* is a story about papermakers and the pride they take in their jobs, but it is for anyone who takes pride in the work they do.

Passing Time is available from Blue Cubicle Press of Plano, Texas. www.bluecubiclepress.com

Also available from Blue Cubile is *Cumberland Valley Chevy,* a part of the *Overtime Series.*

Ron's work has also appeared in *WORK,* www.workliterarymagazine.com

All are available from the author

Ron Roy
72 Elm St.
Berlin, NH 03570
603-752-5105
Rroy10@earthlink.net

Follow Ron on Facebook, *Passing Time*: a novel by Ron Roy.

ISBN 978-0-9840224-6-5